THE Boyfriend COUNTDOWN

A Holi-FATE Novel

The Holiday Match
The Boyfriend Countdown

THE  Boyfriend COUNTDOWN

A Holi-FATE Novel

Tori Samuels

Book design by Samantha Filice

The Boyfriend Countdown / Samuels, Tori
ISBN: 9781738141302

Margo's Playlist

11:11 | Arkells

Feel Like This | Ingrid Andress

Bad For Business | Sabrina Carpenter

Snow On The Beach | Taylor Swift

Take Me Home | Jess Glynne

Good Person | Ingrid Andress

If You Ever Feel Alone | Sainte

Hostage | Billie Eilish

Single On The 25th | Lauren Spencer Smith

Lose My Mind | Dean Lewis

Author's Note

My goal when writing this novel has always been to tell an honest story with raw emotion. I aim to create genuine characters who find themselves unluckily in love around the holidays. While fun, the story includes topics of anxiety and depression in order to process healing. Readers who may be sensitive to these topics, please take note. This novel also includes explicit content in reference to nudity.

I do write in Canadian English, and if some words look a little funny to you, please know they are correct.

Creating a safe and welcome reading experience is important to me. I appreciate you picking up my contemporary romance book with the utmost care to yourself. Enjoy, kind reader.

For those who found their person in the most unexpected
of ways, and to those who are still swiping.

1

A Fresh Start

Dedicated, organized, patient.

These are the words people usually use to describe me, but I never expected *liar* to be added to the list. Never expected the compliments to twist in my favour. No, no one would date a liar.

Really, it's more of a fabrication of events, a moment of untruth. The kind of fib that comes back to bite me in the ass when my big mouth hadn't paused before thought or properly assessed the ramifications of delivering disinformation. Truthfully, if my honesty is worth anything at this point, I'm in too deep. But the pounding in my ears and the emotional fatigue are telling me to keep going.

"Margo, stop pulling your hair at the counter." Mom swats my hand away from my temple as she swerves around me, reaching for a red bell pepper that rolls away from her.

The barstool at the kitchen counter is an excuse to spend time with my mother as she prepares dinner, but suddenly my quiet desk upstairs seems like a better alternative. A month-end report submitted from our newest Junior Accountant sits on my laptop screen, untouched. The customer's account wasn't balanced and I had to reconcile the numbers.

A text message flashes on my screen from *him* and everything inside me thrashes, convinced I'm about to sink with the organ in my chest weighing me down like an anchor.

Sun, Dec 25

SS: Sure, sounds good

7:39 pm

Simple, kind, *panic-inducing*. My blind date agrees to meet.

It's not as if my date is completely anonymous. No, we've talked for twelve days through a holiday dating service called Secret Santa— cute, right? When I signed up, the countdown seemed like an easy commitment and the algorithm gave me a shot at finding a believable fake boyfriend, but as the days ticked down on the calendar, committing to the Christmas reveal made me want to dig in my heels.

There was no denying that the town's advertisements for a local holiday dating service arrived at the perfect moment. The bold posters taped to each streetlight and the ads playing on the radio, posted in the town's

Facebook group, and hung at every grocery store all conspired with me. Already the lie spread through the firm that Margo did, in fact, have a love life. At the time, I had a month until the New Year's gala. Twelve days to persuade the guy to meet me, and then another six days to not only get him to agree to go as my date for the countdown, but to also convince everyone we are in a relationship. I'm a numbers gal, and the calculations lined up.

Day twelve: I feel like I'm jumping from a burning building.

I'm convinced the lie has gone on for too long, but the unread notification pulls my attention to a second unanswered text beneath it. Marked with a timestamp from a few hours ago, the message reminds me that it's now or never.

Harvey Lauder: Janice wants to know the total guest count for New Year's

4:21 pm

My boss Harvey is a man in his fifties with an unfortunate case of resting bitch face. His wife, Janice, is a woman whose involvement in the business serves no purpose but I'm forced to pretend otherwise. Besides, I confirmed the guest count two weeks ago, and there's no real reason for her to know the exact numbers.

Though unanswered, the fire Harvey's text stoked had blazed under my ass, nurtured by my strong desire to overachieve. I have no other choice but to commit. The text might as well be a calendar reminder.

Leave it to me, boring, quiet, *lying* Margo to promise everyone at the firm I'd introduce them to my boyfriend. I needed a plus one, and the first step was meeting the mystery guy on the other end of my phone.

Day twelve: like jumping from a burning building and plummeting into deep waters while a squad of choppers pursue chase.

I stare at the stove clock, unsure what to say to either of the pending messages.

Dad folds the sides of his banana leaf green chilli tamales and Mom stuffs her peppers. Together they follow a rhythm unrelated to the holiday music my little brother blasts in the next room. No one suspects I'm a bad person.

My phone chimes with another message, a prompt from my secret texter confirming the time and place to meet. The stove fan hums in the kitchen but feels as if it thrums directly in my ears. I slap my laptop closed.

I'm actually doing this.

A lie flows fluidly from my mouth because this is what I do now, I deceive. "I have to pop into the office, I forgot a folder."

Mom meets me with her lopsided frown. Dad stares at me for several seconds.

"Raphael hasn't opened presents yet." Mom lets the statement hang in the air, not asking me to stay but hoping the freedom of choice allows me to make the right one.

I don't.

"I'll only be gone for an hour."

The lie isn't hard to sell. It's not as if I have a choice to go offline on most days. As the current Director of

Finance at Lauder Accounting, I spent all of my twenties building myself up for this responsibility. The year-end reports are always hectic. Last-minute receivables and payables complicate the process. Not to mention late night texts from my team asking for a second opinion before submission. If the emails pile up, our clients will miss their deadlines, and new Junior Accountants could submit error-riddled documents that would screw up the entire year-end. They need me. Even on Christmas.

Telling my parents I have to step out on Christmas is the line Mom always warns me never to blur: work and family. And though she nods her understanding, she refuses to lift her attention from where she now smooths Raph's hair for one last photo in front of the tree.

Emotions choke me. There were times Mom and Dad had missed weeknight dinners, leaving Raph and me with Abuela's cooking and Spanish soap operas. My middle school friends snickered when I told them my parents cleaned office buildings at night, but their second job at the time never bothered me; I only felt truly cheated on nights like Valentine's or Halloween. And even though Mom sewed my costumes and Dad brought me home a single red rose, they missed the magic of the evening. I wonder if Raph will remember his older sister the same way.

On my way out, Mom's soft kiss on my temple and Dad's tight squeeze of my shoulder are enough reassurance to make me step over the threshold. They're proud of my success, and Mom thinks I'll gain the promotion I had accidentally let slip to her when my boss announced a buyout of our biggest client.

My parents have no idea I'm about to freeze my ass off Downtown Bolton under a Christmas-lit gazebo waiting for a guy I met online. No photo, no name, not even a recording to hear his voice. I have no idea who he is.

After a quick update dropped in the girl's group chat, I start the engine and throw my car in reverse before I can back out of the plan. When all of this started, my best friend, Jane, warned me to prepare for disappointment. Not that she doubted the dating service, but rather she insisted the whole scheme wouldn't work.

"You can't cram a man into a box you created for him, they barely know their shapes." Her winged liner narrowed her scowl when I showed her the Secret Santa submission form.

"It'll work," I sounded more sure than I felt. I required a believable date and Secret Santa was kind of like online shopping. If I wanted to be a credible applicant for the promotion, Lauder Accounting couldn't know how the mild fib snowballed.

Over the span of the month, I spared few details about my fake relationship, masquerading as a woman who preferred her privacy. I avoided showing people photos of him— they didn't exist, and when they asked what he looked like, I stuck to generic responses like, *super cute with a nice smile.* I hope he meets the low bar I pegged for him.

I used to wait for my firework moment, the one where the man finally claims his lady, kisses her, and causes bursts of light to shine behind her eyelids, the surroundings to blur, and her insides to warm. Everyone knows the scene.

Part of me is still a romantic, but the hardened shell I've grown used to is what keeps my heart protected and listens to Jane. There's only one reason I'm not a romantic anymore, but we don't talk about him.

Disappointment is inevitable, but every text from SS softens the protective layer. He's a real person on the other end of my phone, and the awareness of him makes me careful, kinder, as if responding to his messages atones for how I use him.

Am I insane?

The question rings through my head, but not for the first time since I rushed out of the house.

Up Highway 50, passing the community hockey arena with Christmas lights brightening the large trees, I map the route to Downtown Bolton. I'm missing Raph stealing presents, hoarding the ones with his name on them behind the pillows thinking we won't notice, and Dad filling everyone's glasses, making sure the wine hasn't gotten too far from the lip. We always wait until Christmas night to open presents, somehow convinced this lets the magic linger a little longer.

I am insane.

I shift my car into park, the Tim Horton's in view.

Out in the cold, the magic meets its rival. The darkness shrouds the night into one more mundane. Standing here, I'm empty, void of any thrill because my stomach is full of panic. Facing the street, a question slithers through the gloomy fog in my brain.

What if he doesn't like me?

The intruding thought slips away without hold, curling up in the bed I made for it at the back of my mind. So what if he doesn't? So what if I'm single and waiting at the side of the road in the dark to greet a guy like some kind of drug dealer? This isn't a real meet cute.

Strung around the gazebo, the colourful lights flicker in alternating patterns to give the illusion of the bulbs shifting in dance. On the surface of the cold, the night is beautiful. I do my best not to turn around and go home where Mom and Dad lay out tres leches and Raph whines he wants churros. Gathered together around the tree, they probably pass the sweet desserts that will later feed my dwindling confidence. If my Secret Santa ever shows up. Or if he never does.

I don't know which I prefer. Either option fuels the flutter in my chest, causing the nerves to overflow up my throat. I huff, and the tiny cloud lingers in front of me. I've been standing in the cold for ten minutes, but it's my fault. I'm the one who showed up early.

With families tucked comfortably in their homes, there's no one out to interrupt the soft snow from falling and gathering in my puffy hair, dissolving to make the light brown strands damp. I count the stars to ease my mind and watch as headlights approach. I perk up, wondering if the car plans to stop, wondering if it's him. But the car continues to drive off to whatever holiday plans they have. Seconds pass, and screeching tires and a horn held down with a heavy palm interrupt the stillness of the night, shattering the bit of peace I clutch tightly. I inhale and count to four to hold onto the bit of reason that convinces me to stay.

But I wait under the gazebo, the weight of the lie growing heavier in my stomach.

Honesty.

Something SS gave me that I didn't return.

The chill freezes my fingertips when I pull out my phone to open our conversation. About to tell him I'm unable to meet him, and mentally already sitting in my car and turning on my butt warmer, I do the wrong thing and scroll. Through our half-hearted banter and lame knock-knock jokes, I read the reasons why I should stay. Why he deserves a chance when I should ask him for one instead.

If I could change my answer, or rather if I could change reality, I would say that I signed up looking for a girl who liked me for me and trusted me when I told completely crazy truths like losing my phone or the sun is exploding, he had wrote.

I shake my head, remembering when he lost his phone during our twelve day window. He often texted quirky comparisons, told me about his day, sent me photos of what he was doing. One image of burnt gingerbread cookies earned him a capitalized LOL. Maybe because we have things in common, or maybe because he was a genuine, good guy, but Secret Santa paired us through an algorithm and I have to believe the codes and questions worked well enough to introduce me to a man who checks the right boxes. The New Year's gala depends on it.

Across the street, a car pulls up to the small ice cream parlour. Now closed for the season, the windows are dark and the pink-painted trim accumulates with snow. A woman slams her car door and rounds the hood. The parlour owner. It takes everything inside of me not to run after her requesting a tub of tiger tail ice cream, to resist going home and eating it by the spoonful.

A crunch breaks the silence.

Footsteps behind me interrupt my doubt. Slowly, with my lungs too scared to move, a man clears his throat to announce his presence as I turn. Masculine and deep, the sound echoes.

The secret texter I spoke with for twelve days is *approaching*.

I remember the keys in my pocket too late, the ones I'm supposed to hold between each knuckle as Jane instructed me. My heels dig in and I've run out of time. My chance to panic, question my sanity one last time, fear my safety. Oh no, *what if he's unattractive?* Not that any of this matters, my chance to bail is gone. Besides, talking to him is strictly temporary, a quick fix that needs to last until New Year's Eve.

I gulp and swallow my rationality.

Facing him, my tongue falls heavy in my mouth. He's tall— the first thing I realize only because I won no lottery with my height. In front of me, I have the chance to evaluate him. Dark brown curly hair peeps out from beneath his hat. His pointed nose is red from the cold and his broad shoulders fill his jacket, made with the kind of fabric that tapers down to his waist, showing off his slight swagger.

My breath catches as I take in his strong jaw and his chin dimple. The same chin dimple I texted Jane about a week ago. I remember because I specifically told her I wanted to stick my pinky finger up against it.

I know him.

Correction: I've *met* him.

Recognition blankets his face, slacking his sharp jaw at the same time I notice him. I can practically see our first encounter piece together as his head tilts and his brows knit. The intensity leaves tracks of goosebumps over my body. He remembers me, too.

I hadn't expected to see him again, hadn't expected fleeting niceties to make a comeback. I can't believe it. Because the same person who stuck around to help in a busy parking lot is the same guy who stayed up late texting corny jokes. *This* is insane. But then my feet do a thing I swear I don't tell them to. They try to run. To him. To the stranger.

"I'm Margo." Breathless, my introduction escapes with a side of accusation. His answering smirk dissolves my backbone instantly.

I hug him because he's earned it. That's what I tell myself when my body melts against his. When was the last time I hugged an attractive guy?

In his arms, I feel everything. His hard muscles through the light jacket, wide shoulders I wrap my arms around and dig my nails into. Over his plump bottom lip, his straight teeth beam, and everything about his amused expression is familiar. He radiates the kind of warmth that makes everything fall into place.

Leaning his forehead against mine, I peer into his dark eyes and marvel at the flecks of green. His stare blazes with a heat that mirrors the flush that creeps up my cheeks.

"Hello again, Margo. I'm Richard."

None of this is supposed to happen. I have one week to convince him to come with me to an office New Year's party. One week to convince everyone we're seriously dating.

I collect myself and remember I have a role to play. Stepping back, his dark gaze roams over me, taking me in with a full, slow sweep that leaves my face burning a deeper red.

A seductive smile curves his lips. "Shall we start our first date?"

2
Holiday Favour

This is the man I've been texting? The guy I'm meant to convince the entire firm I've been dating for *months*. The same guy my family *met*. This was not good. No, not good at all.

C'mon Margo, play it cool. You need this to work. He asked you a question.

"Yes, want to head inside?" I point to the Tim Horton's he requested to meet at.

There's some relief knowing we are only grabbing coffee because my stomach cannot handle food right now. Not when having him close keeps tangling my insides.

Last week, SS made his first appearance in my life at a tree farm. A fir had fallen out from our truck and landed on my dad in the parking lot. Stunned with horror, Mom and I feared Dad had hurt his back again, and the man in front of me now was the same person who stepped in to offer assistance. I talked to *him*. I thanked *him*.

Richard is the guy from the tree farm, the *cute* guy who rushed to help Dad when he fell.

Following Richard as he aims for the street, I fight the urge to run to my car as we pass. Ruby, my sad rusted Toyota, looks as if she's frowning with her hanging cracked bumper— courtesy of a snowbank I hit three days ago. If I'm fast enough, he may not notice my disappearance. But I don't want to leave. Not entirely.

"I made a change of plans. I hope that's okay," he says, turning to me and piercing me with a look that says he easily guesses what I'm thinking as I gaze longingly toward my car.

"No coffee?" I fight back my disappointment. At home, I refused Mom's offer when she took coffee orders, reserving stomach space and preserving my bladder for my encounter with the secret texter.

Two steps ahead, Richard has the kind of butt that reminds me he once said he played hockey. His tailored jacket and the curls brushing his collar almost make me stumble.

God, he's attractive.

"If you still want to, we can grab some after." His tone angles like a question and his amusement drops from the lines of his face, second guessing his decision to take control of our date. Regret spikes through my veins. My request to meet was last minute and he managed to string something together to surprise me.

It's our first date and I'm already failing to maintain an easy, go-with-the-flow image. One week, that's how long I require him to hang on. Then this growing ball of nerves can go away and I'll spare Richard my caffeine addiction.

"No!" The word screeches and I wince. "Wherever is fine, honestly."

"We'll grab you a coffee, I promise." He nods, reaching back for my hand. The gesture stiffens me. He must feel me tense because his grip loosens and he opts for lightly gripping my forearm, casually bringing me forward and in step with him. He releases me, but the warmth of his long fingers lingers. My skin tightens where he touched, wanting to savour and hold, but refusing to thaw into comfort.

"Where are we going?" I stare longingly after the Tim's we walk by. He tilts his head back and chuckles, and the rich sound shakes me out of my misery.

"Somewhere I think you'll enjoy," he says, confidently, his lips twitching.

His gaze hasn't left my face, intent on reading every emotion that passes. I can't remember the last time a guy paid this much attention to me, can't remember the last time a guy *cared* to. I study my boots, transfixed by the slush pushing around our feet as we near the crosswalk.

A flicker of light pulls my attention across the street. The small ice cream parlour turns a sign on in the window. *OPEN*, the flashing red and blue shouts in the dead of winter when everyone is with their families and possibly too cold to crave a chilling dessert. The timing makes no sense. Turning towards Richard to remark as much, his crooked mouth manages to hold straight, refusing to reveal what he knows, which admits he does know something.

"Did you," my mouth dries, "Tell me you somehow got them to open." There's no way. Richard called in a favour to the small parlour to open on Christmas.

"Oh, you wanted ice cream?" he asks.

I pivot towards him, fast enough to see the awkwardness leave his voice and morph into his playful grin, one I'm starting to get used to. Embarrassed I jumped to a conclusion by thinking he made a grand gesture, I'm about to apologize. Because who would go through that much effort for a first date? Instead, deep satisfaction blooms inside me at the excitement raising his brows.

"You mentioned you were craving ice cream the other day, so I decided I'd freeze my insides for you."

"How romantic." It totally was, but I'm not going to admit it. Sarcasm will do.

"If I had known it was you, I would have just saved your Dad's life last week and kept the follow-up coffee."

Unable to stop myself, I laugh, and my breath shoots out along with it. I'm always craving ice cream. He remembered and I'm right, he somehow got the small parlour to open. Something warm thumps in my chest. A quick, hard flop that reminds me my heart is listening.

I hear Jane's voice in my mind asking, *is that so bad?*

Yes. Yes, it is.

People hurt you when you let them in, and I refuse to be the person forgotten when someone better comes along because someone better always does. There are 2.9 million people in Toronto, and if this man decides to expand his radius, I'm up against more. Secret Santa matchmaking was a pairing of interests and values, but if Richard was able to sort based on appearance, and flip through a catalogue of women how most dating apps function, I'm not sure he would pick me.

When we first started texting, I asked why Richard signed up for a twelve-day anonymous dating service, and after a few days, he admitted he hadn't. Someone signed him up for a prank. He might not have considered his dating possibilities. Or maybe he was already checking other apps daily.

My stomach tangled into too many knots for me to ask any specifics but with raised brows and a glare that was just so *Jane*, my best friend reminded me I had my own motives for signing up. It was Aubrey, her girlfriend, who said if he gave the service a chance, I should too. He did tell me the truth, and that's around the time my shell first showed signs of softening.

Learning he didn't sign up on a quest for love did raise some alarm. Probably overwhelmed with his guilt, he confessed, and I stared at my phone with blame of my own. But I stayed strong and gave him a chance when I normally would have thrown in the towel. I stuck to the calendar that counted down to our first meeting, and the knots that leashed my heart fell loose to my feet during the late hours we spent texting back and forth. A spin-off game of twenty questions saved me from awkward small talk and let me meet the secret texter on the other side. A man who seemed genuine in getting to know me.

After all, I am the one with the twisted motives. And I owe him my own confession.

I have my friends, my job, rhythm. Single by choice is a distinction I make whenever Aubrey asks why I don't download a dating app myself or when Jane stares off into the distance as soon as her girlfriend leaves a room, lost and a little wistful. Seeing them together, they are enough to make anyone question their single status.

But choosing to stay alone is safe, comfortable, and reliable. Richard is a possibility. If he agrees to come as my date on New Year's, I'll have succeeded in convincing everyone I'm fine, my whole life doesn't revolve around deadlines. Whatever comes after the gala, I'll handle it. I've been through worse.

One day at a time.

"There's only one rule," he pulls me from my thoughts, his gaze is intense on mine as if he somehow reads my internal discussion.

"Please don't tell me this is where you ask me not to fall in love with you." I cross my arms over my puffed chest.

"Hell no, please do." His dark eyes glint and half his mouth lifts upward. My insides are no match for him, and whatever he melts them to, sends colour straight to my ears.

What's going on with me? When was the last time I blushed this much?

"I was about to say, you have to pick what flavour I'm getting."

Damn him for making me smile. "You're totally on."

His jacket strains as he holds open the door for me, and I take in the wide span of his shoulders. With a leg perched on the stoop, he stands taller. His towering frame bends low as I pass, close enough that his breath is on my ear. I shiver. Whatever tickles my spine is different from the chill that fills the parlour from the running fridges.

"No peppermint." His voice is pitched low like a shared joke, somehow making the familiarity of texting him seem intimate. Richard prefers fruity candy canes and basic coffee, but he accepted my recommendation and he tried a peppermint mocha. I hadn't heard any complaints.

The parlour is a simple takeout single-window storefront, the space smaller than my bedroom and not large enough to put distance between myself and Richard. So close, he stands behind me like a heater against my back. If I close my eyes, I imagine how his chest rises and falls, almost touching me. Facing the menu, I repeat the names of the flavours in my mind.

Reindeer Tracks, Rocky Road, Maple Praline.

I struggle to concentrate. Richard looms behind me, sparks shooting off him and piercing through my back right through my torso.

He clears his throat, a deep grunt releasing with a growl that scratches along my insides, coaxing me to turn. My knees lock, and I force my focus to stay on the menu, ignoring the way the air seems to charge and the sweat collecting beneath my hat. My lungs fight for an even rhythm, but my pulse runs.

Get a grip.

Crinkling plastic echoes as footsteps shuffle, reminding us there's someone in the back. And yes, Richard is attractive, but we're not alone.

And if we were?

I push the thought out of my head. I just met him. Or re-met him, I suppose.

"Margo." His voice is like velvet, muted and throaty, making my toes curl. I want to wrap myself in it.

Unprepared for when I turn around, he stands as near as my climbing hormones imagined. My breath catches in my throat. His hands are in his jeans, but he leans, bringing his face closer to mine. From my pom-pom hat to my wet boots, his gaze takes me in with a slow crawl that seems to touch my bare skin beneath my layered jacket. A dark shadow flashes across his face, and he rolls his lips inward. His mouth looks soft. I trail my tongue over my bottom lip and he moves closer, tempting me to meet his gaze.

Oh crap, he saw me do that.

"Hello! You're here! I'm so sorry, I had to reconnect the WiFi to get the store online." A small woman rushes from the back, tying a knot on her apron behind her. "What may I get for you?"

We spring apart, or rather, I do. Richard straightens, and his brows scrunch. The weight of his gaze lands on the back of my head as I step towards the glass to read the flavours for what I assume is the tenth time.

With forced calm, I bend closer to the window. "I'll take a single scoop of tiger tail in a cup. And for him," I turn around and put my hands on my hips, hoping to appear more intimidating to hide my nerves. "Cover your ears, this is a surprise and I want the full reveal when you have the first bite."

Richard shows me his palms, raised in front of him before lifting them to dramatically cover his ears. He closes his eyes and I do my best to ignore how his long lashes brush against his cheekbones. I swallow.

"He is going to have one scoop of this and a second scoop of this one, in a cup please." I don't trust Richard enough not to eavesdrop, so I thump my index finger against the glass. The lady smiles patiently, amused by our methods of flirting.

Two cups are placed on the counter, and I reach for them quickly before Richard glimpses the flavours I picked. I bump his arm and his stare easily locates the spot where I nudged him. His hands dig inside his jacket pocket, and revealing his wallet, he places a large bill on the counter.

"Let me grab you some change," the lady flusters, putting down the debit machine, unprepared to handle cash.

"No, that's not necessary. You came here tonight to help me." He clears his throat, growing uncomfortable by the lady's awe. "I appreciate it."

"This is too generous." Richard steps further away from the bill she holds out to him. After some debate, and not having any change to break the amount, she eventually concedes to his offer. "Have a wonderful evening, and thank you." She glances towards me, sharing an encouraging nod as if to say, *he's a good one.*

That's what I'm worried about.

Once outside, the cold cups pierce through my mitts. Maybe ice cream in the winter isn't ideal, but man does it taste good. Trying to hide the flavours I picked for him, I reject his reach for the second cup.

"Let me hold one before you lose your fingers to frostbite." He lunges but I dodge his efforts with my shoulder. And I won't analyze the spot where his breath is warm on my neck.

"False. They will remain attached until I tell them otherwise." His fights a laugh.

"Would you want to sit in the car?" Realizing how the question sounds, he squints across the street. How can he act confident in one beat and unsure in the next?

"A place where my frozen face will defrost so I can eat? Obviously, I'm in." I already head towards the parking lot.

"Obviously." He repeats, amused, his voice is like warm sheets rubbed over my body.

Get a grip.

Richard is easygoing. He enjoys simple coffee orders, spending time with his friends, and outdoor winter sports most people would complain about after an hour like hockey, tobogganing, and I wouldn't put it past him if he snowboarded.

At the tree farm, I had nothing to go on. He was impossible to track down on social media and I'd be lying if I said I didn't try to find him afterwards. Turns out, searching 'cute guy with curly hair' doesn't return the same results on Instagram the way Google would offer a catalogue of eligible men. Too ashamed to tell Jane I tried to search for the man who helped Dad after his fall, I only mentioned the incident to her in passing, but I might have gone into detail about his good looks.

Richard was my secret. It's not as if I expected to see him again. No, I thought he was one of the many occurrences of a cute guy in my life that I would eventually forget about months later. Except, days passed and here he is. Here he's always been.

I had no description, no picture to reference the guy I talked to when I came here to meet him. Only the location and time. The good-looking guy at the tree farm had no place to fester in my mind because if I told myself fate would bring us together again, then that would mean tonight meant something bigger than an online dating service and a weird coincidence. But Richard strutting towards me had caused my heart to leap and fumble, and even now, walking in front of him, I still haven't managed to pick it back up.

Seeing Richard sparked instant familiarity, a static connection that called me to him, and holds a charge that tugs and pulls at my chest while he shuffles behind me. I'm happy I hold the two ice cream cups. I don't think I'd survive the warmth of his hand in mine again, even if the slip hadn't lasted a full second.

"I'm over here," Richard says. His voice is rough from misuse as if we haven't talked for hours rather than minutes. A silver car flashes its lights, signalling me where to go.

"Let me grab the door." He meets me on my side of the car and pulls at the handle, his shoulders angle towards me and I almost step forward to put myself between his arms.

He closes me inside once my boots clear the threshold. I'm alone, huffing cold clouds of moisture for the span of time it takes him to round the hood of the car and slide in next to me. Fumbling the keys to start the engine, Richard recovers the slip along with his confidence. The car rumbles to life and I force myself to relax in the seat, welcoming the leftover warmth spewing from the vents with the scent of pine air freshener.

"There's a butt warmer," Richard offers, reaching at the same time I move to hit the button with my knuckle. His fingertips brush the back of my hand, flaring along my skin. I pull away, again struck by the lingering sensation still dancing along the spot he touched. His throat bobs and I wonder if it's for the same reason.

"Thanks, my butt appreciates it," I say, forgetting to engage my verbal filter.

He laughs, and the rich sound hits me from all angles, making the car suddenly feel too small. Aware he's watching me, the ice cream mushed at the end of the spoon is suddenly more fascinating. I turn my cup as if another angle will make a difference for my line of attack. The rather large single scoop of orange ice cream with black licorice remains half-frozen, and I steal a lick where it started to lean. He looks away and clears his throat.

"What flavours did you get me?" He nods his chin towards the scoop of green and brown that pile above the cup rim, very clearly not the one I licked.

I rest my ice cream on the dash to free a hand. A new idea forms in my head. "No peeking, you have to guess!" Why does this excite me?

"Are they standard flavours? How am I supposed to guess a flavour that isn't vanilla, chocolate, or strawberry?" His eyes light up with interest, and humour tugs at the corners of his lips.

"Where would the challenge be in that? Don't worry, they're not uncommon." If I'm being honest, maybe this is a little lame, but we need an ice breaker and it's either this or more knock-knock jokes. "C'mon, are you worried your tastebuds are that terrible?"

"I'm worried you're about to find out how boring I am." He analyzes the ice cream and I give him my back, hiding the test from the cheating student.

"No cheating!" I glare at him over my shoulder. The rest of me faces the door.

"And if I get them wrong?"

"I'll leave this car and make a recommendation that ice cream preference should be on the dating questionnaire." I give him an innocent shrug and his brows scrunch. Rubbing his chin, he loses himself to a thought.

Right, Richard didn't fill out his questionnaire, someone else did for him. A confession I shouldn't let myself forget.

"Alright," he says, and it sounds more like he's convincing himself instead of me. "If I get them wrong, you're not leaving this car. You are here to expand my ice cream horizon and also to tell me why you chose that neon orange blob you're eating."

He nods to my melting scoop of tiger tail and I give him my best winning smile.

"Deal."

The heat in the car blares, reminding me outside is winter and letting my melting ice cream forget it. Leaning back relaxed, Richard waves for me to proceed. I gulp. Plucking out the small plastic spoon, I scrape a bit of the green remembering it's his favourite colour. I'm suddenly nervous I picked flavours he's going to hate.

Facing him, I lift the spoon for him to grab the bite, but he leans forward. Keeping his eyes on me, he opens his mouth, slowly accepting my offer. His tongue lays flat beneath the spoon, and closing his mouth around the tip of his tongue, he pulls back. He doesn't look away as he trails a slow lick over his bottom lip. I squeeze my thighs together.

"Pistachio," he announces confidently.

"Yeah." I clear my throat. "Yes."

"The colour helped," he jokes.

Shaking my head, I clear the memory of him accepting the green spoonful. "Round two."

I repeat the motions I did before, but this time I scoop some of the cappuccino flavour. I hold the spoon a little closer, ready to examine how his mouth moves. He purses his lips, letting his tongue swirl around to determine the taste. My own tongue anticipates the flavour, and I lean closer. Calculating the space between us, his pupils widen at the slight shift and the voice inside me roars that I back away.

The air blowing from the vents is thick and dries my throat. Suddenly, the car is too hot. I untie my scarf and unzip my jacket. I don't miss the way his eyes fall to my chest. The warning to move away dies with the burst of satisfaction pumping through me. Feeling bold, I use his spoon to sample my own ice cream taking my time to lick it clean, aware he tracks the movement. The reasonable Margo screams in my head, reminding me why this is a bad idea, but the fuck-it Margo remembers how long it's been since I've been laid.

We sit in silence for a pulse. One pulse beat to remind me why I'm here. I need a date for the company gala. Showing up alone isn't an option. Not again, not this time.

I abandon the spoon, pinning it in his cup on my lap, and do my best at nonchalance when I ask, "So, no plans tonight?"

Accepting the tension intermission, Richard reaches for the cup of ice cream, careful to grab it from me without touching my skin. The barely-there brush of his thumb on the inside of my thigh sends a shiver down my spine.

"Thankfully, no." He runs the spoon over both flavours, mixing the green and brown for his next bite. I turn away when he lifts it to his mouth.

Aware of his compliment, I follow his lead and focus on my cup.

"What about you?" he asks.

"I'm missing my brother open all of the presents. Him claiming everyone's gifts for himself is kind of our tradition." I'm not sure why I shared more than a yes or no answer, but he waits with his dark eyes on my face encouraging me to keep going. "It started when he was small and my Abuela passed away. He was excited to tear the wrapped gifts open and pluck out the tissue paper. No one had the heart to stop him. His excitement was contagious and we all needed some cheering up." That year, Mom and Dad decided not to put up a Christmas tree, but we still agreed to buy each other gifts. Raph hadn't understood why our house didn't have lights like all of our neighbours.

"Your brother, Raphael, right?" He tilts his head, frowning. Regret floods his expression. "You didn't have to miss an evening with your family. We could have met up another time."

"Yes, Raphael. You remember his name," I say, surprised. At the tree farm, Richard gave my brother a candy cane and told some elaborate tale about a snow elf. The story was absolutely terrible, but he lowered himself to my brother's height, intently stared at him as if he could will Raph's sadness away. That was when I first noticed the dimple on his chin.

"Of course." Richard falls silent, and the frown still hasn't left the crease between his brows.

Uncertainty pinches my chest, and I wonder if he notices I have no answer for the rest of what he said. He's not wrong, I didn't have to miss Christmas with my family, but the text from Harvey is safely tucked in my pocket. We lapse into comfortable silence, but I decide I want him to keep talking.

"What happened to all your jokes?" I tease.

"Well, I can't Google them in front of you."

I slam back against the seat and bark a laugh. Satisfaction blooms on Richard's face. Of course, he texted me corny jokes he searched, I did the same after I used up the one Raph told me he heard in school.

"May I?" He points his spoon towards my deflating ice cream. Holding out my cup to let him taste the liquid scoop, I wait for his verdict. "That's," he swallows, "Disgusting. What is that? Black licorice? Who willingly eats that stuff?"

I shove his shoulder and he catches my hand, but I wiggle free from my mitt. With the cotton carcass dangling, he throws it at me playfully. He snickers.

"Tell me about your family, what do they do for Christmas?" I ask.

Richard's parents moved to Florida a few years ago, finally calling it quits against Canadian winters. His brother bought their parent's house where Richard rents the basement. He shows me a photo of him and what looks like a younger version of him by a few years, sitting in front of a tree. Their faces crinkle with laughter and the candid of Richard in a Santa hat does something to my insides.

He needs to stop being cute.

An hour goes by too fast, and my buzzing phone pulls me back to the time. Mom texts wondering when I'll come home from the office, I told her I'd make a quick trip, and now she's putting Raph to bed. As much as I want to sit here and get to know Richard, the night is getting late. I should ask him if he has plans for New Year's and set the date to get this over with, but my gaze flicks to his.

Sure he's attractive, but he's not the stranger I expected. Good looks are easily dodged, but Richard is patient and he isn't put off whenever I pull away. He isn't pushy, he doesn't talk about himself the whole time, he makes an effort, and somehow, the conversation transcending out of the screen softens me further. This isn't someone who'd agree to meet me for the second time at a party without a follow-up. He'll see through me, and rushing things with him will leave an impression I'm unsure I want him to have of me. The concept of securing a meaningless date for New Year's is jarring compared to the ease of tonight.

I worry I'm the one in danger of not letting go after New Year's, but that doesn't stop me from saying, "When I see you again, I'll pick harder flavours for you to guess."

"I'm seeing you again?" He scratches the short hairs of his beard, hiding his chin dimple.

"Oh." Had I misunderstood the evening?

Maybe the conversation was too easy, too familiar because we already met. The kind of comfort that transpires between friends and his willingness not to push because he doesn't see me as more. Richard didn't sign up for dating, and bumping into a girl he already shared an encounter with is a great excuse to say he tried to see what was out there and it ended up being what he already knew. Uneventful and disappointing, no reason to pursue further.

I face forward, turning my nose up to hide my disappointment.

"Tomorrow is not good for me, but how about Tuesday?" He leans. His forearm rests on the centre console, a wicked grin turning up his full lips.

My muscles relax with relief.

Oh yes, this was bad.

3

Unannounced Guests

Taking the elevator up to the twelfth floor, I rehearse the speech I prepared in bed when the minutes ticked well beyond midnight.

The windows on the large grey building are checkered in even increments, separating the business levels from the lower foyer. It comes as no surprise when the elevator doors open to the dull reception area of Lauder Accounting. The advantage of being on the top floor of the short high-rise is the view, opening the cubicle common area with a strip of windows spanning over the city.

I keep my head down on my way to the back hall, for once not entering the room with a purpose or a deadline. The faster I close myself in my office, the faster I can release my building groan.

A soft breath caressing my neck in a small, dark-lit

room. A spark against my knuckles where long, narrow fingers accidentally brush.

My date with Richard replays in my head over and over, somehow still able to jolt through me while I source the bit of fear that pricks in my chest. I want to text Richard, ask him about what he did when he got home and what he plans to do today, but those are the sorts of things someone would ask another person they are interested in, and I'm not into Richard. Right?

He hadn't asked me for a second date until I accidentally let the notion slip. Not that I gave him a chance, but the night came to an end and the conversation loomed at its edge. It wasn't as if he didn't have an opening.

Jane will want to know how last night went, and I haven't decided if I should tell her all the unrepressed details. My two-year dry spell hasn't been all that entertaining for her love of gossip, but if finding a release was my goal I'm sure I'd find a lot wilder candidates. Not men who open ice cream parlours and blindly eat whatever sludge I scoop into their mouths.

I conclude last night really was a date.

Despite how I've gone about finding someone to attend the firm's New Year's party, Richard agreed to meet me. And I had a great time. That's the feeling that stiffened my joints this morning. I woke up happy. Then fear had a way of immediately slamming into me, rocking me off course.

Back and forth, I'm no closer to a conclusion.

Just one week and then this will be over.

My heart flops with the false bravado I feed myself on an empty stomach. Maybe it's not that I'm tricking Richard. We just started on the wrong foot is all. Many people go on a few dates and then disappear.

Okay, but what if last night was a real first date?

I don't know how to do this.

Overwhelmed, I want to cry but all I do is stare at the grey tile runway leading to my office. I'm a dried-up well but something inside me is left unsettled, threatening to overflow. The lid I jammed on my emotions whistles under the tension. I refuse to let Richard distract me. The smile I woke up with, for the split second when I remembered the intensity of his gaze, had hit me like a warning flare luring me off the road, away from the route I already mapped. I swaddle the burning happiness with layers of contempt.

Focus on work, focus on the deadline, and whatever I do, keep my distance from Richard Vixen.

"Hey, Margo. How did last night go?" Bianca, the Junior Accountant I trained in the spring, calls from her desk and my whole body twitches. Wrapped up in my mind, I almost don't see her.

I adjust my grip on my leather laptop case as it slips against the water-repellent material of my jacket. I frown at my hands like they're the last straw, the last bit of annoyance I can take. Whoever designed this Tiffany-blue bag had not tested it with winter clothes. Clenching my jaw, I bite back on life's inconveniences and force my voice to sound cheery.

"Everything went great! Thanks for asking!" I walk faster, my short heels striking the ceramic tiles.

"Can't wait to hear more details about what your parents thought of him. Want to grab lunch?" Unaware I attempt to retreat, she rolls out her chair to keep me in sight. I do my best to look convincing when I smack my head, which is hard to do with expensive technology and a purse in my arms.

"I have a doctor's appointment today," I say as if I just remembered.

"I didn't think the doctor's office opened today." She clicks on her monitor as if verifying today is, in fact, a stat holiday.

"Yes, it's a specialist appointment. Hard to get into." I squint across the long hall of empty desks and let my sentence trail as I move further away from her. Accepting my distraction, she doesn't push more questions. "We'll catch up later. I want to hear all about your holidays!" I call over my shoulder, and my guilt isn't an act.

It's not that I don't like Bianca. She's sweet, smells like raspberry and vanilla, and she's one of the hardest-working accountants at the firm. She probably picks up more hours than most of the senior staff. But, I really don't want to spend my lunch feeding into the lie she had overheard and then helped spread like wildfire.

Richard and I met yesterday, but to everyone else, we've been dating for months. And to Bianca, he met my family last night. The day she found out I was dating, she cornered me in the women's bathroom and squealed she wanted to know all the details. Determined to keep our friendship closer than coworkers, Bianca managed to squeeze out some information. I didn't dare give her a name, I didn't have one, but in saying things weren't serious yet, she asked me if he would meet my family over Christmas. Her big blue eyes were hard to disappoint. Hence, the growing layers to my false love life.

At least part of the lie was kind of true, he did meet my family once. And with the promise of hanging out tomorrow, we are going on dates.

Jane. I need to find Jane.

Not everyone wants to earn overtime, and I'm relieved most of the office is empty. Throwing down my bags and fighting with my jacket, I'm free from the down-filled web and the scarf that causes my hair to static and stick to my cheeks. Hooking up my laptop to the dock and powering on the monitor, I type out a text to Jane.

Mon, Dec 26

Margo Diaz: In the office today?

8:49 am

I pound my keyboard, spelling out the month my parents eloped, the digits of both Raph's and my birthday, the acronym of our families initials in capitals, and ending with an exclamation point. My password takes me into my home screen.

I've been working at the firm for almost ten years and I still haven't gotten around to changing the screensaver. Scrolling down the unread emails, thirty new ones from last night, I click the one marked red for urgent. Two more clicks and I'm reading Harvey's request for a morning *powwow*. I hate how he calls meetings that. He attempts to sound welcoming and young. He could use an edge of nicety, but the same edge morphs into his hard demeanour. Apart from his permanent glower, his sentences always sound chewed and spit out. It doesn't help that Harvey refuses to send meeting requests, not caring about anyone else's schedule because he takes priority. I grab my binder.

Shoving away from my desk, my chair wheels roll over my draped scarf. I huff, forcing the wool free from the plastic tires. Entangled by static and heavy clothes, I glance back at the stock images cycling as my screensaver. A warm beach and palm trees taunt me. I miss Mexico. Maybe one day I'll visit again.

Down the hall past Bianca, who to my relief is on a phone call, I turn the corner and head towards the executive suite. Sheryl, Harvey's receptionist, speaks into a low mic when she sees me. After a short whispered conversation, she signals me in. I offer my thanks and smooth my hair.

Following the route to the familiar cushioned armchair reserved for one-on-one meetings, I pause in the doorway when I discover it occupied. There, in obnoxious dress pants hitched above his ankles, sits Tristan. I collect my dripping expression easily, and that's when I notice the reason for his presence. In the seat next to him sits Logan Hymn, our biggest client and who Lauder Accounting is in negotiations with to finalize a buyout. Hyup Media will expand the firm's qualifications for campaign budgets and predictions. Most of our clients are marketing agencies who outsource us for their contract approvals and month to year end reports. Harvey is smart to expand our services. By acquiring Hyup, we will grow. I just wish Tristan wasn't part of the negotiations, but I suppose the Sales and Marketing Director is relevant.

Lounging in the second chair, Logan shoots me a leer that might have been unnerving if he wasn't in his early forties with dyed blond hair and a spray tan. At least he acknowledges me. The same can't be said for the back of Tristan's head.

I know he hears my entrance, and Harvey is gracious enough to glance in my direction from behind his large desk. They don't halt their conversation for my benefit. Tristan wheezes a sound I recognize as his forced laugh and Logan slaps his knee. There's debate about an unfair goal, mention of a score, and praise for a last name attached to some highlight. After another minute of me standing in the doorway, Harvey ends Logan's rant with the tap of his pen. He pushes back his salt and pepper hair like he might be the retired hockey player they mention. To be honest, I'd consider him good-looking for his age if he wasn't so damn intimidating.

"Glad you could join us, Miss Diaz." Logan shares little pleasure. He talks without looking at me and I bite down the retort that if I knew of the meeting, I'd have come on time, but he's too busy beaming at Tristan like he's some kind of marketing prodigy and an answer to the company buyout.

I place my binder on the desk in the middle of the three men. Moving to grab the chair pushed aside to the corner, I make no effort to hide my awkwardness as I struggle to drag it against the carpeted floor. Bending my knees and shoving from the backrest, I turn around and adjust my grip and heave. The three men watch me but don't move to help. Funny how female power enters the room with heavy lifting but no one halts the discussion of sports long enough to say hello.

"What's the purpose of today's meeting?" I beat right to the point, folding myself into the seat I purposely placed between Tristan and Logan. Staring dead centre at Harvey, I retrieve my notes.

The chair refuses to yield against my weight, and the cushion pushes stiffly into my lower back, but I recline casually as if I am born to sit here and this chair is my birthright. Tristan may succeed at sports talk, but he struggles to communicate employment structure and business goals.

"Powwow," Harvey corrects.

"Yes, the powwow." I nod. Tristan smirks next to me and I do my best to keep my expression neutral.

"Mr. Hymn stopped by this morning and wanted an update on the event details. I admit, I haven't been strict on the requirements. A brief rundown will suffice. I assume the budget has been sorted for the gala?" Harvey is quick to abandon the excitement of the earlier sports talk. He falls into his familiar charge, ready to hammer out numbers with me. A brainstorming flow we've spent a lot of time perfecting since he took me on as an intern in my first year of university.

"Yes, the numbers are well within budget." I slide him the loose page listing expense breakdowns, including costs of the buffet, lighting and audio, plus the hired DJ who threw in an extra hour after midnight.

Observing him, I wait for any flicker of disapproval. Because the event falls on New Year's, the rates are doubled, but Harvey expected this and set aside a hefty budget. Hyup is our biggest client, New Year's is a chance for Harvey to flash his success and to finally close negotiations.

Last week, a memo had been sent out to all employees at Lauder Accounting to announce the buyout. Harvey held a private meeting with Tristan and me to discuss the numbers, but to the rest of the company, he announced the news with confidence.

Tristan leans forward, and for a split second, I wonder how everything would play out if I spoke my mind. *Why are you here, exactly?* I'd ask. Make *him* feel out of place for a change.

He frowns at the spreadsheet I prepared and I wonder how he reads upside-down.

"What's the theme?" Tristan asks with a *tsk*. I grind my molars.

"Theme?" Harvey asks. Tristan catches the two CEO's interest and Logan tilts forward to peer at the paper for answers. If I thought Logan cared enough about the cost of the gala we were throwing him, I would have snatched the sheet right from under all three of their chins.

"Yes, I don't think Margo has announced any theme for the gala?" Tristan turns to me, and I force myself to look at his long boring head, his Owen Wilson nose I once thought gave him character.

Harvey turns to me, crossing his hands on his desk. Logan's attention is on my face. Hyup Media would love the idea of a marketable party theme.

"Does New Year's need a theme? You're celebrating hope for the next year and forgetting the resolutions you failed," I say. My boss frowns at me, unimpressed by my dry joke.

"We want to inspire Hyup." Tristan forgets me. Perching himself at the edge of his seat, he dares to throw out ideas for party themes.

I scowl. He discusses the plans for our New Year's gala in front of Logan to insert himself and prove his value over mine. The task Tristan rejected now catches his attention. It didn't take him long to notice the advantage it'll give me against him for the promotion.

When Harvey first announced the prospect of a New Year's party one month ago, no one volunteered. After a half-hearted speech about recognizing how his young staff may have families and significant others, Harvey offered expenses for babysitters and extended invites for everyone to have a plus one. It's not like I had plans anyway. I'd invite Jane who would then bring Aubrey, and I'd have no problem fitting myself into their slow dance.

But then Harvey called Tristan and me into his office and explained how the company is implementing some big changes in the new year and he relied on us to show our leadership skills, disclosing that we both ran against each other for a promotion. The New Year's party was important, we had to impress Hyup, and this was an opportunity to step up. I stared at the creases wrinkling my boss's forehead, reading through his intimidation and recognizing his desperation.

Before I could remind Harvey of the stack of files he left on my desk, Tristan announced the month wasn't good for him. Oh no, I wasn't getting stuck with the party planning, but I had been too cocky when I reminded him everyone has year-end reports and holiday stress. Tristan lost his usual confidence, the slip lasted only a second but was enough for me to catch.

Like an idiot I stood straighter, readying myself in front of Harvey as he contemplated his two best employees for the promotion. That was before Tristan stiffened his back and announced why his month was busy.

"I'm planning to propose so I'm a little busy, but Margo is single. She can help." Tristan laughed, the airy sound grating beneath my skin.

He was planning his engagement to Stacey. *Stacey with the perm.* At first, I thought the mention of his *proposal of marriage* was an excuse to get out of party planning, but the room slowed as I watched Harvey pat Tristan's back and shake his hand the way men gripped too hard with excitement. Married. *He planned to marry Stacey.*

Without thinking, I stepped forward. Evil-Margo spoke before I could stop her.

"Actually, I'm not single. I have a boyfriend." My voice bit, taking me and the two men off guard. Pulling away from Harvey, the lie already snagged Tristan's sneer as if he expected my defence was fake.

"Oh, really?" Tristan feigned interest.

"Well, we can't wait to meet him at the party. Mark yourself down for a plus one," said Harvey.

I still couldn't figure out why I said what I did and dread dripped cold in my veins when Stacey loudly announced she heard from Tristan I had a boyfriend. With shrill excitement, she approached me in the copy room. Whether her performance was to clear her name or let everyone in the office know everything worked out for the mistress and the ex, her motive cemented the lie.

Somehow, in my shock, it was decided I'd become the party planner.

Tristan promised he wouldn't interfere with the planning, but as the month ticked by, his suggestions grated against my skull and I checked the washroom mirror to make sure my teeth weren't ground smooth.

First came the daily requests for an update on whether I found a venue, then the reminders about the budget. Even though he wasn't in charge, he asked me for updates as if I was his hired assistant rather than his opposition who managed a project he was too busy to do himself.

Almost a month into planning, Tristan asked me at our Christmas office luncheon, "Is there peanut-free dessert?" He reminded me he was allergic as if I didn't remember from the number of times we picked up brownies from the local bakery that specifically baked without peanuts, dairy, and egg. No, Tristan raised the question in front of everyone to doubt my ability to lead. Not only did Harvey frown, not having thought of allergy restrictions himself, he assumed I had the same oversight as well.

An engagement doesn't require a month to plan, anyway. How hard is it to ask a question? Not that I had any experience. There was one time I thought I might get asked the grand question, but then she happened. *Stacey.*

Her fake curls and voice seemed too loud, too happy for a Human Resources cubicle desk. Tristan was in charge of training her. Late evenings, confused emails at night, urgent phone calls on the weekend. I should have known.

His apology meant about as much as the fallen lettuce out of a Big Mac. There was no point in picking up the leftover pieces and trying to shove them back into our lives. Our five-year relationship was done, and the worst part was the entire office knew what happened. Two years later, people got over the drama. The changeover of staff helped with fresh faces not around to experience the two weeks I chose to work hybrid then the months that followed where my hair was unwashed and I swam in my clothes. Then Jane cornered me in the lobby washroom. A lawyer on the third floor and a stranger who didn't know she'd become my best friend, the glue to the pieces of me that were left behind. I was better than a scandal, better than Tristan.

Since the announcement of the promotion, I poured myself deeper into work. The promotion will determine which one of us will lead the team during the transition months and come with the title of Chief Financial Officer and the promise of a raise.

At first, when I graduated, I found a studio apartment near Lauder Accounting. The Murphy bed and single closet fit perfectly into the professional image I dreamed of for myself. Tristan and I planned to share the small space when I eventually built the nerve to tell my parents he would co-sign at the renewal. We broke up one month before then. Probably about the time when Tristan realized he had to pull through on his empty promises and actually commit. Suddenly, the small apartment felt too stifling and I moved back into my childhood bedroom.

"The theme is Old Hollywood." I bring myself back to the present, and slowly the idea unfolds. What place has more scandals than an office romance turned sour by a mistress?

"Old Hollywood?" Harvey repeats, pondering aloud.

"Interesting," Logan echoes.

Fur scarves, glitter decor, large drapes, awards. The vision takes hold.

"Yes, gold and black are always classic for New Year's. Why not make it a little fun? It doesn't require a full costume, not anything fancier than a nice dress and suit people most likely have in their closet." Already the red sequin dress in my own closet comes to mind.

"Alright, I'll let you run with this." Harvey agrees after some thought. Tristan's mouth opens to defend his list of themes, but then he makes the right decision and clamps it shut.

Distracted by the phone on his desk, now ringing for his attention, Harvey waves us off. "Let me know if you need anything else from my end. Logan this will last only a moment if you'll excuse me." His half-hearted offer is appreciated, though we both know I have no intention of requesting any help.

Tristan waits at the door, holding it open. He could have just headed out first to save me from having to thank him. Logan is more appreciative than I am and he offers a bow before retreating down the hall. With his coat draped over his briefcase, his cream suit is out of place against the overcast sky accumulating on the other side of the large windows.

"Old Hollywood, nice one." Tristan smiles towards Sheryl and I fight the urge to hold my finger to my tongue and gag.

"No thanks to you. Why do we require a theme?" I hiss, but he stops me from turning the corner. The building is empty save for those trying to collect extra hours before the end of the year. I count three bent heads.

"Every party has a theme." How dare he look at me as if I hurt his feelings when he just set me up for an ambush?

I glare at where he grips my forearm and he quickly pulls away. I don't know why I look at his bare ring finger. He's the one who proposed over Christmas, he wouldn't wear a ring. No, that's for when he's *married*.

"Yes, well you were too busy to help plan. Therefore, you have no say." I turn the corner, not really caring if he follows or not. Our offices are across the cubicle area from each other, but luckily mine is first. Inside, I kick my door shut behind me. It was just a nudge, and to my disappointment it closes with a soft *click*. It would have felt amazing to let it slam.

For the second time this morning, I am surprised to see my seat occupied. But unlike the unforeseen welcome in Harvey's office, the person who sits behind my desk with her heels almost touching my keyboard is someone I desperately need to see.

"Oh thank God." I flop in the armchair reserved for clients and hang my head off the back.

Jane kicks her feet, letting them drop to the ground to crawl the chair closer to the desk. She perches taller and absentmindedly fidgets with her septum piercing. The twelfth floor is used to the appearance of my black-clad friend. On most days, she rides the elevator up to eat lunch while I click my fingers over my keyboard and sign documents. If I'm honest, I think her visits are her way of making sure I feed myself.

"That's not the reaction I'd expect from someone who had a good date. Was he awful? Wait, was he *old*?"

"What? No, the date was good." I completely forgot about the thrill of last night. The debriefing ruined my morning mood. Wait. Did I just label meeting Richard as a date out loud?

"Harvey requested updates about New Year's and Tristan had to put me on the spot, again." I steer clear of all things Richard and focus on the most pressing problem.

Her low exhale comes out as a whistle. "What happened?"

I summarize how I showed up to the meeting to find Tristan and Logan already there, the guys' exchange of sports talk, and how my budget update turned into me having to wing a party theme. Jane watches with her hands clasped beneath her pointed chin. Her black eyeliner narrows her disappointment into slits. And though we both keep our responses professional, I remember she's the one who helped me burn Tristan's office shirts during a summer bonfire.

"Old Hollywood is a good idea. I have a gold satin dress I'm dying to wear." She shows me her palms, knowing exactly what I am about to ask. "Fine. I just bought it, and I already planned on wearing it to the gala." I snicker.

"Aubrey can design the e-invites and we can email them out as a reminder and put up a poster in the staffroom. Even if someone misses the update, whatever dress they wear will go with the theme, like you said," Jane continues, and for a second she's lost in thought. "Maybe we can get some extra boas for a photo booth. We should have a photo booth."

We.

God, I love her.

"Are you sure Aubrey isn't too busy?" Not wanting to take advantage of their help, I can't deny her girlfriend has amazing graphic and computer design skills that will bring the theme to life.

"Oh, she's fine. She misses the creative element of what she does ever since she took the job as a web developer. I tried to tell her money wasn't a strong enough motivator if it meant straining your eyeballs staring at robot language." Jane waves off the hope of reasoning with her girlfriend.

"I look at Excels all day." I raise a brow. She shrugs, not seeing my point. To her, numbers are a common dialect of robot tongue.

"Anyway, tell me about your date." She bounces where she sits and I return the same enthusiasm.

"Richard," I blurt. And before she asks anything, I dive back in. "The guy from the tree farm last week, his name is Richard."

"Okay and how did you figure this out? Did you somehow run into him again? No! Tell me secret texter guy is tree farm guy?" I'm pretty sure her eyes are the widest I've ever seen them.

"Yes! I still can't believe it. And Jane, he's even better looking in front of my face." I melt further into the armchair.

"Details. Now."

From his adorable curls to our ice cream guessing experience to the open-ended suggestion I'll see him again tomorrow, I spill it all. I'm unable to hold back. The last time I was excited about a man was well, when I dated Tristan, but even then I wouldn't say I gushed about him. He was familiar, and we clicked the way kids who went to high school together then slid into one's Direct Messages often did.

I don't tell Jane about the spark that tickled my skin wherever Richard touched. No, that secret detail is for me. And I'm determined to figure out what it means.

"Do you think he'll want to come to the New Year's party?" she asks when I finish my happy rant. And just like that, reality resurfaces through the dream of Richard.

"I don't know. Won't it be obvious to everyone we just met?" I imagine Tristan and Stacey standing there with pity, judging me.

The worst part of our breakup was everyone was too busy feeling sorry for me that no one cast Tristan as the bad guy or Stacey as the mistress. We weren't married. Dating in your mid-twenties wasn't supposed to be serious to anyone but you.

"I think you're missing the big picture. Tree farm guy is who you've been talking to. Do you hear yourself?

Who cares what anyone else thinks, this is your chance to date someone. How long has it been?"

I don't answer her question and she doesn't expect me to. She knows I haven't dated since my break up.

The thing is, I know Jane is right. Saying I had a boyfriend to avoid the shame of my single life, of being the poor Margo who never moved on from her cheating boyfriend who is now engaged to the girl who broke them up. Yes, I lied. And pretending to have a fake boyfriend to appear less pathetic to my coworkers is worse.

I shouldn't care, but I do. And I will make sure Richard comes to the gala. Now that the jar of emotions is released, I can seal it back tight and focus on keeping the wall between us intact.

4
A New Leaf

The message comes in around noon when I'm about to pack up for the day. The firm hums with stragglers on deadlines, but mostly stays quiet. Most of my year-end reports were submitted last week, clearing up my schedule to make sure the New Year's party runs smoothly.

"You're smiling at your phone," Aubrey says, squinting from behind a laptop screen covered in sticker decals. "Jane mentioned you hit it off with the secret texter."

I flip my phone over to hide the unread message, letting it morph with the alternating blue and grey bubbles that gathered all day yesterday.

"I think we did." The bit of panic I pushed down, spikes, almost reaching my fluttering heart. Suddenly, I'm unsure. Besides, "He only has to agree to come to this gala. And with your amazing artwork, I don't know how anyone will say no." I shake her shoulders.

Clicking on the file she sent me, the poster's washed colours and yellow accents announce the Old Hollywood theme beautifully. The illustration of a woman and man dancing, drawn in the artist's technique of a pinup girl, immediately makes me gape. Key event details outline the page. The small black script lists the venue information and the date is highlighted in vibrant red, hard to miss. Beneath the faceless models, the section written in the style of a review, announces the three-course menu.

"You drew this?" I gawk.

Aubrey's face turns as cherry-red as her hair. "It wasn't much, really! I normally doodle while Jane watches her shows."

"Is she still on a *Teen Wolf* binge?"

"Her love for Stiles makes me question her love of women, to be honest." Laughter bursts out of me. Aubrey pauses. Taken aback by my sudden roar, she releases a chuckle and shakes her head. Her blush deepens.

"You two will take the award for the hottest couple at the gala," I say, with no hint of a lie. She closes her laptop just as I press print.

"I don't know who's inspiring my outfit, but Jane's calling herself a black-haired Monroe in a gold dress." She picks lint off of her sleeve, and the remark is very Jane. "Do you know what you're wearing?"

"I'm the host, I have to play the theme." I already know who's influencing my outfit. The famous Dolores del Río was one of the first Mexican actresses who rose to fame in Hollywood.

Abuela used to rewatch classic movies and, very generously, tell me I was a spitting image of the beautiful star. I saw no resemblance and assumed it was an example of lost translation in her broken English, but Del Río was apparently cursed by love and had failed marriages. Abuela said the actress was struck with bad luck. Del Río did eventually find a man to grow old with, but her misfortune seems all too relatable.

"Right," says Aubrey. "We can all get ready together, it'll be fun."

My throat closes. She doesn't exactly admit getting ready is a buffer in case Richard doesn't agree to go as my date, but the offer drops like a pin in the silent room.

"I'd like that," I say.

She reaches across the desk and squeezes my hand. Standing, she jams her laptop into her knapsack, a jean bag covered in buttons. "Also, I sent you a copy of the email we formatted this morning. All you have to do is forward it."

"Thank you, seriously. You're a lifesaver. If Jane doesn't marry you, I will." My mouth smacks shut after the joke slips out, but if Aubrey catches my stress, she pretends not to notice, hiding her delight with a bell-like chuckle. I can't believe I almost ruined my best friends' surprise.

"I'll talk to you later, Margo."

The door clicks shut behind her and I lunge for my phone.

Margo Diaz: Done now. What's up?

3:22 pm

The bubble next to Richard's name is instant. He's typing a reply, and I pull the phone closer to my face. The jumping dots disappear and I frown. Had he changed his mind? Did I wait too long? Did my silence turn him off?

Before the doubt festers, my screen brightens and *Richard Vixen* is bold across the top. He's calling me.

Taken aback, I haven't considered whether it's a good idea for me to answer, but my thumb already pounds to accept the call.

"Hello?" Richard's rich voice bellows into the silence.

"Er, Richard. Hey!" I bring the phone to my ear. My heart is racing.

"Hello, Mystery Woman." He speaks as if he has a smile on his lips and it is odd I can recognize the change. Wind blows into the mic and I swear I'm *not* imagining how cute he'd look right now with his curls poking out from his hat and his nose red from the cold.

"I'm no longer a mystery," I retort.

"Aren't you?" The voice on the other end of the phone prompts.

I click out of the mail window on the screen just as another notification pops up in the corner. Slouching back, I open the document for last-minute contract changes. I mean, everything is last minute, the firm is closed for the holidays, but my clients know I'll answer, and Richard's voice on the line makes me less in a hurry to pack up.

"No more than the Egyptian pyramids, Bermuda Triangle, or aliens," I say.

"Aliens," he repeats, and I imagine he nods along. "I wasn't sure if I sensed a shade of green in your skin the other night."

"Must have been the light, it washes me out. It's more of an indigo."

Holy shit, am I flirting with him?

"I may need a closer look." His voice comes clearer as if he steps out of a windstorm and takes cover indoors.

"You sure you're willing to unlock the mystery?"

"I'm not scared of you, Margo." His determination rakes against my stomach as if he implies a second meaning.

"You haven't seen my fangs."

Why, why did I say that?

"Hmmm," he pauses. "Nope, still not scared."

"They're sharp."

"I'll take my chances."

"Reeeeally sharp."

"You're not sounding any more convincing when you say it like that," he says.

"Okay, what about you? What makes you one of the *World's Greatest Wonders?*"

"Nothing, I'm ordinary. Not a hair out of place."

I laugh. "With those wild curls? You do not instil confidence."

There's a pause which makes me wonder if I overstepped by commenting on his appearance. Clearly, my green skin was fair game.

"Alright, I do have one secret wonder."

This time when the phone falls silent I bite my nails. What is it? A third nipple? An extra toe? A tail?

"Go on," I say.

"No, I changed my mind." But his voice is anything but timid, he's enjoying leaving me hanging, taunting me.

"Richard: the most normal, ordinary person there is. Nothing for the world to wonder about. Just a man and a bat wing coming out of his ass."

His booming laughter satisfies me. "That would be awesome. Imagine the flight?"

"You'd fly ass first." I shake my head at the visual this gives me.

"Margo: the child made from an alien and vampire affair," mimics Richard.

"Now *that* would be awesome." Our laughter mingles for a moment and I forget about the document opened on my monitor as I lazily shake the mouse around the screen.

"Seriously, though," I say, breaking the comfortable silence. "You mentioned a wonder and it sounded like you had one in mind."

"No, no. It's not something you tell a beautiful girl about." He tries to flatter me, but I'm not about to admit he has an effect.

"Oh shut up and tell me."

His answering chuckle makes my heart whoop. "Alright, Mystery Woman. My wonder is the cute mole on my ass my mom calls her coffee stain."

"Oh my God!" Work forgotten, I pull off my glasses. Resting my head on the back of my wrist, I wipe the tears springing from laughter. "Richard, that's utterly *adorable*!"

"So, you think I have an adorable ass then?" His amusement is clear through the phone.

"Why does she call it a coffee stain?" I ask.

"I don't know. There's some tale that if you have a craving while you're pregnant you touch your ass. She said she craved coffee a lot."

"Wow, this." Honestly, I hadn't expected Richard to call. For our conversation to turn so effortlessly funny. "Richard, I need to see it."

"I'm not showing you my ass, Margo."

"It's for science. One of the *World's Greatest Wonders*, remember?" Not that I expect him to show me, but it's certainly fun reversing the conversation for the upper hand.

"This is one wonder that deserves to remain unsolved." He doesn't sound at all fazed by the conversation's turn.

"Fine," I say, pouting despite myself. "Why did you call, anyway?"

My phone buzzes. "I just sent you a photo, did you get it?"

I pull my phone away from my ear and check our chat. An image of a purple toboggan stares at me. A thrill shoots up my spine. The last time I rode a sled was with Raph, and Mom and Dad pulled us over a flat surface convinced a real hill would scare my brother.

"I'm in! Where are we going?" I wince at how eager I sound.

"Dick's Dam Park, you know where that is?" he asks.

I do. The park is at the bottom of the hill, the valley dividing Bolton and close to the gazebo where we met the other night.

"Give me half an hour."

"Great, I'll see you then," Richard's voice rumbles with pleasure.

"See you." I hang up.

In a daze from what just happened, I clean my glasses and put them back on.

A mole on his butt? The image shouldn't commit itself to my mind, but I have no willpower.

Clicking through my inbox, I find the email Aubrey formatted and populate the BCC with the list I prepared earlier. Checking over the Excel document to make sure I have the right amount of contacts, and that they are accurately entered into the right field, I press send.

I'm happy no one is around to witness how fast I pack up my things.

5
Ups and Downs

In jeans and short leather booties, I failed to realize the problem with my outfit before it was too late. Assuming the only other car in the lot belongs to Richard, I throw on the knit pompom hat from my backseat. My ears thank me when the chill whips at my face.

"New ride?" I nod towards the red pickup with a business logo. Behind him, the vehicle is much larger than the silver car we sat in the other night.

"Work vehicle. The other one is my brother's." Surprising me, he passes me the drink in his hand. "I made you a promise the other night and failed. One peppermint mocha. I drank mine while I was waiting. Sorry."

He tacks his apology at the end, a quick flash of embarrassment to give away his nerves. If I doubted my attraction to him the other day, this smooths over any concerns. Swaying on his heels, Richard's broad shoulders stiffen with false confidence, and all I think about is how it'd feel to climb him like a tree and dig my nails into his back. Even in jeans, I can tell he'd support my weight, carry me before he lays me down, right before…

"Did you want me to drive? It's just up the road." Shattering the forming fantasy, Richard jerks a thumb towards the running engine behind him.

"I," blushing, I force myself to sip the thoughtful beverage he brought me. Lukewarm, it makes the liquid easier to swallow, easier to buy me time. "Yes, you know where we're going. I'll come with you."

"Don't sound too eager." He lifts an eyebrow, questioning my hesitation.

"My experience with you behind the wheel was in a Tim's parking lot while we were parked. You could be a reckless driver for all I know." I refuse to mention my actual concern. The single bench cab and the charge in the air that runs static along my skin.

"I promise I'll go slow." His eyes flash, and my brain falls further into the gutter.

"Not even ten over the limit?" I challenge.

"I'm a model driver."

"Five?"

"Despicable. Those numbers are for people who struggle to maintain a speed."

"*One* over the speed limit?" I raise a brow.

Richard touches an imaginary wound on his chest. "Have you no trust in my driving capabilities?"

"No, and that's the point."

His smile knocks out whatever progress I make for my lungs. "Then let me prove myself."

"By getting in your truck?" I scoff, unsure why I'm giving him a hard time about driving. He's probably an average driver with a semi-clean record and there's really nothing intimidating about his truck. "What if you prove me right, and I spend the whole ride fearing my life? I'll have an expensive therapy bill."

"I'll send you flowers once a week." He moves closer, and the air grows taut.

"What if the flowers are a trigger of the incident?" I don't budge, squaring my shoulder to peer directly into his liquid brown eyes.

"Then I'll write you a card." He's confident.

"I don't think poems will soothe the trauma."

"I never said anything about poetry." His lips twitch at the corners.

"Ah, but then how will I know the true words of your soul?"

He shakes his head. Looking up to the sky as if to ask for help. Whatever sun trickles between the clouds finds his face. With a halo around his sharp jaw and wild curls, Richard belongs in a magazine for winter athletics or GQ.

"I'll come with you on one condition," I bargain.

"And that is?" He's suspicious. As he should be.

"You show me the mole on your butt."

I don't expect him to agree, but the suggestion serves its purpose. Richard's husky laugh shakes his body. The sound is delicious.

"Get in the truck, Margo."

"Fine, only because you bought me a mocha." I strut by him with an exaggerated chin lift. His low chuckle skitters across my skin with pleasure.

Richard leads me to the truck, but damn him for walking to the passenger side, not giving me a moment to recover. Opening the door, he frowns, scratching his temple.

"I didn't realize the truck has no step." He glances at the height of the cab and then towards my sodden booties, his frown deepening further.

"What you mean is: I didn't realize how adorably short you are, Margo."

"No, I noticed that immediately." His grin is wicked and his dark eyes flicker. I force myself to glance away.

"My dad has a truck, I got this." Reaching for the oh-shit bar, I leap with one foot on the mat and grip my drink tight.

A warm pressure circles my waist. Richard's arm wraps around me and my legs give out mid-momentum.

With ease, Richard lifts me into the seat and shakes his head, but there's no missing how his fingers linger on my hip for a beat too long or how his expression tightens, his irises melting into a deeper brown. The spot on my hip tingles from his touch, and I wish he wasn't staring at me. I want to pull up my jacket and shirt to analyze all the parts of my skin he might have pressed against.

Instead, I'm left with traces of him, and I'm not one-hundred percent sure if I made them up. The flex of his forearm against my back, the pop of his lips when his breath made a barely audible hitch. I tuck away the moment to pull apart later.

"Thank you," I force the words.

He clears his throat and drops his head. Without a word, he confirms I'm tucked in, then slams the door. Hammering in my throat, my heart appreciates the seconds without him, but I track his movement through the windshield. His expression wipes clean from tension and I scold my pulse to shut up before he hears.

This is not good.

Up the road, Richard parks the truck and then swings around to open my door. This time, he lets me wiggle myself down alone, providing a wide berth. From the truck bed, he reveals a purple toboggan too small for one person.

"Your chariot." He offers me the rope and I pull the plastic over the snow behind us.

He reaches for my other hand, and I jolt. The familiarity of his long fingers folding around mine is more jarring than the act of hand-holding. When did my body start to recognize his touch? How had I come to expect his comfort?

His skin heats through the thin fabric of his gloves into my mitts. The sensation of him is overwhelming. Springing apart, I cup my drink, stealing a sip to feign ease. Richard's expression is thoughtful, but he doesn't say anything.

Our walk up the hill is silent.

Thankfully the snow is thick and not powdered, my boots have a chance of surviving the day. Still, there is no fight against Mom's voice ringing in my head. In a childhood lecture I heard many times, the warning that if I want to go outside, I have to wear snow pants. The same speech she gives Raph when he insists on building forts in our backyard.

On the top of the hill, Richard presents the toboggan with wide arms, an offer for me to go first. I hide my fear of the many tree obstacles and low burr bushes ahead and give him my best *you're on* face. A low smirk spreads his lips flat.

Sitting, every groove of the hard plastic pushes into my ass. Before I inhale my confidence, Richard crouches low behind me. His hands press flat on my back, readying the shove that will project me down the hill, but rather than launching me, he bends close enough that his head hangs above the crook of my neck.

"I can't wait to hear you scream." He chuckles low, and my insides squeeze.

Then I'm flying.

My knees tuck to accommodate the length of my legs and my hands grip the very unreliable piece of rope like it's a lifeline. The wind whips against my face and the crisp winter burns my nose and throat. And yes, I'm screaming. A whoop of joy springs out of me and I clamp my mouth shut when the sled slows at the bottom of the hill, remembering his last words to me.

I run back up the hill, determined to give him a taste of his own medicine, replaying my options over in my head that slowly lose their confidence when I face him. His expression is amused, reading the flush on my cheeks, his eyes gleam with pleasure.

"Now, now, a good man doesn't let a woman deal her own screams while he watches." My statement is bold, and despite the way my voice is shrill and not at all husky how my inner monologue rehearsed, Richard licks his lower lip. Unable to stop himself, he looks me over, and he takes his time.

"Get in the sled," I order. And honestly, who am I right now?

He bows, accepting the rope I hold out to him. Folding his long legs to fit in the plastic frame, I commit to my next move. Nudging his knees with my boot, Richard lifts his brows, but understanding what I intend, he obliges, shuffling to widen his lap so that I fit.

Good God, I really didn't think this through.

My back flattens against him and between his legs, I feel *everything*. Wrapping one arm around me, Richard shifts closer. His breath is warm against my ear. I grip the rope, tight. Thinking of the pressed, bunched fabric between us, I imagine myself against his body if we weren't in a sled, wearing clothes, on a very public snow trail.

"I have to push," he whispers like it's a warning as if his heads-up is an opening for me to back out. Somehow this jolts my heart.

"I'm told that's how this works. A gentleman wouldn't ask a woman to do all the work."

He says something under his breath that I'm sure sounds like *Lord, help me with this one or Gord, I need my knees done.*

With a thrust that delights me in more ways than one, we are off. With his wide arms wrapped around my waist, Richard tries to maintain space between us, hunching to keep himself from barely brushing against me. But my hormones don't listen to chivalry. My control slips and I push back, moulding myself against his body completely.

The toboggan hits a bump. Unprepared, I jerk the front end. We're falling and my squeal expects the impact of the forgiving plush snow, remembering the many times Dad took me skiing as a kid.

Richard doesn't let go, not even when we roll. Careful to take the brunt of the fall, he tucks me against his body, which is why I'm smiling down at him while he winces in pain. I land on him, one leg thrown over his and his arm snug around my lower back.

Forgetting the snow, my job, the distance I'm supposed to keep between us, I lean closer. Through his jacket, his muscles are hard where my body plumps and squishes with gravity. Richard, my fake boyfriend turned into a very real man, stares up at me. His eyes are a storm in the winter sun.

A million questions deliver in a single look. He tilts his chin.

I pull away, hoisting myself up and off him until I'm back on my feet. Mortified, I glare at the abandoned purple toboggan. Upside down, I see the price tag, unmarked and confirmation he bought it specifically for our date. He wanted to take me out, and my unchecked hormones had one feel of him and insisted I needed to have more. He's like dessert, one taste is not enough, just a mockery of what it's like to have all of him to myself.

Richard quickly stands, swiping the snow off his hat and tugging it back on.

"I'm sorry," I burst. Unsure how to explain what for.

"Margo. Hey." Unable to meet his gaze, I examine where the leather darkens on my toe. He steps closer and lifts his hand. Second guessing if he should touch me, he lets it fall. My heart clenches. *He* did nothing wrong. "Seriously, no need to apologize for… you know." He jerks a thumb behind him as if, in his mind, a version of us still lay in the snow.

There's more for me to apologize for, but as attracted as I am to Richard, as nice as he is, I shouldn't kiss him. I seriously need to get a grip on myself and keep my impulses in check. There are many hot guys.

None that buy a toboggan, bring me a peppermint mocha, and listen to me like I'm the most entertaining person. Surely two years hasn't been that long. Not really. And it's not as if I hadn't taken care of myself. Especially on the night of the tree farm encounter when I came home flushed and downloaded an ebook. I specifically picked the cute cover knowing it was smut.

Staring at my leather booties, now completely dark from the wet snow I bury them into, I shift gears in my mind to slow my heart rate. My cheeks must colour as red as the bottom line on my credit card statement after holiday shopping. Too warm in the middle of winter, I want to dive face-first into the snow. Anything to escape the way Richard watches at me, half-teasing, half-worried.

"I don't have to apologize, huh?"

I bend over. Quick with my hands, I pack together a ball of snow, letting the dampness bleed through my wool knit mittens. Sparing a second to check my aim, I send the cold mass at his chest.

The ball bursts into tiny clumps, crunching against his jacket with an odd sweeping sound the way water hits a tarp in the rain.

"Did you…" He approaches with an expression of pure bewilderment, but I already have the second snowball ready.

Expecting my next move he's fast on his feet, ducking low to dodge the flying blow. The world swirls as he grips my knees, his shoulder connecting lightly between my hips with an efficient maneuver that has me staring at his backside. Air whooshes from my lungs, and I fight the urge.

I pinch his ass.

"Is this your way of showing me your mole?" I chirp.

Richard yowls. He does have an attractive butt. The kind of tight bubble that forms from playing hockey.

"Wow, I wouldn't call it a great *wonder*, but I still need to see that coffee stain." As if sensing my next thought, Richard swings in a circle.

"Mystery Margo, you will not see my ass." He sounds so sure.

Spinning me, I squeal. He's laughing too, but he tucks in his tailbone when I aim for another pinch. Carefully, he plants my feet, but we aren't square. I dive for more ammunition, crouching low just as something hard hits my right ass cheek.

A shriek escapes before I catch it. Holding the pulsing spot, I face him just as snow smushes against my head. He rubs into my hat, letting the snowball break apart and crumble down my face.

"Now we're even." If the sun weren't out, I'd say his grin would have brightened the entire park.

Faking a frown, I cross my arms. He pretends not to notice, but his gaze dips momentarily to where I strategically perch my breasts.

"Don't start a fight you can't finish," I say.

"Believe me, I always finish." One side of his mouth crooks up.

I snap my mouth shut just as a shiver travels through my body. Misreading the reaction, Richard places his arm around my shoulder to soothe me, so casually as if the gesture is natural between us.

"We should get you warmed up."

I'm sure he doesn't mean it how it sounds, but boy do I fight the impulse to correct him. He doesn't need to know the effect he has on me.

My body is alert. My veins run hot and every part of me is burning. Something inside me purrs in response.

"Warm is good," I manage to get the words out as he guides us back to his truck, only stopping to pick up the rope of the plastic sled that played the most subtle wingman.

6
Out with The Old

Richard doesn't bring me back to the parking lot where I left my car. No, the part of me that is Evil-Margo had made the comment she left her mocha on the snow hill to which Nice-Richard refused any objections and promised to get the drink replaced.

"You really don't have to," I say for what is probably the seventeenth time. I definitely said it more than ten.

"No, I want to. I made a promise. Just remind me where this bakery is you mentioned."

I might have said the abandoned peppermint mocha wasn't a big loss because *it's not like it was from Sammy's.* Yes, Evil-Margo struck twice. Behind his steering wheel with his large hands at nine and three, Richard insists I give him the directions to the bakery that won my sugary affection.

Guiding him out of Bolton, Richard is content with keeping up the light conversation. He asks about my

Christmas morning, and I ask about his. We discuss the temperature. He adjusts the air blowing through the vents. The small talk is comfortable, safe as if we mutually decide neither of us will bring up the moment on the snow hill.

This is the part where the regret hits after following an impulsive decision. I shouldn't have leaned in, shouldn't have stared at his plump lips, paused with him beneath me. Sitting in the single cab of his truck, I'm certain animals have more composure when they're stuck in snares. I'm freaking out.

I was caught up in the moment! I want to slam my head against the dash. It's not every day you accidentally land flush on a good-looking man whose eyes drink you in. The same sly, confident man that challenges you, makes you question the moral compass that wobbles off-axis. His gaze packs enough heat to warm every inch of my skin, which explains why I'm coiled up and cold, tense against the chill in the passenger seat.

He hasn't looked at me since we got in the truck.

Light conversation is our buffer, an excuse to disrupt the quiet without drawing attention to the problem. Me, I'm the problem. I almost kissed Richard and just as easily as I pushed myself against him, I pulled away. Yes, the snowball fight was a nice save, but the walk back to the truck echoed the rejection. Each crunch of our feet in the snow might as well have been imitating the sucker punch I threw at his ego. Not that Richard raised any concern, he seemed to understand why I pulled away. That makes one of us.

If I already broke all my distance rules, why not let myself enjoy it? A taste of his bottom lip, the stroke of his tongue against mine. No. Dating Richard is a means to an end. There's no time for a boyfriend with this potential promotion looming. Just the thought of a relationship stiffens my joints.

Thus the cause for Richard's discomfort. I practically ooze regret. I'm convinced my pores release a type of pheromone meant to keep men away.

Just when I think my mouth will erupt with the overflow from my head, Richard slides the truck into a stall by the entrance to the white wood-panelled bakery. Lucky timing.

Still during the holidays, the bakery's lot is packed with vehicles and the line of customers pointing at the desserts in the window no longer maintain the cheer. The week after Christmas is usually two things: jam-packed with visits from family, or quiet because you were smart enough to finish them leading up to the big day. My family has always been quiet around the holidays. Mom's cousins live in Mexico and Dad had only Abuela, until he didn't anymore.

"Margo, I fail to see a peppermint mocha on the menu. Did you lure me here for a distraction?" Richard's voice rasps close to my ear, and without seeing him, I imagine he glances up from thick lashes.

"The only thing I'm luring you to is a dinner to eat your words." Nerves collect in my throat, making my voice squeeze an octave too high. I turn around, and his eyes crinkle with amusement.

All brown curls without his hat, Richard's head sticks out above the crowd. The rustic lights that are more suitable for a mineshaft send a glow that catches the angles of his long nose and sharp jaw. Swaying back to peer at the chalkboard menu, Richard unknowingly shifts to clear my view of the rest of the bakery. The small movement is enough for me to notice a familiar face.

Tristan's profile is as easy to spot in a bakery as it is in the office. As if Harvey is here calling both our names into his office, Tristan's head snaps in my direction. The woman behind the counter calls us forward.

My pulse beats loud in my ears. The woman's expression seems to stretch and wobble, a funhouse with coffee-scented air and the delicious waft of freshly baked bread. Tristan is here like the Ghost of Christmas Past ready to show me my mistakes.

Ignoring the repercussions, forgetting the distance I'm supposed to keep between me and the beautiful man next to me, all the reasons why I signed up for an anonymous matchmaking service burst into my mind.

Tristan is here.

I grab Richard's hand, looping my fingers through his as we take a step forward, together. Avoiding the pressure boring into my back from across the bakery, I greet the lady in front of us.

"Two peppermint white mochas please." I force myself to look forward, but my brain betrays me, sending a signal to my heart and neck to turn in Richard's direction.

The timid corners of his mouth attempt to recover his shock, and he squeezes my hand just as the strain of judgement leaves the spot between my shoulders. I try to tune out Tristan's presence in the room completely. Tiny circles are drawn over my thumb and I'm finding the point of the lie hard to reason.

Richard's warmth ignites against my palm, thawing through my veins. In the middle of a bustling crowd, I'm tethered to one place. For the first time in years, I'm not in a rush to get home. The binder in my car no longer shines as a beacon calling me back. The night is left wide for possibilities and there's no motivation for me to complete everything by tomorrow. Go-with-the-flow Margo has the chance to make an appearance.

Besides, holding his hand is… nice.

I let go.

My job. The promotion. Tristan.

Everything falls together, but not in a neat organized structure. Where one thing shifts, the others follow suit. Unable to stop the motion, they connect in a way hard to determine the start and end of each. Holding hands with a man in a bakery isn't how I spend my evenings. It would be naive to let the familiarity of him take root. My palm already tingles in protest, craving his touch. The spot his thumb rubbed, pulses in disagreement, shouting at me. But the man across the room is proof that this will fail.

My wallet, where is it? Richard's brows pinch and something flashes across his face too quickly for me to read.

"I'm sorry, how much is it?" Why does my voice sound like *that*?

"It's okay, I got it." Richard slides his card to the lady, accepting the machine to insert his pin.

His long fingers type the code slowly and I should turn away, avoid having him think I plan to rob him, but I enjoy observing how they move. Almost musically, patient. My face burns and I'm grateful when the woman directs us to the side counter.

Quiet, I peer around the room, reassuring myself Tristan is gone. Richard observes each face as if he's doing the same, somehow knowing the cause of my anxiety without me having to say it.

I thought we were safe here. *Sammy's* was one place I got in the breakup. It was practically my sanctuary.

Yes, the bakery has the best peanut-free, vegan desserts. And yes, Tristan and Stacey are happily bettering the planet with their strict diet while I consume sweet beverages anywhere without qualms, but this place is mine. How long has he been coming here?

Evil-Margo chooses now to pipe in. *Good, let Tristan see me with Richard. Let him witness I can be happy.* I silence her.

"I heard you say white mocha, what is that?" Richard rolls on his heels, his hands are safely in his pockets.

"Delicious. That's all you need to know." I cross my arms, fighting to stay serious.

He accepts the drinks from the counter when our order is called and offers me one. "You have yet to lead me astray, Mystery Woman."

No, I wouldn't want to do that.

Holding open the door, we're back in the cold. I shiver, but it's not from the wind. Tracing my finger around the lid, I keep my head low and fight the urge to scan the parking lot for a familiar black sedan, but it's no use. I locate Tristan's retreating head immediately.

The passenger window rolls down, and there she is. Stacey reaches for the bag her fiancé holds out and the way they move is natural, a habit they had years of practicing. I struggle to turn away.

As if sensing me, Stacey looks up. Even across the lot, I see her expression narrow. She waves.

"Go on, take a sip," I say, turning back to Richard with forced cheer, but the rest of me is stiff. The petty part of my ego amps up the act and hopes sound travels clear across the parking lot.

But I lift my chin, and like magnets, I'm caught in Richard's gaze. He stares at me as if he means to ask, *Is everything okay?* The silence carries our wordless conversation, and my body loosens, and my lungs relax. I shouldn't care about what Stacey thinks. I buried that anger long ago. Slowly, my smile no longer pins into place but is a sigh of contentment. *Yes, I'm fine now.*

"Excuse me!" Someone calls, taking me too long to realize she means to grab my attention.

"Yes?" I swallow a hot mouthful of my mocha, and it burns my esophagus the whole way down.

"Would you mind taking a picture of us?" The girl asks. She has to be in her early twenties.

In a white ankle-length jacket and large puffy earmuffs, her pose is trained, making her snow royalty next to her winter prince in front of the rustic bakery. He holds her against him and stares down with his pride on full display. My throat closes.

"Here you go." I swallow and pass her back her phone. "I took a few. They all look amazing, but let me know if I have to take more."

She swipes through the photos, pleased. "They're great, thank you! Want me to take one of you two?"

A pause beats when I glance toward Richard. His mouth purses with the insinuation of a challenge, reading my discomfort and beating me to an answer before I chicken out.

"That's great, thanks!" Richard pats his chest pocket, but no, he's not leaving with this photo.

"Here, use my phone!" I rush towards the girl and Richard grunts behind me.

I gulp. Richard moves closer, angling us to use the bakery as our backdrop. Unsure how to stand next to him, I lift my arms, dangling them between us awkwardly while staring at his hips. Richard spares no hesitation and scoops me up against him, his grip securing my lower back and his other hand cupping my neck. His fingers wrap in the hair at my nape, sending a tingle down to my toes. For a moment, I'm suspended in a place where all I see is him.

His woodsy scent, muddled with the sweet aroma of bread and coffee, clouds my mind. A haze of nostalgia creeps over me, and the familiarity is hard to place but welcomes me home anyway. He's the voice that rang with every text chime, the face to scenarios I dreamed up. If winter freezes everything around us, Richard captures the moment.

"You're sending me the photo, Margo," he whispers, his words close to my ear.

I laugh through the shiver. Pulling away, his darkened gaze peers up through his full lashes.

"That's presumptuous."

His lofty grin returns. "I'm in it. I get custody."

"It's on my phone," I argue.

"Technology came a long way. Did you know the screen you carry has the ability to send messages?" He speaks with a faux mix of disbelief and incredulous surprise, but he is adorable and all I manage in response is to swat his arm.

He catches my fingers, rubbing a thumb beneath all four, splaying them across the zipper of his jacket. I consider what his chest might feel like, hard beneath my hand, small hairs lining down…

"You two are cute!" A voice breaks through the haze. "Seriously, I took like fifty million candids. You'll love them!"

I hadn't noticed Richard watching me as I gape at our fingers, tracing the places his thumb left little stars dancing along my skin. We break apart and I manage to tell the girl my thanks as she returns my phone. My face is on fire and I know I shouldn't look at the photos, that I shouldn't care how me and Richard look side by side or what she meant by cute, but I unlock my phone and start swiping.

Twelve photos. I have twelve photos of Richard and me. If I flip through them fast enough I almost put together a fragmented video of the moment played between us. Seeing us from the outside, how my smile is wide from laughing, my head tilts back to peer up at him. Caught in his stare, I was content to stand there and he kept looking. In all the photos, his gaze followed my face.

I'm aware Richard stands behind me, observing the way I flip and pause. He stiffens, probably noticing when I stop breathing. In a swift movement, he plucks the phone from my grip. My mind is delayed, fuzzy from what I see. Myself, with emotion in my expression I'm not ready to digest.

Richard sends every single photo to himself. A quiet ding rings in his pocket.

Retrieving our drinks from the ledge we sat them on, we let our crunching feet fill the silence. Our hands dangle between us, almost touching but with enough of a gap to keep me from being pulled in. The thrum of energy fights, and I'm tempted to reach for him again, to test the limits of his warmth and where it'll travel inside me. Curious, my knuckles bump his and like a direct access to my veins, my pulse quickens.

"Mmm, Margo!" Richard pulls the cup from his mouth, turning the drink in his hands to examine it from all angles.

Lingering next to the door of the truck, Richard leans forward as if he desires to share his excitement only with me. His lips are glossed from the mocha he licks off.

"Good right?" I cock my head in victory, aware I ogle his mouth.

Opening the door, his dropped gaze does something to my insides when he says, "I can think of something better."

He closes me into the truck and I steal the moment to talk down my pulse, but it's sprinting, ready to leap.

"I'm sorry this place is a little out of town," I manage to say when he starts the engine.

"It's all good. I no longer blame you for forgetting the dirt in a cup I tried to pass off as a mocha. My drink was nothing like this. What's the secret, unicorn blood?" He steals another sip of his drink while pulling the seat belt across his broad torso.

"Gross." I scrunch my nose and he turns to face me and actually winks, the kind that's all humour and free from doubt. My stomach flops. "But you admit you blamed me?"

"At first I didn't," says Richard, thoughtful as he watches the road. "But now there's evidence against you." I laugh, shaking my head at how easy it is to fall back into a rhythm with him.

"Besides, I have to thank you for showing me them. I'm not a flavoured coffee person," he goes on.

"Dessert coffee is basically the point of fall and Christmas." I whirl in my seat, my back against the door, facing him with unexpected excitement. 'Dessert coffee' is basically any type of caffeinated beverage that is sweet and tastes like a hug.

"I'm happy pumpkin-spiced lattes are off the menu." He shudders. Paused at a stop sign, he sees I'm about to object. "You got me making peppermint mochas at home, I refuse to drink pumpkin-perfumed beverages."

The silhouettes of trees are black against the dark navy sky, but somehow I make out his every feature in the glow of the radio screen.

"First of all, they're delicious and I feel attacked." I hold up a single digit. He scratches his jaw, turning his attention back to the road and I force myself to swallow.

Why did I find that hot?

"And second of all," I continue, two fingers up. "No one said you have to *make* peppermint mochas. You developed the addiction yourself. That's on you for having no self-control."

He scoffs. "I'm not paying ten dollars for a drink I can make myself."

"I bet yours taste like trash."

The car jerks to a standstill. Granted, we're at a red light, but the stop isn't graceful.

He turns to me, sticking me with the blow of his brown eyes, rimmed with flecks of green. I'm staring, I can't turn away.

"You have no idea how delicious my peppermint mochas are."

"Okay? Prove it." I challenge, forgetting the drink that sits hot in my hands.

"You asked for it. And when you're wrong…" He grips the steering wheel tighter while he waits for the light to change.

"I doubt I will be. You're a dessert coffee newbie." I sit back, smug.

"Oh, how wrong you are."

"And yet, I hear no attempts to prove otherwise."

"Yeah? Come over. I'll show you." He bites the tip of his tongue between his teeth.

I'm wrong about something. It isn't just the contact of his skin that warms my insides.

"Fine." I bite, and Richard's mouth curls.

7
In with The New

Did I just convince this man to make me a peppermint mocha?

My heart flutters knowing where Richard takes me. With his parents living in Florida, there's a very real possibility of privacy when we arrive. I straighten in the passenger seat of his truck, fighting against the growing nerves and the way my body anticipates what it means to be alone with him.

My brain works overtime to compensate for the innuendos my ovaries make. Somehow, my conscience concludes that there are no rules against hooking up with a good-looking guy.

Am I about to hook up with Richard?

Jane would encourage the possibility. Aubrey would want to know every detail and label tonight as an adventure. Time passes both fast and slow while my heart and head wrestle. I'm pretty sure it's not with each other, it's like they tripped and got tangled in my fallopian tubes.

I had exactly one fling in my life. I was in university and tried to date the guy after, suggesting we go for breakfast and got confused when my texts went unanswered. Spoiler: he did not want to date.

My body jitters with nerves over the idea of making a second attempt. Again, I weigh the pros of giving in to a night of spontaneity. It's not unreasonable to crave a man who fills the frame of his pickup, holds the steering wheel with the grip I recall against the back of my neck, who draws my mouth closer to his in an agonizing lure.

It's been too long since a man ran his hands over my body, held my waist, and pressed my hips to his. Taking care of myself is nothing compared to the image of Richard bracing himself over me, forearms flexed next to my head.

Realizing my mind wanders, I widen my focus, trying to pay attention to the road and where he drives. Did Richard ask me something? I rummage through my thoughts to recall the last thing we said.

Flushed and bothered, I prepare myself for what will actually happen when we arrive. It's just coffee. He'll stay on his respectable side of the kitchen. I assume he'll stand far away from the place I'll sit. We will talk about abrasive topics, like the time I cut open my knee on a can of corn and swore I saw my bone, and he'll tell me something equally disgusting.

I do my best to reason why I allowed two years to pass without so much as a fling. The idea seems stupid to me when I'm staring at Richard's curled knuckles on the wheel, his biceps flexing. My mouth is dry and no amount of sips from my peppermint white mocha will quench the thirst growing low in my belly.

Casual hookups are hard when you require trust for intimacy. Before Tristan, the mindset of not trusting anyone to stick around reconfirmed the insecurity that I wasn't good enough to stick around *for*. And when he stayed and invested years into my life, I thought I could break the odds. Sometimes it sucks when your gut is right.

There's nothing wrong with those who find their fun and are able to enjoy themselves. I secretly envy them, but my wiring stems from my heart. And Tristan broke that.

Richard pulls into the driveway of a modest house, and I'm surprised my head doesn't hit the roof with how ramrod straight I fling back into the seat. Turning off the engine, a quiet falls over the truck. Words fail to find a way out. Richard stares at the garage with concern, which of course sends my insides into a whole other frenzy. Does he regret bringing me to his home?

Embarrassment etches clear between the arch of his brows. "My brother isn't here."

His admission drops like a stone in my stomach. We really are alone, and he has the sensibility to appear uncomfortable. Yes, Tristan broke my confidence as well as my judgement of men, but something about Richard softens my reserve.

I touch his arm and ignore the shock finding a path to my heart. He clutches the truck keys tight in his hand as if digging them into his palms pulls him from the shadows dipping his features. Turning his hand over in mine, I slowly peel back his fingers, laying my palm flat on his. The key to our night is a decision to make between the both of us.

"Do you think your peppermint mochas are so bad he ran away?" My joke is terrible and corny, but my false concern causes him to snort which accomplishes everything I intend and more.

"You're still doubting me?" He shakes his head and pops open the door.

Before he comes to my side of the truck, I jump down. Part of me requires the small decision to remind myself I'm in control. I'm my own person.

Down the side of the house to the back entrance, I marvel at the lights carved into the underside of each step. Like a runway to the yard, I watch my feet, praying that this isn't the day I fall down the stairs in front of a gorgeous man.

He rents the basement, he explains. And I nod, it's all I manage to do because the butterflies travel from my stomach and fill my throat when Richard turns the key.

The apartment is dark, save for whatever the yard lights manage to sneak in from the windows. A kitchen fit for a single man in his twenties bleeds into the small entrance, and in the adjoining area is a round table for four, the back of a large couch to split the area, then a television screen the size of my body if I laid down in front of it.

"Why are your walls grey?" I blurt. The patches of brown behind the couch are warmer than the dull rock colour that covers every surface, including the cabinets above the stove.

God, I'm nervous.

Truly the grey doesn't bother me. The shaker cabinet doors make a stance on modern decor, and the colour definitely screams 'someone masculine lives here', but the painter in me hadn't associated a dull shade with such a warm man.

I've never judged someone's place before, not after my university dorm— a townhouse split into three floors with bedrooms on the ground level and a communal kitchen for all eleven housemates. The paint patches catch my attention the way a dog at the side of a street might make me slow down while driving, but my question slipped out before I had the chance to phrase myself better.

"Sorry, that was rude. It's not the colour I imagined." I point at the abandoned brush strokes.

"You've thought about my walls?" He quirks a brow, his voice teasing. My brain fumbles any words, taking my attention to my boots.

"My mom never settled on a colour. I simply settled." He goes on, more serious when he combs back his hair. "A grey basement isn't the ideal coffee shop, but I promise my peppermint mocha will transport you."

"Outside to where winter cheer lives?" Why is sarcasm my defence flirt method? I wring my fingers together and clear my throat. "Sorry. But seriously, your place is nice."

The couch has throw pillows and a complimenting coffee table, and the kitchen is mostly clean aside from the leftover pizza box on the counter. There's no visible laundry on the floor or dirty dishes in the sink. The basement back window would let in a decent amount of sunlight during the day. Not that I plan to stay long enough to see the sun hit his apartment.

"No offence taken. And thanks." Richard shrugs, sliding out of his winter coat.

Air does not enter my lungs fast enough. Every time I met up with Richard was outside and in a thick layer of water-repellent polyester. Nothing could prepare me for a black long-sleeve that hugs the curves of his arms and stretches over his chest, falling loose to hide his tight abdomen. Thank you to the designer for the small break and the granite island between us, because if the shirt was tight the entire way down… I pace, turning my attention away before he notices.

Untying my scarf and removing my jacket, I throw them over the nearest barstool then kick off my heels, the leather still wet and splotched from the snow. My button-up dress shirt and black stretchy jeans scream office wear.

Richard stretches to open a cupboard above the stove, and the shirt manages to hug his shoulder blades in a soft caress that makes me jealous. He moves around the kitchen with comfortable ease, gathering his ingredients from the fridge and cabinets as if the rhythm is familiar to him. I drop my elbows against the white granite countertop, fascinated by his movements, captured by his grace. He froths milk in a metal cup and swipes his hand over the steam nozzle— a gesture I'll think about later. Pouring chocolate and a translucent liquid into a clear glass, Richard uses a spoon to keep the layers separate. I chew on the inside of my cheek with the realization that he knows what he's doing.

"What if this peppermint mocha is the worst I ever had?"

"Everything I do will blow your mind." He tosses me a rare wink. He's joking, but something inside me grows hungry and demands to test his statement.

"Cocky, are we?"

"You have no idea."

He pours a shot of espresso over the frothed milk, and I know he's showing off. With careful hands and a steady rhythm, the drink looks as if it belongs in a café catalogue. The knowledge does nothing to ease the saliva accumulating in the gutters of my mouth.

Richard slides me the mocha, stopping the glass in front of me and letting our knuckles touch. He doesn't pull away, and the familiar lick of a flame dances against my skin.

I trace my fingers up the tall glass, aware that he watches the movement. "If this is bad, you owe me a fourth peppermint mocha from a café of my choice."

"If this is good, you owe me a kiss."

The pool in my lower belly expands. His brow raises and I'm distracted by how his thick forearms flex against the counter, bringing him near. The almost-kiss in the snow shouldn't have happened, and I desperately need to pull the brakes on anything more. The organ that flops in my chest warns me to stop. But I move the glass to my mouth, letting him observe how my lips press against the rim.

Damn. It's a good mocha.

"Good?" He hasn't looked away from my mouth.

I shrug, placing the drink down although I want to keep sipping it. Warm peppermint with just the right amount of chocolate swirl together with notes of winter and bliss. A hug on the inside, the mocha demands to be savoured. Instead, I abandon the beverage and bite my tongue, hoping to convince him I'm not all that impressed.

"It's okay."

"Bullshit," he gruffs.

I shrug. "You promised me the best I've ever had, and you fell short. Sorry."

He knows I'm lying when I steal another taste. Not that I keep a list of Best Peppermint Mochas or anything to compare to, but a good dessert coffee is hard to beat and Richard's comes close.

"And what is wrong with it?" One of his dark brows shoots up beneath his curls— the kind I want to twist all ten of my fingers into.

"It's simply too small." It's the first thing I think of. The drink is made in a fancy glass, not a large mug I'd place on my desk and sample through the long hours of a work day, enjoying the taste even when cold. It's a drink meant for aesthetics that happens to also taste delicious. Definitely the kind of coffee that costs closer to ten dollars.

"I assure you, I've never faced that problem." His lids fall heavy with a lustful intensity.

"Ah, but my review is based on personal expectations."

"Keep them high, Babe." His eyes flash, and he leans closer. "I'll meet every one."

The way he says 'Babe' pops off his lips. A nonchalant answer distracting all my nerve endings. I hadn't expected him to be a 'Babe' guy, but my toes curl at the name.

Bending forward, I let my chest rest on the counter, somewhat hoping to give him a preview of my cleavage over the two undone buttons on my blouse. To my satisfaction, his eyes dip low.

He struts around the island in three long strides, his hands finding my waist, fingers twisting me to face him and curling into the bunched fabric of my shirt. The storm clouds rolling over his features make my body defiant against every warning firing in my head.

"How's the mocha?" he asks again. His voice is low, drawing my chin upwards.

"Good." And damn, my response comes out breathless. "Did you— you never told me you knew how to make fancy drinks?"

"If you like surprises, I have another." He stares down at me and my body presses closer.

"Oh. Well, I wouldn't say I enjoy surprises. Christmas is my least favourite holiday. I'm not a gift person. Never sat through a gift exchange without having to top the present next year or on their next birthday or some other holiday exchange. Really it's a problem because I start to judge people's attention to detail based on what they get me, and then I'll think they don't care if it's something simple and will collect dust or completely generic I assume there's no thought. Not that I expect gifts, I don't care for them. I know a lot of people say that but I mean it. I hate the five-second pause of awkwardness when everyone runs a quick calculation of what they got and the plastered fake cheer."

"Margo."

I'm rambling. "Yes, sorry. I know that's not what you meant."

I can't meet his stare. I know exactly what he means.

"You owe me a kiss." He drops his chin, bringing our noses to the same level, almost touching.

Standing in his arms, I lean my head away and my hips press forward against his. The warmth of his body against mine is as delicious as the mocha. Like winter and bliss. The corner of his mouth curls up tauntingly.

"You didn't blow my mind." I jut my chin towards the drink, trying to keep us both on the same topic, but he gently removes one hand away from my waist.

I'm about to argue, claim I miss where his fingers started to burn five lines into my hip, but a firm pinch catches my chin. His thumb presses gently in the centre, forcing me to meet his gaze.

"You want your mind blown? I can do that."

I'd say he was the epitome of confidence, the kind of guy who knows how to make seductive promises, but his chest rises and falls in quick breaths admitting his struggle for control. His tight grip, holding me against him, belly to belly, as his large body hunches and presses above mine, guarantees he will do everything in his power to do exactly what he just said. Staring into my eyes as if they anchor him, he lowers his nose, watching me with an unspoken question. In his grip, I dip my face, letting him feel the nod despite the ringing in my ears.

He moves to close the gap, the bit of space that hung too heavy and stretched too far. The same impulse from earlier in the snow is back, and although I was insanely aware of the cold seeping into our moment, I miss the relief. Every part of me is on fire.

He fills the rest of the distance, and I don't want to wait. I push up against him and bite his bottom lip, delicately between my teeth. A nibble, really. Enough to taste the plump skin I've been thinking about since I saw him at the tree farm. He groans, his arm tightening around my waist as his other hand cups the back of my head.

He pulls my body flush against his and I nudge his lips open, asking him to let my tongue taste his fully. Lingering peppermint swirls through my mouth, and my hands roam over him everywhere. The build-up of need, the instant attraction, the part of me that requests *more, more, more*. Tension builds between my hips. The hesitant kiss turns demanding, and his arms flex behind my back, pulling me closer, holding me against the spot I crave. I moan and he tenses, breaking the spell.

A *thunk* hits the glass door. It takes me a second to consider the sound, where it comes from and why it's here.

Another loud beat drums at the entrance. Fists? No, someone smacks the glass with an open palm.

"Fuck," Richard sighs, pulling away to glare at the door from where we entangle, tucked in the corner of the kitchen. "Sorry."

To my disappointment, he releases me. He presses a kiss to my temple in apology. The sheer softness of the touch is as if he subconsciously decides to reassure me. The gesture is natural, an instinct. He doesn't balk at what he does. He adjusts his waistband and leaves to answer whoever interrupts us. The movement is oddly seductive. I melt into the tingling feeling that echoes where his lips were. My body misses the press of his, but the physical response confuses me.

I force the lump in my throat down. Unsure whether I should follow Richard or remain hidden. I hesitate and reach for the mocha to busy my hands.

A loud voice booms in greeting following the heavy thump of boots into the basement. I try to eavesdrop, listening to hear if Richard will whisper some warning to leave or uncomfortably make up an excuse to send whoever is at the door away.

"Yeah, but I have no chips left. You ate them," Richard scolds, but listening to his feigned anger, I recognize the hum of affection in his voice. The same softness he spoke to me with in the car on our first date and again while we tobogganed.

"Nah. This time I came for your Netflix," the unknown voice responds.

Are they coming in? I stand straighter.

Just as I debate hiding in the cupboard beneath the sink, a wide-shouldered man struts into the kitchen. He's shorter than Richard but built with more muscle. A toque hangs off the back of his head, propping up a gelled peak of hair. Behind him, a short man with rich brown skin, grins with unexpected warmth.

The two strangers freeze. Richard stands behind them. And if Richard looked perplexed like his broad-shoulder friend or giddy like the shorter shadow of the group, he gives away nothing in his laugh. Utterly relaxed, Richard pats the two newcomers on the back, then steps through where they stand in shock.

At my side, he watches me from the corner of his eye, his interest genuine and his hand finding the dip of my tailbone, offering me the strength I seek without voicing a word. Too many responses bounce in my skull, but none come out. My body refuses to relax against where he props me.

We had kissed. His *friends* are *here*.

"Margo, this is Eric and Armen." He points to the scowling behemoth then the one who hasn't stopped grinning.

Eric frowns, not impressed with Richard's amusement. More mad at the prank-like introduction than at my presence because when he faces me, his smile is huge and it's sheer instinct to return it. Somehow, his expression reminds me of Jane and Aubrey morphed into one.

"Hi Margo," he purrs. "Richard you dick, you could have warned us there's a beautiful woman in your house."

"Ah, but Netflix and chill wouldn't have been the same without you," I say. The response leaks from my lips and blooms on Armen's cheeks before he chuckles and punches Eric's arm.

Richard trails a palm over his face, but from where I stand next to him, I see his amusement. He wants to contain his laughter and a part of me is proud I made the joke. If Eric and Armen are his friends, close enough to casually show up to steal his Netflix, then I want to make a good impression.

"Don't worry, Sweetheart. There's always a spot for one more." Eric wiggles his brows, and I scrunch my nose up at him in a playful scowl.

"Dude," Richard glances between me and the guys, now realizing the flaw in this plan.

"Relax, bro." Eric comes up to me and offers a closed fist for me to pound. I have to release the mocha, my rock and anchor to reality, to tap my knuckles to his. "Nice to meet you, Margo. Our man has been glued to his phone the last couple of weeks. Glad it was you on the other end instead of—"

Richard clears his throat at the same time his palm returns to the small of my lower back. The circle motions distract me, pulling me from whatever Eric means to confess. Does Richard worry his friend will embarrass him? A curious glance earns me a shrug, but he doesn't deny his friend's statement and his fingers continue to draw along my clothes.

Richard really did want to text me and get to know me. Anonymous dating was an option for him to meet someone, and he took advantage of the situation to see how it went regardless of the prank. Was it Eric and Armen who signed him up as a joke? I tuck away the details of Eric's remark to analyze later.

"Hey Margo, I'm Armen." He hesitantly introduces himself again, and I fight the urge to hug him. He's not much taller than me, and his polite tone melts the last bits of tension from my spine.

"Hey, nice to meet you."

"What are you drinking?" Armen peers at the glass on the counter, now halfway done from my nervous drinking. "Peppermint mochas? Richard. You brought her here and made her *peppermint mochas?*"

"Is that a problem?" Confusion coats Richard's expression as he second-guesses what he has done. I want to reassure him and tell him that I'm enjoying the beverage despite my earlier claims.

"That's our thing!" Armen wails. He maneuvers around us, grabbing the empty metal cup with leftover milk which only deepens his frown. He mutters something under his breath, clearly disappointed in being left out.

Eric mumbles, "Better than bringing her here to Netflix and chill."

"No, that's reserved for you." Richard shoots back.

"You know it, Sweetheart." Eric winks at his friend and I shake my head at the whole exchange.

These guys are close, there's no doubting their chemistry. And as Armen fills the cup with new milk and places a glass on the counter with chocolate syrup and a bottle labelled 'Peppermint', it confirms my suspicion that they willingly share an openness that extends to physical space and personal time.

"So, how did you all become friends?" I ask.

Though Richard means to knead out any tension along my spine, every bit of pressure pulls me from the room. I want his soft touches to press harder, work out the kinks in not only my body but the racing bits of my mind that remain hyperaware of each stroke. I want to curl against him, familiarize his hands, release the doubts my brain shouts, warning me that none of this is meant to feel nice.

"Me and Dick over here used to play hockey, but we've been friends since grade school. Armen came along in university," says Eric. Somehow he made it halfway to the fridge without me noticing.

It's just a hand, Margo. Ignore it.

"What did you go to university for?" My question is directed to Richard, realizing we didn't break through the first level of dating questions before we started making out. I step away from him, casually leaning against the counter in what I hope is a nonchalant way of avoiding his touch. If he notes the change, he reveals no reaction.

"Business," he waves away the question. "Now I do carpentry. My dad used to have a supply store so my life pretty much went in full circle."

He doesn't appear disappointed by the events, if anything he seems thrilled.

"Arthur keeping you busy?" Eric slides Richard a beer just as Armen pours his shot of espresso over a spoon. Armen scowls as the layers of his drink combine to brown.

"Yes," Richard's voice clips with a slight bite, and I peer at him. Confused by the change of his adoration when he announced he is a carpenter to the instant guard he thrusts in Eric's direction.

Eric beams, picking up on a hidden meaning in Richard's defence I don't know enough about to catch. Curiosity fills me as the two men enter a stare-off. I add Arthur to my list of things to ask Richard about.

"Friends from grade school is impressive," I interject. "Do you all live in town?"

"No, I'm in Vaughan but I'm house-sitting at my parents' place." Eric turns to me, enjoying the edge he put Richard on.

"Oh, that's nice." I nod, wracking my mind for anything else to say. Vaughan is the next city over, not too far from Bolton and an easy drive to visit a friend to steal their Netflix. "What Netflix show have you come to bum off Richard?"

"There's never just one. Eric is too cheap to subscribe himself," pitches Armen. He takes a swig from his mocha, reminding me I have my own.

"That I will not deny." Eric points at Armen, but then his attention turns to me and I'm struck by the intense glower he pins me under. Richard senses the change and straightens. "What about you, Margo? Tell us about yourself."

"Eric," Richard growls.

"No, no. It's okay." I step further away from Richard, not letting his presence cloud my mind.

His friends care about him and root for his happiness. From the way they barged in here, they give off the impression of family more than buddies. Since grade school, Eric had said. They might as well be blood-related.

What do I tell them? I'm Margo Diaz, a Director of Finance who constantly faces off with her cheating ex. That the pressure of work and a promotion and being good enough to finally prove to the asshole that I'm better than him had made me a liar out of desperation? Richard and I might have spoken for two weeks but I've been hyping the fake version of him to my office for a full month. I committed fraud over a relationship. He's my fake-boyfriend-turned-real.

My intentions were misguided, but Richard standing calm and patient with a curious, reassuring gaze, is enough proof that I'm glad I did it. All of it.

I'm unsure what to say about myself, but for some reason, this is where I start, "I moved from Mexico when I was young and my Abuela was the one who taught me math in the kitchen while my parents worked nights cleaning offices. Money was a constant equation that determined what we could afford to do and where we could go. I wanted to help, to understand, and now I'm an accountant." I stare at my hands around the base of the drink on the counter.

For a long time, my family has been my light, my source of who I am. They're supportive in ways I could never give back. Earning enough to contribute to groceries was my first goal, but then I took on the job of filing their taxes and understood they needed more. They saved a lot for my schooling and hadn't asked for a penny in return. When I moved back home, I slowly started to find ways to give back. Grander gifts, more clothes for Raph, signing him up for sports and bringing him to each game. When Abuela passed, she left the hole of a caregiver and role model, but that pain lessened whenever I mimicked her kindness, baked her recipes, followed my heart.

"My parents came over with theirs before I was born. I grew up here, but they always remind me to be grateful for their sacrifices." Armen offers me a small nod.

"Nayiri and Aram have my heart, Bro." Eric slaps Armen on the back. "Seriously, Margo. You need to try their cooking."

And just like that, the strain in the kitchen slacks, returning to its natural state of hearty jokes and comfortable conversation. Hours pass, and we never do make it to the living room to watch Netflix. Eric hammers me with questions and Armen intervenes in the conversation to reiterate my welcome and how they're happy I'm here. We settle around the counter, exchanging insults and truths. The whole time Richard listens, his gaze heats the side of my face as he waits for my response. He hangs on my every word, shifting closer whenever I spare honesty that climbs from a chasm deep inside me.

"11:11!" Armen announces, pointing at the clock over the stove. "Shit, make a wish!"

"Man, you're serious?" Eric's jaw drops in disbelief.

"Make it good," Richard whispers low in my ear. I jolt at the nearness of him. Somehow, I hadn't felt him move closer.

"I'm more of a 12:34 person. It's aesthetically pleasing and balanced." I crook a smile up at him, turning my face and our noses almost touch.

"Nerd." He shakes his head, but something in the movement tells me he expected my response. "Make a wish, Margo," he croons.

Glancing at the men crowded around the granite island, Eric and Armen now discussing their three wishes if they met a genie and Richard content with witnessing my thoughts flicker over my expression, my insides flutter. These people, openly ready to accept me and get to know me, are comfortable, kind, and fun. I fit in here, and that scares me. How easily can this image break? Will Armen stop defusing awkward topics, Eric stop caring to learn who I am, Richard stop hanging from my every word?

I forgot. Forgot what it was like to belong, to laugh, to care about someone. For years I avoided glances from men who might have shown interest, refused dates, and stayed home. I told myself it was for my own protection. It was better to remain alone because my family would never leave me and work filled my spare time, leaving no room to miss out.

But Richard, with his full lips, chin dimple, and curls that shape his handsome face is also honest, a great listener, and committed to making me feel like I belong. Every attempt he's made since we anonymously texted has been to reassure me that this can work. We matched online for a reason. We're compatible on some scale.

Whether we make it to New Year's for the gala is no longer my fear because if we don't make it at all, it will hurt more. A seed of hope burrows deep in my chest.

I close my eyes and make my 11:11 wish; one I avoided feeling for a long time: *happiness.*

8
The Ball Drop

I want to hold tweezers to the seed of hope that plants itself inside me. Yank it out and squish it in toilet paper before I flush like it's some type of bug.

The clock on my laptop reads well past noon and I still haven't replied. When my phone buzzed this morning with a text from Richard, I smiled.

And that's the problem.

Relying on a man for any bit of happiness is a betrayal of the vow I made myself. The vow that promised no guy will give me something they have the power to take away. And happiness fell into that category.

Tristan threatened my position at Lauder Accounting with his pity and underhanded support that suggested I wasn't up to the job. Missing days at the office after our breakup hadn't helped prove my ability as a Team Lead at the time, but I got Tristan the job dammit. For him to say I wasn't capable was like a knife to the throat after he already stabbed my heart. It was Jane who shook me and said to get my shit together because I was spiralling and everyone could see. Heck, she didn't even work on our floor and she noticed the change just from bumping into me in the lobby. One day, she overheard someone in the elevator let slip that Harvey considered letting me go, and that bit of insight had fuelled me to get back up. I'd be damned if I let a guy bring me so low, I lost everything I worked for.

No guy is going to have the upper hand.

Not again.

But Richard is different.

He reads my body language and he moves with me in unison. And his laugh, the loud bellow that surges from him when I say something funny causes me to question all the times I bit back responses in meetings and at family dinners. He encourages me to share and documents the details of what I say. Listening is heartening, and his gentle nudges for me to continue were next-level powerful.

How many times has Tristan spoken over me in meetings? Has Harvey sided with Tristan whenever a client is a male-owned company? His ideas, my implementation, that's how it always works. But the credit is given to the man who invented the plan, not the woman who sees it through.

Richard relinquishes control, happy to let me steer. Even if we fly over a snowbank and topple down together. With Richard, I take chances, I put myself first to test my boundaries, and he steps aside as if to say *after you.*

My fingers stumble with the memory of our kiss.

Unlocking my phone, I read his message for the twentieth time based on an estimate averaging about once every half-hour. No response I brainstorm is good enough to type.

All I have to do is say hello back, but to reply with a small greeting after all these changes fall into motion is a slap to the delusion of more. Part of me wants to explain my intentions for signing up and confess that my workplace thinks we've been dating for over a month. The other part of me says it doesn't matter how or why I signed up, I saw through the dating timeline, was myself despite trying a little too hard in some places, and then met him in person. Everything plays out naturally, and who cares what my office thinks about us anyway? What are two extra weeks added to our timeline? He, himself, had been signed up for a prank. A reminder I'll keep repeating to justify my intent. After all, how serious can he really be if he wasn't actually searching for a relationship?

I pound my pointer finger against the mouse and hard press the X on all the open tabs on the large monitor. They swipe down over my screen. One of my closings came back with an adjustment, but I handled that two hours ago. Across from my office, through the window that gives me the best view of Tristan's door, I stare at the Old Hollywood New Year's poster which hangs in neutral browns, golds, and red.

After meeting his friends, Richard had driven me back to where I parked before we tobogganed. The night was dark and he waited for me to enter my car, turn over the engine, then counted the minutes as the old heater fought against the cold to warm up. He continued to watch me through his rolled-down window, and although mine was frozen shut, I mimed for him to go home and waved goodbye. He hadn't driven away. His truck continued to pollute the air next to me until I switched into gear. His headlights followed me up the South Hill until I turned and drove past his street. Brazen confidence tugged at my expression, wondering if I left him curious about how close we lived, one subdivision apart.

Nothing online prepared me to meet him in person. Not the angle of his cheekbones, his intense stare ready to pull apart my every emotion, the confident way he inserts himself near me. His instinct to be present should rally trust, but the alarm in my head warns me to keep my distance.

He already shows up as if he knows me, and maybe he does, we've been talking enough to establish a foundation. Core beliefs and timing, that's what Aubrey sings whenever the topic of me finding someone comes up in conversation. Maybe Richard has enough similarities to make us a match. We did match, but is timing based on the timeline of our life or just the coincidence of fate and being somewhere at the exact right moment? The tree farm being the most obvious.

Am I ready to let someone in?

The New Year's gala poster mocks me.

If I show up alone, I'll have to face Tristan and Stacey's engagement. I'm the ex who hasn't moved on, forced to watch her cheating boyfriend find his happily ever after. And it's not that I still care about Tristan. I feel nothing aside from common coworker rivalry and slight emotional betrayal, but him getting engaged wasn't about him marrying her and his future wife not being me. No, it was that I was left behind while he got it all. The girl, the family, but not my promotion.

He's not getting that raise or any title on his name plaque aside from Mrs. Okay, maybe the analogy would work better if he was a married woman going from *Miss.* to *Mrs.*, but the new promotion is mine. It's the least he can leave me with.

And this is why I have to break things off with Richard before either of us gets hurt. He doesn't deserve the role of a pawn in my power move to impress our biggest client during a buyout, or to stand next to me in front of the entire staff at Lauder Accounting to prove that I have my shit together outside of the office.

But maybe I want him there. Maybe I want to see him in a suit, see his hunger devour me in my red sequin dress.

The light in Tristan's office flicks off, and before he opens the door with his predictable briefcase in his clutch and jacket slung over his forearm, I'm pushing away from my desk. I yank the knob with enough force that it bumps into the wall behind me. Furrowed brows, Tristan leers at me.

His buzzed head, shaved face, and stiff shoulders pull me through the rows of empty cubicle desks. How did I ever find this man intimidating? Gone is the comfort I spent years convincing myself had the potential for forever. Everything about him puts me on edge and turns my stomach acid-sour.

He dumped me and then gunned for my job. Made me the unstable ex. And though years passed, he hasn't stopped trying to undermine my ideas, talk over me, and invite people out to grab drinks while I stayed back at the office. With the promotion in view, I refuse to let him hinder my credibility. Not when I worked hard to redeem myself, to make sure my perfect attendance, overtime, client reviews, and performance spoke for themselves. Harvey was a numbers guy, and my team's closings and year-end retention remain higher than anyone else's.

"Margo, I didn't realize you were here." That's a lie, we rode the same elevator this morning. But maybe it's my fault he forgot the ride up with me. I worked hard to pretend I didn't exist, willing myself invisible whenever he was around.

"Just finishing last-minute prep for the event."

"And you require my help with the final details?" His question is void of any lilt. He's convinced he's useful to me or that I'm useless on my own, whichever it is.

"No, I just wanted to make sure that you understood your role. You will attend as a guest and follow the seating arrangement." A chart I haven't yet organized, but now that it's on my mind, I already know exactly where he and Stacey will sit. Preferably next to the washrooms.

He frowns. "I'm sure Harvey will make sure the introductions are made correctly."

"Hyup is my account. As you made clear, it's been a busy month for you. I'd appreciate it if you didn't disrupt my organization." Hot liquid sloshes up my throat, but I maintain a tone that gives nothing away.

"I'm sure your plans would benefit from my feedback. You know, since marketing isn't your department," says Tristan. I want to growl, to hiss, to let the lashing animal inside of me lunge for him. "Besides, my engagement went smoothly. From this point on, all hands are on deck."

I bristle. He proposed. I knew he intended to ask Stacey to marry him over the break, but I hadn't seen her in the office or the ring. His confirmation is used like a weapon. Stacey said yes, and now he has the time to swoop in at the last minute to steal the recognition out from under where my feet point toe-to-toe with his.

As the Director of Sales and Marketing, Tristan fills in the blanks where my analyses of client campaign success and production are out of scope. Our departments are meant to work together. As part of the Lauder Accounting board, we provide the overall picture and piece together the success of our brand and present it to Harvey. We manage different tasks, but there's the constant debate that his marketing and sales are what drive client success and production, but setting up a client is less work than maintaining them. He may hook them with his fancy PowerPoints and show up with a leather briefcase and popped collar, but I'm who reels them in. I'm the one who makes sure my team follows up, schedules meetings, renews contracts, and submits plans for the New Year.

"You'll stay out of my way." I drop my voice, and I'm impressed I hold my ground.

"Will I? Harvey will love having the full board to welcome Hyup. Logan and I exchange memes, he will expect me nearby." Tristan sighs, placing down his briefcase to shrug on his jacket, a thin cotton duster unfit for winter.

They exchange memes?

"I mean it, I've spent the month pulling strings to put the last-minute details together." I intend to warn him, but somehow, worry creeps in and my words come out as a plea. He can't take credit for everything, surely Harvey will see.

"I signed off on all marketing expenses, my signature says otherwise." He retrieves his briefcase and peers down his crooked nose at me. His pity boils my insides, but then I hear what he says.

"Your signature." I balk. "Your sign-off is required, it proves nothing." Except it does. It's a paper trail to prove his involvement.

"Margo, you didn't have a theme until a day ago." Again, he shakes his head like I'm hopeless. "Are we done here? Stacey wants me home for dinner." He walks away.

"Who needs a theme for a *New Year's Party*!" I yell at his back.

Glad no one is around to witness my temper, I storm into my office and slam the door. Home for dinner, I snort. Counting my breaths, willing myself to rein in my tears before they fall, I wait twenty minutes until I assume the parking garage is clear from his stupid electric BMW.

Flicking off the switches, the office falls into the dim glow of the emergency lights. The sunset paints the stretch orange through the large windows. With my laptop tucked under my armpit, my purse thrown over my shoulder, and my scarf hung loose around my neck, I deem myself ready to embark on a safe exit. Tapping the elevator call button, I watch the analogue numbers count up as the lift carries to the floor of Lauder Accounting.

Entering, I check my hair on the reflective surface. Wow, the winter weather has not been kind to my curls. Leaning closer, I pick at the zit forming on my chin, a loud tattle for the bit of chocolate I keep hidden in the top drawer of my desk.

Someone clears their throat and my spine stiffens. Pulling away from my reflection, another body enters the elevator before it closes to launch us to the ground floor.

Dressed in a sand-coloured suit, off-trend in comparison to the common maroon, navy, and sage shades of winter, Logan leans against the wall across from me. Of course, Tristan exits and the owner of Hyup traps me in an elevator.

What is going on today?

Logan's nose crinkles, zoning in on my chin where I'm sure the bit of skin is red with a bead of blood. His quiet judgement presses on the lift as if it carries enough weight to plummet us right to the basement floor. Does the building have a basement?

"Logan— Mister Hymn, I hadn't realized anyone else was in the building." I adjust the strap of my purse on my shoulder.

"Figured as much." He pulls his phone free from his chest pocket and starts to scroll. Is there service in elevators?

"Last minute budget changes for the New Year?" I ask. My attempt at conversation falls about as flat as my back presses against the elevator wall, demanding as much space from the man who has the power to determine the length of my career.

"Shouldn't I ask you that?" Logan's glare shoots up from his phone but he refuses to lift his chin. Probably sharing memes with Tristan.

I've managed the Hyup Media account for just over a year. Before me, six other accountants stood in as consultants, each of them taken off the account as a request from Logan. I heard rumours about his habit of fudging numbers and moving budgets to accommodate campaigns with low returns, blaming the loss on a bad investment or oversight. In short, he is a nightmare. And his marketing company lost a lot of money, putting his clients at risk. It made sense for Harvey to buy Hyup Media out and act as their saviour while also expanding Lauder Accounting in the process.

For months, Logan strutted into our firm with the air of royalty as if he did Harvey a favour by losing all his money. In hindsight, he did. We will gain Hyup Media's clients and branch into the realm of analytics, tracking, and other reports most agencies don't know how to read when they set up their campaigns. But Logan fails to admit how big of a chunk he lost in his company. He certainly doesn't act like a man swimming in the red.

"If I knew you were in the building, I could have pulled your file and put together some predictions. Tristan looked into the success of your recent campaign."

What was it called? Why am I drawing a blank? This isn't happening.

Logan sneers with the hunger of a shark. He knows my use of the word *success* is a stretch. "Jolly Jokers! It just finished on Boxing Day, but I'll request a presentation right away."

"Thanks," says Logan with careful disinterest. His stare pins me deeper into the metal corner. "Tristan is a commendable employee. I'm glad to have him on my account."

I ignore the jab. Our marketing department is small. Established at the time when I submitted Tristan's resume for the position. He doesn't have accounts, he and his team work with all Lauder Accounting clients. Logan knows I'm his representative, understands he lost a lot of money and the savings I've given him in the last year still weren't enough to fix his mistakes.

The numbers flashing above the door continue to count down. Four more floors, I'll reach the ground level and take the separate stairs to the parking garage. If I didn't know that Logan hires himself a private driver everywhere he goes, I would have camped out at the security desk to give myself some time to avoid an awkward encounter on the way to my car. Cornered in an elevator is about as much as I'm able to handle.

"Lauder Accounting has a great reputation in the industry. We are happy to put together anything you need." My throat is stiff like my response, robotic as if I recite a scripted telephone automation.

"Of course," Logan muses as if he's aware of an oversight I miss.

Finally, the elevator dings. The flashing arrow stops, fading to black just as the doors open. I hang back, clenching my laptop bag to my chest and stiffening my shoulders, waiting for Logan to exit first.

He's slow to put away his phone as if he values my discomfort. The golden metal glow makes his fake tan appear more copper than orange and his hair the colour of dried-out hay. Again, I wonder why he chooses such a light-coloured suit. He looks like a soaked breadstick.

Logan straightens himself, buttoning up his blazer and lifting his chin. Following his lead, I pull myself back when he suddenly stops. His hand smacks flat on the frame of the door, preventing it from closing us in. This close, the harsh musk of his cologne burns my nose. Logan peers over his shoulder and down at me.

"We'll see who comes out on top when the ball drops, Miss Diaz. I hope you're bringing your A-game, I'd hate for you to fumble."

Logan leaves. His strut is a little bouncy as he pushes aside the glass to meet the car he called. Once he's safely folded into the backseat, I exhale.

Had Logan implied he didn't think I deserve the promotion? He complimented Tristan and made me feel inadequate. Me, who has been the one person to handle his account, handle him, and he implies I will fumble?

We'll see who comes out on top when the ball drops. Does Logan mean Harvey will announce the promotion on New Year's or that the gala is a test of sorts? With only a few days to go, my work can speak for itself or I can use this gala to my advantage as one last edge.

Each step down the stairs to my car is a ring of annoyance. Because of me, Hyup Media ended the year without losing more money. Where is Tristan's contribution aside from brand meetings? The platforms of my boots slam into the concrete, dreaming of the chance to flatten the sole of my shoe against the face of my competition and the man responsible for the rivalry.

Tristan. Logan. Tristan. Logan. Left. Right. Left. Right.

I can't let either of them win.

— ☐☐☑ —

Blasting *11:11* by *Arkells* on my drive home, hoping to find the calm I left behind yesterday, I belt the lyrics in desperation. The happy alternative-rock tune is too catchy not to sing, but my choked words miss every note.

The song reminds me of Richard, which somehow reminds me of Tristan and the verbal spar we had in the office earlier. I keep the encounter with Logan safely at bay, not ready to analyze his taunts and the underlying threat.

So what if Tristan is engaged?

If anything, his new commitment means he's less available for overtime as he starts a family. Mom, Dad, and Raphael are my family.

Maybe if I focused on meeting people, I could have been closer to a proposal myself. I shake my head before the topic of my single life sticks.

I'm twenty-seven, there's still time. Besides, Jane and Aubrey already designated fun aunt duties to me. My friends love me, support me, and cheer me up in the same manner a husband and kids might bring joy to married women. The same way Eric and Armen show up on Richard's doorstep for some bro time.

I lower the music as I wait at a red light. My phone is heavy in my jacket pocket, pinned between the seatbelt and my thigh with a message I opened and never replied to. Driving by Richard's street does something to my insides.

But focusing on Richard is a bad idea. Not having a date is the least of my worries.

Tristan schemes to insert himself in my big moment and Logan is aware. Worse, Tristan plans to piggyback on all the connections I made while planning and has no shame. The theme he suggested in front of Harvey and Logan will have his fingerprints on it. When Hyup Media enters the party, dazzled by the decor and the prints Aubrey helped me create, Tristan will boost his marketing team. Dammit, I knew I should have invoiced Aubrey despite her insisting she'd do it for free out of boredom.

Invoices. I tap my steering wheel as an idea forms. If I expense the gala decor and submit my receipts after the New Year, Tristan will have less to claim in terms of design. All purchases relating to the theme he wanted will remain connected only to me.

I pull into my driveway, prepared to visit my idea board on my wall to make a shopping list. I'm going to make the best damn Old Hollywood night and prove that the Marketing Department has nothing on my ability to produce. I'll dazzle Hyup and reap the rewards right in front of Tristan.

"The promotion is mine."

9
When One Door Closes

Mom insisted that I made sure not to come home late. Yet here I am at the door, waiting for her. I'm somewhat of a winter chauffeur (minus any form of compensation), and whenever she has to go to the grocery store to replenish the fridge, I'm her first call. She hates driving when there's snow on the road. As soon as I received my license and proved to her I'm a reliable driver, the weekly ritual became our mother-daughter time. Mom asks me what I want to eat, I scroll through emails on my phone.

A cupboard thuds closed upstairs and a few minutes later the hairdryer turns on. Debating if I should get comfortable, I'm turned off by the effort it takes to untie my boots. Scooting my feet along the carpet until the back of my knees bump the armchair in the front living room, I let my ass fall against the cushion, careful to leave my legs suspended and my wet boots away from the hardwood and rug.

In the kitchen, Raph hunches over his winter break homework at the dinner table, which means I'm not allowed to turn on the TV. Mom never lets us watch anything while he has to focus. I rethink my decision of leaving my phone in the car. The house is quiet aside from the hum of the hairdryer and the tick of a clock nearby. But the silence is my victory, and I chose to escape the text I didn't know how to reply to.

The promotion takes priority. Richard is the key to proving to Tristan that he hasn't won. I'm more qualified and have someone on my arm. He didn't break me. But to make it to New Year's, I have to keep focused on the plan. And I worry that if I grow to expect Richard's name attached to phone chimes, grow used to having him around, I'll fall victim to believing this is something more.

Already, thoughts of him stormed in my mind, jolted through me like lightning. I refuse to test my luck when it's safer to take cover. The promotion is my goal.

Outside, the hot sun glints off the snow, warning winter is not yet at its worst. Through the open curtain, the neighbour's car spews black smog from the exhaust, groaning against the chill with the same sound I make in the morning while I wait for Ruby to warm up. I loosen a sigh.

I really need to repair my bumper.

The Ofrenda we set up in November still stands on the low coffee table in the corner. Images of Abuela hang on the walls leading to the large frame at the centre of the display. Dried marigolds and candles circle the photo of my smiling grandmother, the moment captured on her seventy-sixth birthday. The last celebration before she passed.

At the edge of the table, next to a shot of tequila, sits a candy cane Raph shared with her photo a few days ago. He always likes to leave her sweets. My brother doesn't remember much of our Abuela but when Dad explained the honour of leaving gifts to the dead, Raph had taken to sharing his favourite snacks.

I remember the busy streets and vibrant colours of my first home during Día de Muertos. Abuela had painted my face and lit a candle to remember the aunt I never met. The plush flower displays distracted me and made me twirl my skirts. Different from the sadness that chokes me now.

I miss Mexico. I still replay what my small toes in orange sandals felt like in the shallow waves of water, the fresh taste of cutting open coconuts from the trees outside our door, smell Abuela's perfume while she carried me whenever the sand surprised me with a critter and I'd cry.

Glancing around, hardly anything traces back to our first home. I moved here when I was no older than Raph's age now but I remember the armoire that stood in a front hall and the smell of the sun-heated wood when I'd crawl over the lower drawers and curled up inside. Careful not to damage the book Dad had given me, too thick and with font too small for me to understand, I'd flip through the pages huddled beneath the hanging fabric. I wanted to know as much as my dad. He taught

English at the local high school and the way Mom and him swapped fluently back to Spanish fascinated me.

Dad did his best to teach me when I was young, but moving to Canada had been the ultimate language test when I entered the school system. Dad and Mom insisted on only talking to me in English to help me learn, and when Raph was born the swap between languages lessened. I would have never dreamed that my native tongue would fade from my memory with time.

It was without fail that Abuela would find me in the armoire. She'd swing open both wooden doors and pretend to shuffle through the hanging clothes to search for me.

"Where is *mi chiquita hermosa*?" she would say, and I knew from her surprise and crinkling eyes, she played with me.

In the tiny slit of light, I'd hide all the collected books along the back wall, stack them in different ways while I waited for her to notice I was missing. Dad and Mom spent their days at work, and Abuela never allowed me to slip out of sight. Thinking back, my slither from the couch, army crawl along the floor, and tip-toe out of the room were too obvious for her to miss, but she played along. She left me waiting, but never for too long. And once I was found, she would take a hanger, hold it against her collarbone to place the blouse on full display against her body, asking me, "You like it?" I'd laugh, cross-legged on the floor, while she made silly faces.

I miss my Abuela. I miss the armoire.

The wardrobe was too big to relocate to Canada. We didn't keep any of our old furniture, and the carvings of flowers on the wide wooden doors would have been a statement piece in our modern decor.

"Are you alright, *Mi Cielo*?" Dad pops his head into the room. He looks at my dangling feet and ignores how close they are to the clean floors. His silence is in exchange for me not ratting on the five Oreos he carries in his hands.

"I'm fine, just trying to remember Mexico." I drop my cheek on the couch and he stands sideways now that the floor is at my ear. "Will you ever go back to visit?"

He moves closer and I don't miss how his shoulders hunch and his steps are slower. His back has bothered him since the tree fell on him at the farm. He pretends he's fine, but not even my headphones, the whole upstairs floor, and Taylor Swift hide the long sigh he draws when he sits down on the couch. Luckily, the college he teaches at reopens in another week. Their favourite Spanish professor will have time to rest, and Mom got him new orthotics for Christmas.

"Some day, when Raphael is older." He answers my question and hands me an Oreo.

Raph has never seen Mexico. He wouldn't know the smell of the water, know what places had the best tacos or what a fresh banana leaf tamale tastes like.

"I wonder if our old house looks the same." I twist open the cookie. A quick search on Google Street View would answer my curiosity, but a part of me is too worried I'll shatter the memory I spent so much time protecting and making sure I didn't forget.

"The area has changed since we were there." Dad pops a whole cookie into his mouth. I want to ask what he remembers, if *he* has searched Google Street View, but then Mom wisps down the stairs in a long cardigan and a face smooth from any signs of age. She checks on Raph's homework which gives Dad the chance to lean closer in secret.

"I do have good news," he flattens my hair with a heavy palm over my forehead. I perk up. "Your gift will be ready to pick up this weekend."

"Oh, it's okay. I wasn't worried. Mom got me a bunch of work clothes." I wave him off but appreciate how he smooths all the static strands around my forehead.

"But I wanted to get you something, too. I'm sorry it's late." Dad wears a forced frown, which piques my curiosity back up. He may apologize for being late, but he doesn't appear sorry at all. Before I ask for a clue, Mom turns into the room.

"Margo, don't put your boots on the clean floor!" Mom swats my knees and waves for me to sit up. Turning to my father to scold him for not telling me to take off my boots, she sees the last cookie in his hand. "*Dios*, what are you eating? You know you can't eat cookies! The doctor said to watch your sugars." Then her glare is back on me, accusing me of doing a bad job at not telling Dad to put down the Oreos.

"What am I to do with you!" Mom goes on, not specifying which one of us she references. Throwing up her hands, she heads for the door. She would have stormed out, but she stops to tie a heavy knit scarf around her neck and retrieves her jacket. "What are you waiting for? Let's go." She points at the door like I'm the one who was late getting here.

Dad spares a sheepish smile for me over Mom's shoulder. Before I can question him further about the late gift, he's already faking a run toward the kitchen. "Maybe Raphael will want some cookies."

"Don't you dare. Not before dinner!" Mom yells, but Dad's wispy laugh trails behind him into the next room.

"The car is probably cold now," I mutter on our way out the door. "You're buying us coffee."

She fluffs her straight black hair, not yet a victim to the cold, dry air. Digging into her purse, she pulls free a Starbucks gift card.

"Coffee is on Leanne," she beams, proud that her cheap boss got her something useful as a gift. Still no comparison to the cookie platter Mom spent two nights baking.

— ▢▢☑ —

The parking lot is hectic for an evening afternoon and I opt for dropping Mom off at the front doors before finding a spot. This is good, this buys me time to reply to the waiting text message I rehearsed at every stoplight.

> **Margo Diaz:** Hey! Crazy day. Can you believe it's snowing again?
>
> 6:37 pm

Yes, that's the best I come up with.

Dammit, Margo. Why did you bring up the weather?

It's better than talking about other things, like admitting I'm in constant competition with my ex, everyone at work thinks we've been dating for a month, or our kiss yesterday.

Did that really happen only yesterday?

Already I miss feeling him close to me. How insane is that? My hormones need to get in line. One kiss and my body is already wired and craving.

I huff a breath and beat my head against my steering wheel.

"Get it together, Margo. You've gone on dates before."

Before. As in, before I met Tristan and thought I never had to enter the dating pool again. The same pool my colleagues complain is full of trash and to tread carefully so I don't drown. I wanted to circle the edge, dip my toe in and test the temperature of the water, but I dove in head first. And the water was cold, a fresh wave of reality waking me from whatever dream I convinced myself to live in.

Richard Vixen: How dare it snow in the winter

6:43 pm

Margo Diaz: The audacity

6:44 pm

Richard Vixen: How was your day?

6:44 pm

A simple question. Curious or caring? My day started with a weird wake-up call. The alarm sounded the same as every day, but this morning it only took one ring for me to sit straight in bed. I was ready, the sound was no longer dreadful.

It was Richard's text that provided clarity for why I woke up excited.

Richard's name broke apart my tired face like the sun through the clouds.

Walking across the parking lot, my phone is hot in my pocket. Why is the question hard to answer? I spoke to him anonymously for weeks, yet now I'm panicking.

Mom waits for me at the entrance with a cart that already has some bags of chips in the top basket. These will sit in the cupboard and mysteriously disappear in a week, without anyone calling me to share. Next is the fruit. We skip the berries that are out of season until we shift to vegetables. It's when Mom is inspecting the corn that I hear my name.

"Margo!" Bianca strolls her cart faster down the aisle. It's weird seeing her outside of her usual blazer and blue light glasses, weird that she's not sitting behind a desk. I forgot she lived in Bolton.

Bianca is a few years younger than me and spunky. Her soaked Converse and fingerless gloves give me the impression she listens to soft alternative rock. It makes me love her more.

"Hey, Bianca." I wrap my hands around Mom's bicep to turn her to my friend, already knowing she expects an introduction. "This is my Mom."

"Super nice to meet you, Mama Diaz!" And man, if I ever assumed her excitement was a front to keep clients happy, I'm happy I'm wrong. Her customer service voice is just her personality. "Oh, I'm craving corn. I can't remember the last time I didn't make something out of a can."

Mom scrunches her nose, but Bianca's personality is winning her over. "Food out of a can is no good. Come over one day, and I'll cook for you."

Bianca glows at the invite but then her face drops and she shoots me a glance as if to apologize. She's asked me out for drinks many times, but by the time I clock out, the sun has set and I'm already counting the hours until I have to return to the office. Sometimes I debate the comfort of my desk, if sleeping on the dark wood will show dedication or earn me a reprimand. Instead, I settle for stacking my folders and the comfort of my bedroom, turning on the lamp and laptop in a place where drooling on my desk isn't frowned upon.

Do I feel guilty that Bianca has been around for months and I managed to dodge her every effort to hang out? Absolutely. Is she super cool and totally friend material? Also yes. But my job leaves little time for another friend. And yes again, I realize that makes me sound pathetic and like a total bitch.

"Bianca, you should come. Mom makes the best tortillas from scratch." I squeeze Mom's shoulders for emphasis, earning surprise from both women.

"That would— yes. Sounds awesome." She turns to ask Mom about the ingredients and the baking process. Mom answers heartily, but I know she holds back on giving specifics. Her recipes are secret, not even I've earned them yet.

"Thank you, Mrs. Diaz," says Bianca as she steers her cart away. She pauses as if forgetting something.

"Oh, you never told me how the other night went."

I freeze. Every muscle in my body protests movement. I can't even blink. She couldn't possibly think asking me about Richard in front of my mom is a good idea. I spare a second to realize, *of course she does.* To Bianca, Richard and my mom have met, he's not a secret. Normal people don't have secret boyfriends.

Stealing a glance at my mother who scowls, betrayed I withhold important information from her, I plaster on my bravado. "It was good."

I pray Bianca picks up on the warning I flash her with flat lips and wide eyes, but my communication of *this is not the place, spare me now and I'll tell you later* is lost because Bianca is speaking to Mom.

"Do you like him?" she asks. And there's no chance to intervene.

Mom isn't dumb, and she pieces the question together easily. Bianca thinks I introduced Richard to my mom over Christmas, and Mom now arrives at the conclusion that I'm seeing someone and lacked the decency to introduce her to him.

My mother maintains composure, which can't be said for me. The hint of disappointment is noticeable in her stiff laugh lines and the way she doesn't look directly at me, but Mom isn't one to cause a scene and she keeps up the conversation with Bianca. No, her reprimand is reserved for the car drive home.

"Yes," Mom lies, partially because I'm shaking my head, begging her to keep herself poised. The charade is one she recognizes from my teen years when I signalled her to play it cool, not to embarrass me in front of my friends. She catches the movement in her peripherals.

Bianca squeezes my wrist, sending a cloud of her raspberry vanilla perfume through my muddled panic, unaware of my unease and Mom's forced sincerity. Satisfied with the small admittance, Bianca cheers her excitement.

"Seriously, I'm excited to meet him at the gala!"

My stomach drops. Not only am I forced to explain all of this to my mother, Bianca spills how I promised to introduce Richard at the New Year's gala. I already hear Mom's lecture about bringing a boy to meet my friends before my own parents. My blood pressure spikes and the produce aisle narrows.

Bianca says her goodbyes and declares we will grab drinks this week, promising that she won't take no for an answer this time. I like her, I do. It's not her fault she spread the lie I told her.

"*Mija*, you never told me you were seeing someone!" Mom bursts once the bags are loaded in the trunk and my seatbelt is buckled— her confirmation that I'm strapped in and too powerless to escape.

"Mom, it's nothing."

"This friend thinks it's something."

"We had a few dates." *And have been texting anonymously through a dating service, and you actually met him last week at the tree farm when he pulled the tree off Dad.*

I say nothing else. It's hard to get the words I *do* share out.

"We must have him over, *sí?* What does he like to eat?"

"Ma, seriously."

"Nonsense. It's the first boy you've seen since…" She doesn't finish the thought.

Mom stopped hoping I'll surprise her by bringing someone home. Two years had exhausted her daydream of me starting my own family, declaring twenty-seven old in the same insult that deemed me undateable. She believes I can truly have it all. A successful career, a husband, kids. She sees I'm no longer broken, but put together with a papier-mâché of my life's scraps, and she still wishes differently.

"I know."

The car falls silent.

"He likes you?" she whispers, a small coax not to scare me.

"I think so."

"And you like him?"

That's the question I hoped to avoid. Richard is great to talk to, he's comfortable and I haven't felt the draw to filter myself. Maybe it's because I didn't take the dating service seriously and was shopping for a man, but I was myself with no pressure and he's into me. More than that, he's hopeful. He asks me about myself, wants to hear about my day, and moves where I need him without any prompt as if he is aware of me enough to read what I'm feeling.

Tiny stars shoot across my skin where he held my lower back, pressed his lips against my forehead, and trailed his thumb over my knuckle as if little remnants of him stay behind.

If the night we met was a date, if I want to call it one, then why is my brain fighting against the idea of happiness, ready to expel it like poison?

"I think so," I repeat. A weight releases with my next exhale.

"And this work party, he's going?"

"I haven't asked him yet." I drag a palm over my face and Mom senses my distress.

"*Mi Chiquita*, you must ask him."

"I will. I just think it's too soon." I release the truth with the same vigour as the cold winter air that pours through the crack I open in the window. I want to tell her everything, admit that I lied and said I was dating someone to avoid pity, and how Tristan is engaged. Mom was there through the years with my first boyfriend and those that stretched after him.

"I've watched you work hard over the last few years, but let me tell you something. Work is not all there is." I open my mouth but she silences me with a palm. Her lecture to never blur the line between work and family is one I'm familiar with. "I know, I encouraged you to find a good job, to be self-sufficient. I take responsibility for pushing you hard and I'm proud of what you've done, but work is not love, work is how you provide for those you love. There is a difference. It's good to keep busy, but don't run forever." Mom's gentle fingers pinch my hair behind my ear.

I sniffle and blink rapidly at the licence plate on the truck in front of me. Her words pound into the hard shell in my chest and wiggle into the cracks, expanding them to leave space for the good.

Had I filled all my time with extra paperwork to avoid facing a future I hadn't expected? When I was with Tristan, I thought we would end up in the house we spent long nights describing. I assumed by now that I'd be a year into having a family we agreed we would start at twenty-six. I expected to be married. When that vision shattered, I hadn't considered a new dream. Jane and Aubrey gave me focus, made sure I didn't fall behind on my deadlines and brought me back to life through our friendship. I lost contact with the friends Tristan inherited in our split, and the void that was my cheating ex became stuffed with my job until I made a makeshift sealer.

Without realizing it, I unintentionally missed opportunities outside of the firm. I closed myself into my office to protect my heart.

Work is not love. Could I one day love Richard?

I remember the photo of us on my phone. The captured moment where life felt effortless and my smile natural.

Who cares if the timeline is all wrong? No one ever counts the months of other people's relationships. And if they do, then they can mind their own business. Talking to Richard, hanging out with him, there's a chance. And I deserve to take it.

10
Meet Cute

"And a double double," I say to the lady who punches in my order on the other side of the counter.

Mom and I decided to forego our Starbucks run. I wasn't in the mood to upset my stomach more after the truth-vomit I spewed and we had already driven in the opposite direction. But once we walked through the door, Dad asked where the coffee was.

Now I'm standing at the front of the Tim's line holding the secret apple fritter he texted me to buy him. Knowing I'll have to conceal it upon entrance, I jam the donut into my pocket and ignore how I might squish the glaze. I really shouldn't indulge his bad habits.

Tapping my card on the debit machine to pay, the hairs on my neck rise. The air shifts and a weight probes at the back of my head.

"Thank you," I step aside to the pick-up counter, but as I turn, I see him.

Richard leans against the wall with his arms crossed over his chest. Wearing a vest, his muscles are on full display. The tight long-sleeve hugs his forearms and biceps, and his bemusement tells me he witnessed me shove an apple fritter into my pocket.

Across the room, I read his question clearly. *What on Earth are you doing?* he asks, dubiously.

Nothing, I swear. My response blurts in our unspoken conversation when I drop the zipper.

My fingers knot together, and he steps up to the counter to place his order, his eyes not leaving their corners as he watches me. In wide construction boots and baggy thermal pants that ride low on his hips, no one should look this good in construction clothes.

"Margo," his gaze sweeps with amusement when he steps to my side to wait for his order.

"Richard, hi." I bite my lip. "Sorry, today's been a little crazy. My boss has me planning a Hollywood New Year's party to impress a client and my mom needed me to bring her to the store after work. Then we decided not to get coffee, but when we got home my dad said he thought we would bring him one. I offered to go back out because Mom hates driving when the roads are bad. My dad also wanted a donut, which you saw me stuff into my pocket. Wait, is it worse if the donut is mine or if the donut I bought for my father is squished in my pocket?"

I turn to him for a serious answer, but he's fighting off a laugh. Oh God, I really don't owe him an explanation. He didn't ask me for one and I puked my conscience in a Tim Horton's line.

Where are my coffees?

"A hundred percent worse that your dad's donut is shoved in your pocket. That's just not nice."

"Shit," I mumble, twisting to inspect the zipper on my pocket and to free the squished dessert.

His fingertips brush the back of my hand and I pause, staring at where he stops me. The soft-touch tickles, but in a way that makes me want to curl up and tell him not to stop, like back scratches or when someone plays with my hair.

"I'm sure it's fine." His whisper is as smooth as his touch. He still hasn't pulled away. "A New Year's party. That doesn't sound like a job for someone in accounting. How's that going?"

"It's not," I huff. "I mean, I don't only play with numbers, part of my job is client retention and analyzing sales performance. An important client we're negotiating with is coming to the gala and my boss came up with this grand idea to impress him with the biggest event of the year. I'm on the board and he always asks me for stuff because he knows I struggle to say no. Plus there's this promotion. Anyway, sorry. Long story short is that it's stressful and I only recently decided on a theme and now I need to think of last-minute decorations that will incorporate it."

"Sounds like a lot less fun than I thought." He frowns. "Is there anyone else helping you, like a committee?"

"No, just me." I jerk a thumb at myself to bring home the point.

My phone vibrates and I shuffle to free the device from my pocket. Reading the pending message, I fight back a snort.

Harvey Lauder: Janice wants to know if you bought party favours?

6:43 pm

"Great. Now I need adult loot bags," I mutter.

"Well, what about individual cookies?" Richard suggests, reading the text over my shoulder. It's not his fault I hold the phone at a convenient height for him to see. "The café across the street has unreal sweets. I'm sure she has all the tools to make them into specific shapes and she's good with receiving last-minute orders." He turns to the floor-to-ceiling windows and nods towards the awning of the small café still decked out in Christmas decor.

The place is new, and a local business would appreciate the order. The founders of the dating service I met Richard on are housed out of the small storefront. I heard the owner has her Master's in Computer Science and develops apps. She made the algorithm. A tech-gal and a baker, she sounds awesome.

"I may take your suggestion. Everyone enjoys fancy cookies."

"Especially chewy and gooey ones." His eyes flash with a hint of amusement. Oh, how right he is.

"Hey, do you want to…" he continues, pointing at the booth. But then the Coffee God smites me because someone calls out my order and slides a tray of three coffees. "Right, you are on a mission to deliver a squished donut."

"No, what did you have in mind? I can drop them off at home. There are no bars over my windows or anything, I'm allowed to go out." Trying not to sound too eager to clear my schedule for him, I plaster on my most innocent expression: batting my lashes with the small pucker of my lips. He blinks. And I can't decide if I succeed or make a terrible expression I'll have to test out in the mirror when I get home.

"This New Year's gala you're planning, I have an idea that might help."

"Your walls are grey, what do you know about decorating?"

He bends low and places his hands on his knees. At eye level, he mocks my height but his forced scowl illuminates how much fun he's having. Up close, I see his lashes and the small freckles that dot his nose. His chin dimple is on full display.

"Listen, you're going to accept my offer. It's unfair that all of this is on you. Your boss shouldn't have asked just one person to do everything and I can tell you're not someone who normally asks for help. I won't take no for an answer. Drop your coffees off at home and then your cute ass is meeting me."

No one has willingly offered their help, or demanded I accept their offer. Sure Jane and Aubrey assist with small tasks such as design work and printing out the verified guest list, but no one asked about all the other planning elements unless they required a budget breakdown. Richard's right, it isn't fair that this is on me. Party planning isn't in my job description, and my extra hours at the office aren't just motivated by money, there's always something to do, always something waiting because I've made it a habit to pick up the slack and cross-check all proposals, SOWs and contracts. I made myself available.

But… *cute* ass?

"Okay." I nod, not taking my stare off his.

Satisfied with my response, he checks the time on his phone and then reaches for the coffee that is called out. "We have an hour. How soon can you meet me?"

"As soon as I drop these off, I can get you. I have no problem driving if you tell me where we're going."

"No need, I'll come pick you up."

He takes down my address and I don't question a thing.

— □□☑ —

As soon as I thump the three coffees on the kitchen counter, I announce I'm going out. Mom rightly assumes it's with the man I mentioned earlier and rushes to the front window, expecting to see Richard waiting there on the front stoop.

Ten minutes pass and I've been staring at Mom's teeth, her smile slowly losing ease. I'm betting her face will develop its first wrinkle. She refuses to sip her coffee and I hold back the barb that Richard can't smell the caffeine on her breath from his truck.

Me, on the other hand, I brushed my teeth.

Twice.

When headlights pull into my driveway, I swat my mom's arm to move her away from the window.

"Stop, you're going to embarrass me."

"A young man comes to pick up my daughter and I can't have a peek?" Her mouth is flat and it is curiosity that drives her displeasure, not an actual insult. Mom is a gossip. She and Jane together are like Carrie and Miranda.

"I don't get why he doesn't introduce himself. Back in my day, a gentleman came to the door to ask permission to take out someone's daughter." Dad shakes his head. His apple fritter donut is hidden in the top drawer of his desk where he has me hide his snacks. It's the one place Mom doesn't check.

"Dad," I groan. "I have to go. It's not serious and you would both scare him away."

Mom scoffs and I kiss her temple. Walking by Raph, who sits on the floor as the only one paying attention to the television, I ruffle his hair. "Be good, Raph. Tomorrow I'm taking you out for a treat." My brother beams at me with perfect dimples in his round cheeks.

As I lock the door with the help of the headlights, I wonder what Mom and Dad will think of Richard, if they remember him from the tree farm. Will Raph?

Skipping down the interlock, the weight of my parent's stare presses between my shoulder blades. This is potentially my first relationship after Tristan and as excited as they are, I know they worry. And I worry, too.

I like Richard. And that terrifies me.

11
Party Crasher

I want to say I'm not surprised that a man takes me to the hardware store on a date, but then I would sound as if I'm stereotyping. I mean, no other guy has actually taken me to a hardware store on a date before.

Richard pushes the flat-bottom buggy, a cart with a ring to stack wood and other large items. He offers to steer and I wave him ahead since I have no clue where we're going or what we're picking up. He announced he had a plan to help with the gala, but I second guess giving him complete control before begging for details.

Richard tosses a pack of nails onto the flatbed and I start to wonder if I'm on a personal errand or if he's gathering materials for me. I mean, we're not building something, right?

My experience with a hammer is nonexistent unless you count knowing how to pick one out of a toolbox. Not that I'm completely useless with general labour, I'm just always scared I'll hit my fingers, but a screwdriver, that's a tool I'm on board with.

Strutting down the aisles with a rhythmless whistle, Richard stacks plywood and some 2x4 framing lumber. Grabbing one end, he confirms the wood is straight, and then slides the beam over the rest. I should help or at least offer to, I know I should, but if it weren't for my fear of splinters there's something about watching his muscles flex. I never realized how underrated vests were.

He's stacking a lot of wood. His palm loosely glides one beam against the other, a little rough, unfazed by the slivers sticking out or the weight. I hold myself back from stating that if he plans to frame a new building for the gala, a shelter has already been booked and paid for.

Shuffling my feet, hating that I'm useless, I cut off his whistling.

"Are you eventually going to tell me what all of this is for?" I try to maintain curiosity without letting my impatience leak, and know I'm failing.

"For the New Year's gala, I thought we could build a large Hollywood sign for photos. You know, all the letters spread out? We can even add lights."

Wow.

His vision paints across my brain and already plants itself on the room map before I decide against it. The large letters will span the banquet hall by the raffle tables. Bright lights will add a glow without overpowering the space, feeding into the dark atmospheric lighting. The yellow-tinged bulbs will add to the rustic ambiance. A tasteful backdrop and a great photo op, the Hollywood sign will turn into a showpiece. Something unavailable to buy anywhere else, uniquely custom to our gala. It's a great idea, and I'm sad it's not mine.

"And you're able to build this?"

"It's what I do, Babe." He winks with another piece of 2x4 in his hands. His muscles strain and I have to force myself to blink. Babe. My heart enjoys the pet name a little too much.

"Okay, but I'm not letting you build anything alone."

"Of course not," he chuckles, and I can't tell if he means *I appreciate your hospitality* or if he just expected me to argue.

He pushes the cart down another aisle. I follow asking, "Where to next?"

"We find a paint colour."

"Oh."

This I'm equipped to do. I used to love painting, which is why colour coordinating is part of my organization methods. My Excels are the easiest to read in our office with matching cells and titles. I even include a legend to make sure my team understands my coded system. Anything is better than black and white. Annotating books with post-its, highlighters, matching thin-tip ink flow pens. I live for that shit.

The wall of paint squares stands in front of me. A gradient array of blues, greys, whites, creams, and yellows. Each colour separates into tiers of shades and highlights. The greens are broken up by bold earthy jades, faded olives, and washed-out sage with popular pastels fanning the top.

Browsing the stretch of colour options, I walk the length as if I know what Pantone I'm seeking. Spoiler:

I have no idea. I wonder if anyone has painted a wall orange.

Footsteps pad in the next aisle, dragging louder and a bit too fast to match the tune of my relaxed pulse. Almost as if the last-minute shopper rushes while I selfishly debate paint. Richard lifted the heavy wood, I'm capable of deciding on one potential square.

I turn to Richard just as the footsteps on a mission round the corner. Caught in a silent stare down, my mouth partially open and forgetting what I was about to say, life pinches me between my somewhat-fake boyfriend and my ex.

Tristan's shock widens his expression at the sight of me, but when he notices I'm not alone, he scowls as if he's unimpressed with my behaviour. How dare I stand with a man in the paint section of a hardware store?

Anyone else might ignore their ex, pretend they don't see them and laugh a little too loud in a conversation they distractedly continue, but Tristan's feet stop walking and my shoulders instantly square in defence. I have two options, which are to go along with ignoring Tristan or apparently, lunge toward the man he measures.

Closing the distance, I reach for Richard. My nerves crawl up my throat and my knees rock unsteadily. At first, he stiffens at my sudden change, spiking the same alarm that threw my body towards him. I'm not sure why I jumped for him. Am I protecting myself, the lie, or Richard?

As if his body recognizes my panic, Richard lifts his arm to safely tuck me beneath. His brows arch up to his curls, but his palm is warm against mine, his thumb running a distracting line over my knuckles. I wonder if he realizes he's doing it.

"Tristan, hey," I say, and Richard shifts closer, maneuvering us for him to stand slightly in front.

"Margo," Tristan speaks my name with disappointment but his attention is on the six-foot man with his arm around me.

"This is Richard, my…" my throat dries. I glance up at Richard and his eyes watch me from their corners. A smug smirk pinches the side of his mouth. I look away. It's like I'm back in the office forcing a lie through smiling teeth declaring I have a boyfriend.

When Tristan announced his proposal, it brought back the pain I spent years outgrowing. No longer able to hurt me, the memory of rejection breeds a constant fear that it can happen again. Tristan moved on unscathed while I still wear the scars around my heart. When he shared news about his engagement, I wanted him to realize I was better off without him. I wanted to prove I could move on, too. I created an imaginary relationship to reach his level of happiness because deep down I know Tristan is happy without me no matter how much time I wasted waiting for karma.

But here's the thing, I lied about moving on. Some part of me already decided to date someone new. Regardless of the situation or cause, somewhere inside my brain, I determined it was time to let go because why wasn't I dating? Why lie about moving on if I actually have the chance to move on? And Richard, the man I matched with, he's a real possibility.

"Boyfriend," Richard says, snapping me back to the paint aisle.

Two blinks that's what I allow myself to get my entire body to cooperate. Richard called himself my boyfriend and all my veins thrum in response.

"We've met." Tristan is curt.

"What?" I straighten. Does he mean from a glimpse at the bakery?

"You played hockey at St. Mike's, right?" Tristan glares. "I played varsity at RFH."

"Ah shit, it is you. Hey, sorry. Been awhile." I sneak a glance and Richard's mouth fights a remark at the mention of their high school teams. Somewhat relieved they both don't start hugging, I loosen the breath I held. Neither of the men move.

"Well, nice to see you," Tristan mumbles, trying hard to not pay attention to us, and revealing he believes the exact opposite.

"Sure man. Any friend of Margo's is a friend of mine." Richard flashes Tristan a grin, his gaze twinkling dangerously, enjoying the show the way a lion might watch a gazelle before attacking.

Encouraged by Tristan's discomfort, Richard pulls me against him, my back pressing to the hard wall of his stomach while his fingers run warm streaks up my arms. The sensation of heat blooming across my every surface is intensified as his large hands cup my shoulders and slowly trace back down.

Richard's touch is gentle despite the show. He strategically pries me away from the person who made me flee from the paint wall. His large body fills in the gaps where his thoughts are unable to piece together the full truth.

An instinct to soften the tension, I tell myself.

Unrelated to Tristan shaking his head while searching for an escape, I smile too wide to appear natural. I can't think properly with Richard's hands rubbing over me. Did he sense my discomfort and step in as my *boyfriend* to make a show or was his rescue in response to recognizing Tristan? The men obviously know each other and whether Richard recognized him first is hard to guess. Or does Richard truly mean he's my boyfriend? Back when I dated Tristan, some sort of question or discussion would determine the label of a relationship. But Richard filled in the gap without hesitation.

Tristan's unease intensifies when Richard finds new places to touch me. My hips, my waist, my ribs. The intimacy of each stroke is too private in the audience of my ex.

"Anyway, I just came here for some caulking." Tristan continues past the paint, and I start to believe we are freed from his presence, but then Richard snorts.

"We already called dibs on this aisle."

I'm sure my jaw unhinges at the joke. Blush painfully reaches the surface of my cheeks and I have no clue whether I should laugh or duck behind the department desk.

"Richard, *honey*, he said *caulking* not…" *cock*. I fake a laugh, unable to say the word aloud. The sound comes out too loud and off-kilter.

"Oh! My bad. Makes more sense. I was wondering what he planned to do alone, but I think I'm starting to develop a paint aisle fetish myself." He wiggles his brows teasingly and the full force of his humour sheds any earlier discomfort. Richard happily adopts the role of my protector. All discomfort finds and hangs on Tristan.

"Right, I'm going." Tristan waves the sealant tube in the air before he leaves the aisle and Richard offers a mock salute, two fingers pressed to his temple.

"Tris Piss," Richard says under his breath and shakes his head once we're alone. He still hasn't dropped his arm from my waist. "That guy was shit at hockey."

"Really? You played hockey against Tristan?" My lungs clench, trying to sniff the threat for what it means that they know each other. From the frigid display, I assume they remain out of touch.

"Eric dared him to lick the toilet seat cover during one of our tournaments and he actually did it!" Richard's chuckle rumbles low in his chest, but the sensation is lost.

"No!" I gasp. "He did not!"

"He did." Richard watches me from the top of his straight nose, his lips twisting at the corner, enjoying my surprise.

Laughing, I shake my head up at the man responsible. "You're a troublemaker, Richard Vixen."

Richard faces me and bends low, letting his next whisper carry to my core. "You have no idea."

Staring at each other, the amusement wipes away too soon as the moment plays back, caught in the static air between us. Slacking my jaw and pinching the spot on his forehead, everything slams into us at once. Tristan saw us together, cementing the lie I wanted to fix like a fossil caught between a rock and a hard place.

He called himself my boyfriend. He knew Tristan.

Dating a mystery man was meant to be temporary, a quick fix I could later correct by saying we didn't work out, which isn't another lie. I'd make sure Richard and I didn't progress far into the new year. But the lie develops roots, sinking into the real parts of me. Isn't having Tristan as a witness good for my story?

But Mom and Jane are right, I have a chance at something good. Richard is no longer a lie I want to fake, and by announcing he's my boyfriend he fed into the story I no longer wish to tell. At least, not under false pretense. Everything from the tree farm to now is too real to taint with the fabricated version I told.

I step away, no longer able to face the man who exceeded what I secretly hoped for.

"Thank you."

"Hey," Richard drops his voice. "Want to tell me what that was about? Aside from Tristan acting like someone just ran over his feet, I mean. I saw the way you reacted when he showed up. I'm sorry if I overstepped. I don't want to get you in trouble. He wasn't a relative, right? Did I just fuck up?"

I laugh but it holds no merit. "He's my ex." Richard stills, and I force myself to amend the statement. "It's been two years and he still makes me self-conscious."

His shoulders soften slightly but haven't returned fully to the casual ease he normally carries. "Tris Piss makes you self-conscious?"

"Well, when I knew him in high school, no one called him that."

A shadow crosses over his features. "Eric wouldn't let him live it down. If I had known he made you feel like that, I don't think I would have either."

"In high school, Tristan barely paid attention to me. He was a few grades older." A sound similar to a growl comes from Richard. "We started dating in university. He runs the Marketing and Sales department at my firm. We're up for the same promotion."

I shrug as if it's no big deal I work with the man who single handedly ruined my self-confidence. The irony of taking part in Tristan's hiring and having him as my competition weighs on me through every board meeting. The voice in my head that sings, *you did this to yourself* is hard to ignore.

Richard is quiet, chewing his lip in a manner that tempts me to taste it. But I stand where I am, wondering what he thinks of my minor confession.

"Margo, want to know what I thought when I first met you? I thought, *This woman has her shit together.* I saw you with your brother and then when that tree fell, you ran for your dad. You probably would have lifted the tree yourself, but I thought, *If this woman is going to let anyone help her, it's going to be me.* You were confident. I know little about your job, I'll admit that, but I feel like I know you, and that guy has no right to make you feel less than amazing." His words, carefully spoken but plucked with such honesty, ring through me.

"He's engaged to the woman he cheated on me with," I confess. It's weird to say the words aloud, but somehow they bring relief. They don't hurt as much as I expected.

Richard curses. "You know what comes first in your life and I bet you were willing to put that jackass ahead of it all. He was just too dumb to see it."

I pride myself on organizing my days and I love my family. Sometimes the two blur, but in such a short time, Richard sees this. And when one encounter with Tristan managed to knock my balance, Richard stepped up to catch me.

He watches me as if he plans to dive and cover my body from any pending threat. His curls are wild like his expression and his fists clenched at his sides. The tension roils him, and again I wonder if this is because of me or the Tristan he used to know. Lightheaded, I turn back to the Pantone squares.

Picking up a colour I have no interest in, I try not to track the sound of his shuffles behind me. The phantom pressure of his touch on my hips still feels as if he holds me. Seconds pass but my pulse still races.

"My first real relationship was like sleepwalking," Richard says to break the silence. His voice is low, a confession for only me. "I spent every day walking through the motions and doing my best to say very little. When I finally left her, I was ready to build a relationship out of a daydream. In return, I went for someone who didn't know what they wanted and tried to fit them into what I thought I needed." Richard's voice is grave. He lets his honesty sink in, sharing with me an outline of his past two relationships. "Tristan didn't know what he had, Margo. That has nothing to do with who you are."

His words hit me in places I stopped feeling long ago. He hammers against the shield I built and some pieces break free. Spinning on my heels, I search for his warmth, wrapping myself against him, inhaling his cedar wood and spice scent.

"I guess whoever signed you up for Secret Santa, you showed them." My voice is rough, and making the joke sounds more like a sad omission into his armpit. He releases me.

"Yeah," he says. His mouth closes and the muscles on his jaw pop.

I wait, but no other reassurance comes. The silence beats on. Somehow, we shift into a stream of awkward swaying limbs, caught in the limbo of once standing in comfort but having no idea how to disengage. I pull further away, confirming the end of the moment we just shared. I return to browsing the colour palette wall.

Yeah, I agree or *yeah, end of discussion?*

My mind fogs, distorting the choices in front of me until shades become shadows. Tristan didn't know what he had, but maybe neither do I. Richard instinctively stepped up. We're in a hardware store gathering materials to build a large decorative sign for the promotion he hadn't understood the extent of. Even after I explained Tristan is who I'm up against, Richard hadn't batted an eye at the mention of my past relationship, only acting more determined to help because of my depleting confidence. He's here and he's making an effort. What more reassurance do I require?

"Our theme is gold and yellows with a splash of red, but I wonder if we should keep it neutral." I step towards the yellow section, forcing myself to focus. The colours are too bright and lack the shimmer to match the gold I envision.

Richard is silent as I glower at the options, two squares, one in each hand. I allow him some space to collect himself, unsure if I want him to return to his smug self or the man who just said I'm amazing.

Maybe picking a red first will be easier. I step to the other side and start the next battle.

"I can't decide, what do you think?" I hold my breath.

"Great choices, but…"

I hadn't noticed he stepped behind me, but he's here and my every nerve is aware of where he stands. His body frames my entire back and where he dips his face close to my shoulder for a better look, my skin tingles as if my hair pores strain and stretch to reach for him. One arm circles around me to touch the abandoned yellow paint square, tilting the colour into the light for him to compare and bringing me closer to his chest. My lungs fight for air.

"I think you should get all five." A simple answer to avoid the question. I'm both impressed and too stunned to feel annoyed.

Just get them all!

"We can't get them all," I say.

"Why not? And we will need a can of primer." He snatches the squares away, the two yellows: one mustard and one close to neon, a deep red, a burgundy, and a pale cream.

Steering the cart to the counter, he shows the department lady our choices. But we never actually choose. Our decision is to avoid a decision.

As the paint cans shake and mix, Richard turns his full attention to me. "I'm sure we'll use all the paint if that's your concern."

I shift my gaze between both of his eyes, searching for any hidden uncertainty or reserve, but Richard is just as eased as the day I met him for what I thought was coffee. We stare at each other, the air charged between us.

"It's not that." I don't know what it is.

"I can tell you're thinking too hard about something that shouldn't be stressful." He cocks his head to the side. And he's right, but I refuse to admit it aloud, scared we mean different things.

"Thank you for helping me."

He watches me closely, letting my praise hang in the silence until I overthink what I say and how I say it. I'm deflecting and he recognizes the bit of emotion I let seep into my nonchalant expression. Richard is good at reading people. That's my only conclusion because to admit he is good at reading me will unleash a frenzy of whatever flaps in my stomach.

"You don't have to thank me, Margo," Richard says, finally snapping the tight strain between us.

Lifting my chin, and because I'm shorter and require extra leverage to meet his stare dead on, I hitch a step onto the cart. My boots leave a scuff of water from the extra snow caught in the sole, but I ignore the wet spot and straighten. Standing on the plywood and stacked lumber, I grip the bar between us. Our noses are almost the same height and I'm close enough that I can count his lashes.

A rich brown too rare to match any colour on the wall behind us, I let myself dissect the flecks of green and amber that swirl around his wide pupils. He takes me in as I fill up his view, and the best part is how he cares little to turn away.

"Thank you," I repeat, sternly. I hold his attention, open my expression for him to believe I mean the two words and for him to see how grateful I am for his help. Not only coming up with a great decoration idea but also coming to my aid in front of Tristan while distracting me enough to forget why I'm insecure in the first place.

He swallows, his Adam's apple bobbing and our faces moving closer. The movement of muscle on his thick throat is oddly sexy. My fingers grip the metal bar to hold myself upright in case I teeter too far.

"You're," he leans closer for emphasis, "Welcome."

His lips form the words widely. He glances at my mouth, and my breath catches.

"Your paint is ready." The lady slams a can onto the counter, followed by the rapid heavy placement of five more. She leaves to pull the aisle gates closed, annoyed by the last-minute customers and hoping to veer off anymore from entering her department.

Richard doesn't move and his brows are close enough together, they might as well form one. He's debating if he should still kiss me, but the hammering of the cans reverberates in the silence. A reminder we are not alone.

I pull away, straightening on the cart.

"Come to the New Year's gala with me," I throw out the invite before I waste time talking myself out of one.

My plan to ask him was just that: ask him. I hadn't mapped out where it would happen or how. I hadn't rehearsed what I wanted to say. I hadn't thought about the execution at all.

The voice at the back of my mind shouts, *It's not a coincidence you're unprepared!* Maybe I hadn't intended on asking him. Maybe I didn't expect Richard to have an interest in me. Maybe I anticipated rejection and embarrassment all along.

Rarely am I unprepared for a presentation and not planning how I'd ask Richard is my subconscious admitting I never truly believed I'd pull all of this off. Part of me held back on the idea of bringing someone to a work event and presenting them to my staff and boss if they weren't a man I respected.

I don't let myself blink while I wait for Richard's response. I'm swimming in brown and green and for once, I don't imagine myself drowning.

"Yeah, I'd like that." His voice rumbles low.

He trails his fingertips over my temple then moves my hair to tuck it behind my ear. Lingering with his palm at the crook of my neck, a welcomed pressure against the nook, he considers me. I think of how he pulled me on top of him in the snow, kissed me in his kitchen and parted my lips for a taste, hoping he will do it all again. A fever overtakes me from craving the same nearness.

He drops his hand and my heart goes with it. I swallow and hop down, hoping the hard ground will make my legs more sturdy. The silence eats at the words I debate saying while we pay and then exit the store.

"Have you ever cart surfed?" Richard asks. He moves to collect the paint cans, placing them in the bed of the truck. The wind nips, and I wrap my jacket closed over my chest.

"No." I squint at him. The silent night knocked too loud against everything Richard and I built. I'm relieved by his effort to answer the barrelling awkwardness before my thoughts had the chance of spiralling.

I asked him to the gala. He said yes. We almost kissed *again*.

"Well, hop on." He angles the cart to the empty lot and the store entrance. Hesitantly, I obey, but keep my eyes narrowed.

Excitement breaks across his face, the change is as instant as the wind pushing against my back. My mouth is almost levelled with his, but he's concentrated elsewhere.

"Hold on tight. Lucky for you, I'm experienced." He pushes faster.

No second is spared to consider his intentions. Richard runs and my hair flies forward from the rush of air as the small tires roll. My balance wobbles and he hooks his fingers over mine to secure me to the bar. His grin is permanent and his callused grip strong as he navigates us through the night. His gaze never leaves my face.

We'll see who gets the New Year's kiss and who kisses the promotion goodbye.

Party Favours

People see me with my brother and assume I had him at a young age, but it's Mom who had *me* at a young age.

Walking the streets downtown, Raphael's mitt-bundled hand cups mine and we swing with the rhythm of his small feet. Left-right, forward-back. Whenever he catches someone carrying a dessert box, he perches on his toes to peer inside. His jaw is agape, tracking each gift bag and all the wrapped goodies over his thick scarf, which I knotted just beneath his nose.

"Mmm-margo," he sputters my name as he's done since he's started speaking. Mom wonders if Raph will develop a nervous stutter but Dad, the language coach, isn't concerned. My brother has a habit of extending certain letters in words when he's excited as if he's trying to sing sentences, which I'm almost positive he picked up from me.

"Yes, Raph?"

"Are we almost there yeeeeet?" His alto voice picks up with his pace.

"Wow, wow, wow. Slow down, the ground is icy!" I tug his small hand until he's next to me again. "We're going just right over there, do you see the pretty window display?"

He bobs his chin towards the glass window with the giant red throne and the snowflake streamers that hang from the ceiling. I laugh when he pulls me again, but this time I let him steer us to the café, the place Richard recommended I check out for cookies.

I'm shocked and a little exhilarated I took the day off to eat cookies, but they are for the gala so really I'm on the job. I have my qualified taste tester with me.

The bell over the door chimes with an old mistletoe dangling above us. Cinnamon fills the small entrance lined with shelves of handmade local artisan products. The scent is comfortable and not at all sweet as if the owner brightens her restaurant with essential oils and a diffuser. Different from the peppermint I smelt during Christmas, I relax in the aroma as I step up to the counter.

The cute decor extends to the chalk written menu hanging on the wall with glitter snowflakes and subtle blue lights that twinkle around the display. I mentally promise to set aside more time to visit the small café. The shop waits at the back of my head each time I drive by, but it's about finding the break to stop.

The last time I was here, I read a dating ad in the newspaper. After seeing it several more times on the town's Facebook page, I caved and came in to scan the

QR code on the counter after I placed my order. While I waited for my mocha, my online ticket to the Secret Santa matchmaking service pulled up on my screen. If I had known Richard was on the other side, if he never text me or if I never signed up, would meeting at the tree farm have been enough? Would we have crossed paths in other ways while both living in Bolton?

Because I have a secret: I never came to pick up my Secret Santa match. I chickened out.

If Richard hadn't texted me first, I wouldn't have known who the service selected for me to blind date. I wouldn't have gotten to know him at all, and he would have forever lived on in my mind as the gorgeous man with the cute butt-dimple chin who I met once in a parking lot.

I'm not one for fate, but whatever pushed me in Richard's direction, I'm thankful. All the bits of the universe that gave me a second chance to see him, deserve my praise.

Raph's face presses against the dessert display and I wait for the barista to turn around. The short man portions sauces and some powder. He nods at the scale and he records the number in a binder. Not wanting to interrupt the man's counts, knowing how frustrating it is to lose the numbers in your mind, I occupy myself with my phone.

I shoot back texts to employee questions and skim through client emails, flagging the requests that require more thorough research. The usual drive that itches my fingers to reply is absent. I scroll for one name.

Margo Diaz: I'm at the café! I'm asking about the cookies you suggested. Maybe party planning is your calling?

11:17 am

Richard Vixen: Absolutely not. What are you doing later?

11:18 am

Margo Diaz: Depends. What do you have in mind?

11:19 am

Richard Vixen: I plan to build your O

11:18 am

I scoff, choking on whatever air was trying to make its way into my nose. Did he just insinuate a hookup? Again, the press of my back against Richard's hard stomach comes to mind. The soft glide of his touch along my bare skin is hard to shake. I blush.

Peeking up, I make sure the man behind the counter hasn't chosen to turn and greet me yet. He counts the line of coffee bags on the shelf above him, organized based on the boldness of their brew. I duck back to my phone and type ferociously.

Margo Diaz: That sir, remains as another one of the World's Greatest Wonders and not a discussion to have in a café line!

11:21 am

> **Richard Vixen:** I meant the O in the Hollywood letters, Margo.
>
> 11:22 am

> **Richard Vixen:** I just finished the H
>
> 11:22 am

Oh. Not giving him the satisfaction of an explanation, knowing damn well he's smiling at his phone right now, I hammer out another text.

> **Margo Diaz:** Pick me up from my place in a couple of hours?
>
> 11:24 am

> **Richard Vixen:** Done
>
> 11:24 am

> **Richard Vixen:** But don't worry, I'll help you reach the peak of the O
>
> 11:26 am

> **Margo Diaz:** Shut up
>
> 11:26 am

His reply is an instant ding in my pocket and the happy sound pushes the corners of my mouth up. I'm the corniest cliche: Girl smiles at her phone when boy's name pops up on the screen.

Lame. When did I become that person?

"Hello," says someone on the other side of the café. The swinging door to the kitchen closes behind a girl with platinum blond hair and she shoots a glare towards the counter, but something in her expression softens when she sees the barista bent over the binder. "I hope you haven't been waiting long."

"No, no. It's okay." I try to get the words out just as Raph says, "Only like forever!"

The barista turns around at the sound of voices, and two things happen at once. One, I'm embarrassed by my brother, which causes me to pull him closer against me where I promise to keep him in line. And two, the man behind the counter recognizes who I am in a way someone might recognize a person from high school. And then his focus drops to Raph and his excitement falls in the same direction. In his defence, he's careful to catch the change and maintain his mild curiosity, even if the cover-up is too slow to go unnoticed.

"Hey Margo," Armen greets me, but his attention is glued to Raph. His guarded expression is different from the openness that welcomed me in a basement apartment a few days ago. He probably wonders if Richard knows I have a son.

"Hi Armen, this is my brother, Raphael. We're here to taste-test some cookies. Aren't we buddy?" I emphasize brother, making it clear we came from the same uterus. Raph shrugs against my arms but I keep him tight against me. I already notice the handprints on the dessert window.

"I'm sorry, I thought," Armen's face turns an adorable shade of deep red. "Nora, this is Margo, who Richard matched with."

"Oh, you're the new girl." Nora crosses her arms, sweeping me with a head tilt that labels me as the dirt someone would brush aside.

I stiffen. What does *that* mean?

Backbone pinched straight, I glance at Richard's friend. Armen clears his throat. "Nora, want to call Allison from the back?"

The platinum blonde who's clearly in charge squints in thought, but she decides to let it go and follows Armen's suggestion. Shoving back into the kitchen, the door wobbles loud in the silence Nora leaves behind. She knows Richard and from her response, I assume not in a good way.

Mentally I check over the cracks in my guard, ready to reinforce the wall before anyone else slips in. But that's a response I'd have a month ago, this week's Margo is doing her best to brush off what Nora said. Richard hasn't given me any reason to worry.

You're the new girl. Nora's voice pings in my head.

"It's nice seeing you again! The other night was fun. I hope we didn't scare you off," Armen calls me back to him.

He leans his elbows on the counter and waves to Raph, who gives him a confident peace sign. I'm happy to see Richard's friend again, glad his welcoming energy extends to the café, and he remembers me and my name. I'd be mortified if he hadn't. Because if Nora meant Richard has a revolving door of women, Armen might not remember all their names, and there's a small chance he'd introduce each woman in conversation, right? He could have announced me by name and left the conversation at that. He didn't have to bring Richard into this at all.

"I worried I scared you away after oversharing!" I say a little too forced, but Armen holds out a small menu, and my grip on Raph tightens. "We're not here for drinks. Richard told me about these cookies, but he hadn't mentioned you worked here."

I wonder why. If Richard has something to hide, he wouldn't risk having me near his friends, but here Armen is, openly greeting me in public without any hint of guilt. Maybe Richard thought I wouldn't remember Armen and that's why he didn't think it important to share.

"Just helping out here and there. He probably didn't realize I'd be in." He shoots a glance at the kitchen door where Nora left through. "My company changes to skeleton hours over the break. I load cargo and drive the transport trucks everyone hates getting stuck behind. Isn't that right little man? But you don't hate trucks do you?" He peers over the counter at Raph and mimes holding a steering wheel.

My brother and I step forward in one movement. I have yet to uncross my arms from around Raph, but he stopped fighting me. He's too busy nodding his head, showing he takes Armen's full-time job seriously.

I like Armen, I decide. He's the kind of guy you'd want your boyfriend to be friends with.

Not that Richard is my boyfriend. *Don't get too comfortable*, the voice in my head warns, still trying to work out Nora's comment. A new girl would imply he has an old girl, or many.

"Hey, Raphael!" Armen stage whispers. "We have some leftover reindeer cookies. Do you want to take them home with you? Free of charge."

My brother turns his chin up to me, a silent ask for my approval. "Armen, we really can't accept—"

"No way! Better you take them away from me. I keep eating these things." Armen bends down to retrieve a box and slides his stash over the counter. Stacks of individually wrapped sugar cookies fill to the cardboard edge.

Forget Raph's health, Dad's sweet tooth doesn't stand a chance.

Lifting a cookie for careful examination, the clear ingredient sticker on the back confirms they are peanut free. The cute design of antlers and a red nose are exactly the style I'm looking for.

"Wow, these cookies are amazing." I let Raph take the reindeer from me. "Just one, okay?"

"Did Richard not tell you where he learned to make a mean mocha?" Armen jokingly shakes his head when I do the same. "He's the one who taught me. Right on this big guy." He pats the large espresso machine.

"What!" My mouth drops. Richard worked here? Why hadn't he told me?

"Yeah." He nods, his eyes narrowing slightly, seeing something in my expression that turns him hesitant. He adds, "They needed extra help over the holidays."

Armen sorts the cookies in the box, moving them around to make all the columns even in height. Is Richard embarrassed he worked at a café? Nonsense. Helping out a small shop at Christmas time is a good thing. It's something I would have done if I were available. But why did Richard act as if he barely knew this place?

"Hey, sorry to keep you waiting." A woman enters from the back, trading places with Nora. I assume she's Allison.

Her black hair and multiple cartilage piercings, laced knee-high boots and black off-the-shoulder shirt, give her an edgy-chic vibe. There's no denying she's stunning. It's even more impressive to know she's the brains behind Secret Santa, the woman who created the algorithm and questionnaire. I read somewhere that two sisters ran the café, and without wanting to stare, I have little time to compare her features to Nora's to connect the similarities.

"You asked for me?" Allison greets Armen.

"I just had a few concerns with the counts, but Margo is here for you."

Allison comes to the counter, dropping her attention to the little boy and then scrutinizing my face, trying to guess where she knows me from. Quickly realizing we've never met, her expression moves to one of confusion, probably wondering why I'm here requesting her specifically. I can't say I recognize her either. Her age is close to mine, and I would have remembered her style, so similar to Jane's I'm sure they'd get along. I shouldn't feel as shocked as I am. Then something deep and toxic spikes inside me, realizing she's another of Richard's friends. Someone he helped out when the café got busy.

"She would like some desserts made, I think? Richard recommended you," says Armen. He turns to me, realizing he never asked for the full details of my visit. Raph reaches for a second cookie and I'm too out of my depth to stop him.

At the mention of Richard, Allison's face brightens. Obviously, Nora decided not to lead with me being his *new girl*.

"Richard. We miss him here," says Allison, fondly.

"Yes, Armen mentioned Richard worked here." I stare at my twined fingers and swallow my jealousy.

"More than worked," Nora says, passing the table. An armful of to-go coffee cups wrapped in a plastic sleeve hangs over her shoulder.

"Ignore her." Waves Allison, dismissing the back of her sister's platinum blonde head.

I have no idea how to respond. I'm blindsided and confused as if I somehow showed up to a meeting without reading the previous minutes or today's agenda. Richard hasn't told me anything about his time at the café. He worked here but mentioned the cookies casually as if he only tasted them rather than handed them out personally.

Richard and I are not familiar enough for me to offer some half-hearted reply on his behalf. I'm not in the position to say, *He misses you, too.* And if he does, my ego isn't strong enough to handle speaking those words to her blemish-free skin and perfect button nose.

Luckily, Allison guides us to a small table after leaving our orders with Armen. "Free of charge," he announces and Allison doesn't appear bothered.

After introducing herself and explaining how her café combines her passions, baking being one on top of computer science, she shows me her portfolio of cookie designs. To Raph's delight, he gets to sample different desserts in the window, but I've already decided on the peanut-free sugar recipe. Raph approves, delighted from his time here and equally excited about his large box of reindeer cookies to take home.

"You have a variety of shapes to pick from. Leave everything with me and I'll send you some concepts tonight to go over. I'll have to move fast with only a few days."

"No, I trust you and your designs. You have the full range as long as they stick to the theme."

"Are you sure?" she asks, and it's obvious not many customers give her the freedom to create, but Richard trusts her which means I do, too.

Aside from walking into the café unprepared to enter a piece of Richard's life, brainstorming cookies with Allison came naturally. She dove in with the same enthusiasm Aubrey has when she discusses her art and her next freelance design job. Allison enjoys what she does and whoever she is to Richard only seems to make her more willing to reassure my order is handled with care.

After giving me her quote and hammering down a few last specifics, Raph and I leave, and I'm confident with having Allison in charge of the task. Thanks to Richard, I'll have cookies for each guest that will match the Old Hollywood theme and get me one step closer to securing that promotion.

13

Night Out

"Okay, what you mean to say is that he's basically perfect?" Jane's dry voice echoes on speaker while I fix my make-up.

"Yay!" I hear Aubrey cheer in the background of the call.

"I didn't say perfect." I frown, which causes the edges of my red lipstick to blotch the corners of my mouth.

Armen's uncertainty when he announced Richard used to help at the café confused me. Especially Nora's comment replaying in my head the last couple of hours. *You're the new girl.*

"He's building large letters for your work event. They might as well spell 'love of your life'." Jane's dry voice sounds disappointed— in me not in the details of yesterday. I finally catch her up on my date at the hardware store, but I haven't told her about Nora and

Allison. Partially because I know she'll tell me I'm creating excuses. I haven't decided if theoretical Jane is right.

"And he said yes to being your date!" Aubrey's voice is close to the mic, and I imagine her grabbing her girlfriend's wrist to bring the phone up to her mouth. In the background, their exhaust fan runs loud causing feedback that sounds like a truck's engine. Jane was in court all day, and called on her drive home, only to have me start over when Aubrey overheard the topic of Richard.

"How do any of these things mean he's perfect?" I throw up my arms, and the gesture is lost on the phone call. Alone in the washroom, my reflection and I share a knowing look.

I'm doing my best to remain neutral, to tell myself whatever happens, happens. But Jane and Aubrey's thrill shake away any leftover doubt. Why can't I let this play out and feel excited? A man is building me letters for New Year's for crying out loud!

A text vibrates my phone, lighting up the screen on my counter. "He's here. I have to go!"

"This girl wastes time telling us she doesn't think he's perfect as if we'll believe her lies," mutters Jane.

"Have fu-uuun!" sings Aubrey.

"Not too much fun," Jane lectures.

"Yes, too much fun. It's been forever since—"

"Bye!" I hang up before the debate continues on speaker for my whole house to hear. Richard is outside and I have no time to waste.

With a quick kiss to my parent's foreheads, I'm out the door and in the comfort of the truck. The smell of the leather seats is familiar, carrying notes of cedar wood that wholly belongs to Richard. He tosses me a smile that melts my insides, the kind of reassuring glance that turns into a stare the moment we lock eyes. I see all the reasons why I should trust him and my unease lifts slightly.

He lowers the radio. "How was your day?" he asks, tucking a lock of hair behind my ear and plucking out the last bits of uncertainty. If he has anything to hide, surely he wouldn't have sent me to the café.

"Good, Allison seemed excited to get the order. And Armen was there."

Richard pulls out from the driveway. He focuses on the mirror, but his amusement is obvious.

"Man, this guy." His exasperated sigh mixes with admiration.

"He said he helps out the café," I hedge, but I shouldn't.

"He helps out *Nora*," Richard retorts.

"You don't mean," Nora, the dolled up sister with the icy attitude and Armen the man with the soul of a puppy. "He likes her?"

"He denies it, but that's my guess." Richard shrugs. "Good that Allison is willing to bake for you. I'm sure she appreciates the business."

An unfamiliar indifference rolls off Richard, and before I overthink his tone or tear apart the words, he removes one hand from the wheel and slides it across the cab to take hold of mine. I don't pull away, appreciating the confident way he reaches for me and admiring how

I've come to expect his touch without flinching. And then we're on our way.

The trees thicken the further we drive from town and the houses grow wider apart. Snow begins to accumulate, shining in the headlights. Richard is bringing me to the shop where we'll build the Hollywood letters, and there's a buzz in my body that makes it hard for me to sit still. He's showing me where he works, sharing a bit of his life and trusting me to come along.

Richard confidently explains the game plan of how we'll construct the letters based on the first one he did this morning. He already drew out the designs and grabbed all the tools. He goes into some other details I try to keep up with but fail to understand.

Holy crap he has a gorgeous side profile.

I never guessed a side view could have this effect on me. And he's wearing that vest, his one arm held straight on the wheel putting all the dimples of his muscles on full display. A lick of lust lights and dries the back of my throat.

"Arnold and Louisa are away visiting family up north so I was thinking we could go back to my place for dinner and order in?"

His place. My mind instantly goes back to our kiss in the kitchen that felt like months ago, my attention drops and snags on his flexed arm. Wondering if I'll get another chance to have his strength wrapped around my waist, his hands guiding my hips… I'm grateful Richard's attention is safely kept on the road. He doesn't witness the way I start to pant.

"Arnold and who? Who is Arnold?" *Pay attention, Margo.* Had Richard mentioned them earlier while I daydreamed about licking his Adam's apple?

"Oh sorry, I thought I mentioned them. Arnold is the guy your— he's the guy who owns the farm. The one who owned a supply store with my dad." His lips flatten into a line, and I really hope I haven't disappointed him for not remembering.

"Of course!" I force cheer into my voice. Eric mentioned an Arnold. "Maybe I'll meet them next time."

"Yeah." Richard bobs his head, thinking. Then he adds, "I'd like that."

Butterflies swarm in my stomach. He tosses his head in my direction, a short glance from the road, but enough for me to catch a gleam in his eyes. The small sense of being part of his life wakes a craving inside me. Desire swims and sloshes in my veins. Rationality fights against the desire to crawl over the centre console to straddle his lap. I want to demand he stares at me for hours. His warm callused hands raking up and down every inch of me while I watch his brown gaze darken, fighting the urge that builds in us both. It's the sheer strength of the seat belt that forces me to stay in my seat. Without it, I would have probably already lunged across the truck.

"We're here."

His voice is low, firm as if the tension in the car lies thick in his throat. Had I accidentally given off some type of pheromone? Or maybe the quiet drive through the lot and past the house in the silent snow-covered field reminds him we were alone, isolated, and together.

Richard throws the truck into park outside of a large barn. Before I turn to say something to him, he's gone. He leaps out as if he's in need of escape and the comfort of open air. I frown, until I catch the bob of his hat around the hood.

His face is in the window, the pure image of mischief as he yanks the door open. A gust of wind blows in and eliminates any of the leftover comfort that lingered in the cab.

"No, no, no. Close the door. I changed my mind, I'll stay in here."

"Oh yeah?" He raises his brows, wickedly.

"Yup, it's decided. I'll spend my day off in your truck, enjoying the butt warmers." I attempt to pull the door back closed but Richard doesn't budge.

"I'll warm that cute ass," he reaches for the seat, one arm hooking beneath my knees and the other snaking around my waist.

"Richard, don't you dare. Stop!" He carries me, newlywed style, and kicks the door shut behind him. I have no time to process the cute ass comment.

"If you want to stay warm, Baby, you're staying with me."

He tightens his grip, holding me closer against his chest, and I have no complaints. The warmth is nice as if he has it built into— I catch the glow of a red light on his left breast.

"Is your vest heated?" My jaw falls as if it has a loose hinge.

"Yup." And man does he appear smug.

"That's cheating!" This whole time I have been layering up, dressed like a marshmallow when he struts around with well-defined arm muscles and a clear view of his thick neck, pointed jaw, and wide shoulders.

"If you want to warm up, I can think of a few other ways to give you my body heat." His serious expression fights against the innuendo, and his brows shoot up, now lost in his curls.

"Oh, shut up." I smack his chest and he laughs. Though the joke is clear, the blush that stretches to my hairline cannot be reasoned with.

Our walk to the shed door is short, and Richard places me on my feet to unlock the latch and enter a pin-code. Once inside, the smell of cut wood wafts through the large area. A long table is at the centre, hooked with tools and wires pulled from each available plug. And thankfully the shed is heated. Stay in here long enough, I'll forget about the winter that knocks at the door.

Richard moves towards the pile of lumber I recognize from yesterday's excursion. Next to the haul are the piled paint cans, and beside those, are rolled-up sheets of paper which Richard begins to lay out on the table.

"Come here, I want to show you my plan," Richard calls, and my feet willingly answer him.

Hesitant to peek at his drawings, I stand with enough space to feign understanding. Lines drawn over grid paper illustrate the dimensions for each letter.

"Wow," I breathe. The drawings must have taken him hours. Did he stay up late to sketch these?

Of course, some part of me guessed constructing the letters might require some measuring and accuracy. I just hadn't thought beyond the essentials, hadn't realized what that meant for Richard and how much time he willingly put in.

"You're kind of my muse," he peeks at me from under long lashes. The dip of his chin is more feral as he tracks my movements.

"How so?" I try hard to keep my expression blank.

"You inspired the height of the letters."

"Fuck off."

I intend to angrily stomp away from the table, the drawings, and the man who gives me heart palpitations, but his fingers catch my wrist. Trailing down over the back of my hand to twine through mine, he spins me with the momentum of a practiced dancer. I'm against his chest, his pulse beats under my palm. Through his vest, I'm certain it's galloping like mine.

"You're the perfect size." His voice is low and his gaze roams my face, dropping to look down the length of my body.

My every nerve responds like a live wire. Hot in my veins, my blood rises to the surface of my skin, calling him to touch me. There are many remarks I debate making about size, but my stomach flops and my thighs press together with each thought.

Suspended against him and all the time in the world, I let myself stare at him. The back of my mind fills with half-hearted taunts from Jane and Aubrey, their jokes to have fun, but not too much. Not caring to pull away and feign embarrassment, I risk all of my ego to take in his every detail. His gaze drops to my lips, painted red like a stop sign to do just that, invite him to stare.

There's something bold and taunting about wearing a good red lipstick.

Not yet ready to give in, I reluctantly risk our rhythm to untangle myself from him. There are too many factors, and every pore and cell of my body protests each despite moving away. I should remind myself why I'm here, barricade my heart, and finish the task, but every step with Richard no longer feels choreographed. I'm not sure if it ever was.

Our closeness, the attraction thrumming between us, none of this can be faked. And I want to linger in it a little longer. I want to turn off the part of my mind that ignores my gut. Staring into Richard's dark eyes, I follow the spike of adrenaline mixed with an unfamiliar emotion I waste no time trying to name. I inhale a lungful, willing my heart to catch its breath.

"My height, huh?" I cross my arms to intimidate him, but all that does is bring his attention lower. And dammit, I like his focus on me.

Feeding off his attention, I slowly unzip my jacket. He leans against the table with his forearms folded over his chest, a mirror to my attempt at being stern, but his stance is the complete opposite. Blasé and at ease with his hip resting against the edge, he watches the teeth of my zipper as I pull lower and lower.

Dressed in jeans and a long turtleneck that makes me appear bustier, I hadn't considered the fabric hugging my hips. All my curves are hidden by the large puff of my jacket, but as I free my arms, I turn, giving him a view of my *cute ass* as I walk to the hanger by the door. His stare is on me, every part of me is aware of it.

Spinning, I'm impressed by the way my hair flips onto my shoulders, landing with perfect volume and coverage to contour my round cheeks. Richard's chin is low, tracking each step as I strut the length of the room, careful to keep myself out of reach.

"If I inspire you," I ask, aiming towards the large rectangle hidden underneath a sheet, some other project he hopes to protect from dust or damage. "Then what else stimulates you."

I trail my fingers along the sheet, sneaking him a flirty glance. Richard's eyes glue to my fingers, watching them move up and down. He stands straighter, guessing that I intend to pull the curtain.

"Margo, leave the sheet," he warns, but his voice is strained.

"Why? Someone tall must have inspired this one?" I peer up at the height of the rectangle-shaped project.

I give the sheet a little tug and I'm certain fear flashes across his face, but then his mask smooths into a playful sneer. Trusting my instinct, because I don't want to get him in trouble or damage whatever is beneath the covering, I abandon the game and tilt my head to consider him. His shoulders relax a fraction, but we're caught in a standoff.

"If size is a big concern of yours, I have other ways of satisfying your curiosity," his voice is rich and deep. My toes curl at the suggestion.

It's been a long time since length was an option. My insides are coming undone and I'm not sure how I manage to hold myself together to respond.

"I'm not concerned."

The words are loaded. Loud enough in the barn to carry over and slam into him, exactly the way I want his body, over and over. He sees it on my face because he drops his arms, anticipating the long strides I take back to the table.

I reach for his neck at the same time his hands pull my hips against his. And if I thought the kiss in his kitchen was fireworks then everything inside me explodes in this moment. He brings me closer, and the kiss isn't gentle. Nudging my mouth open, our tongues collide in a frenzy of pent-up need. Richard reaches for me as if the days between our first sweet kiss and now had starved him.

His lips move with mine, widening hungrily, and I groan, a low sound that I hadn't expected, but Richard leans further into me, arching my back. His hands lower, squishing my thighs then circling back to my ass.

"This perfect fucking ass." He squeezes me into his palms. Breaking the kiss, I try to steal a breath, but he's not done.

In a smooth motion, he reaches and hooks his hands behind my thighs. I don't realize I'm in the air until the wooden table is beneath me. He places me down gently and stands between my open legs, pressing himself against me. The smoothness of the movement deserves my full attention, but I'm too occupied, trying to get closer to him as if we don't wear layers of clothes. His mouth is on my throat and his tongue strokes every right spot. A hand in my hair, he pulls my face back, letting me fall into bliss while his other arm circles my lower back to keep my body where he wants me, his hips rubbing gentle, delicious circles. And yes, yes I feel him right there. Right where I need him.

I hook my legs around his hips, bringing him closer, demanding.

"Don't stop," I let the words escape.

Any guy would be happy to hear those words.

Any guy who is clearly not Richard.

He stops.

The hard imprint of him still presses against me and I was so close, so close to an edge I haven't crossed with a man in a long time. And I willingly planned to toss myself over, still clothed and sitting in a barn. I might as well have fallen into a pile of snow because the blood in my veins runs ice cold at the realization. Noticing the change, Richard loosens his grip on my hair. His other hand splayed on my lower back, he cradles me as if he might break if he decides to let go.

"Margo," he swallows, making sure I'm paying attention to him. But of course I am, I can't look away. Despite the growing embarrassment building pressure against my eyes, I don't want to admit my fear. A part of me is scared of the Margo he just unleashed.

I wait for the speech that will confirm we got carried away, how I misread what he wants, or that this is where he'll establish this is all he wants. I force my chin to stay level with his. My lips still burn with the sensation of him.

"Not like this, okay?" He waits for me to answer and it takes me more seconds than he expects because he keeps talking to fill the silence he caused.

Not like this?

"You deserve more than a quick fuck. No, I intend to take my time with you. Make sure I savour you. Your ass, your tits, that mouth. I'm going to make sure you enjoy it."

Holy shit.

Screw the barn and the table and his stupid etiquette because when he pulls away to give me space, I'm pretty sure I'm about to die and combust… reverse that, combust and die! He helps me down from the table and my legs wobble. A lingering kiss on my temple then my lips, he watches my face to make sure both are okay. They're not. I want more.

"How about we get some work done," suggests Richard, misreading my silence.

I nod, not fully trusting my voice. I clear my throat, "Yeah— yes, show me the drawings again?"

I turn to the now crumpled pages. Delight shoots through me when Richard places his palms against the table on either side of me. A shaky breath moves through my hair, and I no longer see the lines on the papers. Fuelled with built-up passion, I barely hear what he says when his chin brushes my ear, and his still-hard length presses against my ass.

"Believe me, it's my pleasure." His voice rumbles low and I'm certain I'll climax just from those words.

Eventually, my pulse manages to calm down and we spend the evening measuring out wooden pieces. Richard saws the lumber to the appropriate height. He wasn't kidding, the letters are five feet and just as tall as me. And when he hands me a hammer, I stare at his offer and request we use the power drill instead. I splinter the wood on my first try, and Richard guides me to move the screw further from the edge.

There's something about Richard patiently instructing me, and how he hasn't grabbed the drill from my hands to do everything himself. His directions are encouraging, and to my surprise, he hasn't benched me. He's perfectly at ease holding the wood and teaching me what to do. He doesn't show off by making me watch, he's content with me learning even though I'm sure building the letters would go by a lot quicker if he does them himself.

By the time my stomach growls, we have HOLLY.

"I'll finish up the rest. Let's get you fed." Richard disconnects the battery from the drill and slides it onto the charging block.

Hearing him, my growing hunger grumbles again in agreement. He holds open my jacket by the shoulders, allowing me to slip my arms in one at a time, but he keeps me in front of him, turning me to reach for the zipper. Slowly he rises, bundling me up to my chin, he leaves his hand on my collarbone.

"You okay to come over?"

He's providing me an out. I have many excuses to give.

My mom expects me home for dinner.

I have work to catch up on.

Sorry, plans with the girls.

Anything to avoid the remnants of the buzz that thrums between us.

"Yes, I'm okay to come," I whisper, and my lower belly pulses its agreement.

"Alright," he loosens the breath he held. Nodding, he steps away, taking the warmth with him. "Let's go."

He stops to grab the paint cans, his muscles flexing to hold three in each hand. I don't mind the view but, "Why are you bringing home the paint?"

"Because finishing these letters I can do, but picking the wrong colour I want no blame for." He winks to let me know he's joking. "We can test them on my wall."

Imagining a streak of red and yellow next to the swatches of brown that already exist on his grey walls shouldn't thrill me this much.

Shaking my head, I open the door... right into a snowstorm.

14
Night In

"Mom, I know. It's okay, I'm safe."

Mom is frantic on the other side of the phone. In all her years living in Canada, she hasn't learned to trust the winter roads and storms make her nervous.

"Yes, I won't go out." The door to the barn creeks open and Richard comes in balancing plastic containers stacked to his chin. Blankets are tossed over his shoulder and pillows are pressed beneath his armpits. We lock eyes, and it just happens. I lie to my mom. "Yes, we're just watching movies. Jane will bring me to the office tomorrow. Anyway, dinner is ready. I'll check in later. Love you."

I wait for her response before I hang up.

Richard places his haul on top of the table, revealing the containers clouded with condensation I assume are warm leftovers. He doesn't ask me to explain who I was on the phone with, but it's obvious I didn't tell them I'm with him.

"My mom," I say, because suddenly it's important he knows I'm not ashamed of him. "She wouldn't approve of me spending the night here."

Not with a boy at least. But that's the part that sounds pathetic. I'm twenty-seven and I'm incapable of sharing details about my love life with my parents. Even when I lived away from home, we ran strictly on a need-to-know bases. It's for their protection. Let them keep the innocent image of me intact for as long as possible.

"Hey, you don't see me calling my parents to tell them where I am. It's nice that you checked in." He unclasps a lid to reveal the contents in one of the containers.

"That's different, you don't live with them and they live in Florida." He shrugs, failing to see my point.

"I've only recently started making the habit to call them everyday," he says, and there's something in his tone suggesting more. Then my nose catches the scent to one of his fridge finds. "I wanted you to try Louisa's cooking in its glory, but her leftovers are still amazing."

Delicious spices waft from the warm stew and garlic green beans. Whatever is in the rest of the containers, I care little to check. Grabbing a fork, I claim my dinner. Richard accepts his consolation potatoes and fish with dignity.

"I should text my brother. I called Arnold when I was in the house to let them know I was raiding their fridge. Louisa says the guest bedroom is already made." He stops there, the concept of sharing a bed dawning on him.

I force down a chunk of cooked carrots. "That's—that's really nice of them."

"Yeah, they're the best." His crow's feet crinkle with admiration.

I need to step away, clear my head. Everything about this man is comfortable. He teaches me how to build things without overly explaining or making me feel inadequate, which is different from the work environment I'm used to. Richard enjoys showing me what to do and gets a thrill from sharing his knowledge with me. And his adoration for his friends, his father's old business partner and his wife, his brother, his parents. Richard is caring and kind, and I'm not used to any of this. I've spent years convincing myself I'm fine alone, that having it all is impossible despite Mom's hopes for me to find a husband and start a family. My career was my child to drive around for, it kept me up well into the night, and I worried about it every waking hour. But Richard brings me mochas, offers to help without wanting anything in return just to make my life easier, he constantly thinks of new activities, and makes time for me. Somehow, he's already inserted himself in my life and I can't imagine him not being here, next to me, in the middle of a snowstorm, in a small barn on the outskirts of town.

Nudging a paint can with my toe— no shocker, it stays exactly where it is— I use the space to shake off the tension. Richard is my match. There's no denying it.

"Well, I'm all fed and ready for the second wind. Did you want to test the paint colours?" I ask, and Richard pivots on the stool, content in savouring my every movement while he finishes his dinner. "Oh sorry, I don't want to rush you."

He drops the fork and wipes his hands on his pants, drawing my attention to his thick thighs. Why am I over here when a perfectly good lap is over there?

Cool it, Margo. We're here for business.

"No worries, I wanted to test the colours and figure out what shades you want where. I'll spray them tomorrow," says Richard.

"Are you saying I'm no help?" I cross my arms.

"I'm saying," He stands and crosses the barn and stops, lowering his head and his mouth is inches from mine. "That to spend my night alone with you working on measuring out WOOD is a waste of time when I can show you instead." A seductive grin spreads across his face.

"Oh, you want to work me yourself then?" I retort before I catch the words that spring into my mind. I have no idea where this is coming from, but he's standing in front of me with wide shoulders and thick legs, and all I imagine is climbing him like a tree.

"That." He pauses to think and his expression turns serious, his eyes tumble like storm clouds. "But let's get one thing clear. If you're sweating, it's because of me. If you're grunting, it's not because you're hitting a nail into a piece of wood, it's going to be my name on your lips and me hammering into you. How's that sound?"

Between my legs pulses and I force myself to swallow. I meet his stare dead on. "I believe I'm the one who's leading the job."

"Then I'll cater to your every command."

He drops down to his knees and I gasp, but the touch I wait for doesn't come. Richard opens the paint cans, one by one, popping the tops off with smooth efficiency. Meeting my gaze, I see everything I'm feeling mirrored in him. The growing need we pushed down earlier screams louder as if it fights against the storm outside, reminding us that inside is just him and me, alone.

He sticks his pointer and middle finger into the paint, circling the rim in a slow motion that makes me ache. I can't move. I'm frozen with desire. I want him to touch me, every cell in my body demands him to.

"Where Margo?" he asks, as if reading my thoughts. "Where do you want me to touch you?" I bite my lip and with his wet fingers, he draws a slow lazy line down my arm, a soft tickle that burns every pore in its wake. "Here?"

I nod my head, biting down harder to avoid telling him how good his touch feels. He dips his two fingers back in the paint with a *come here* motion.

"What about here?" He cups my thigh with his large palm, bringing me closer. He peers at me from the floor, a direct line up my body over every curve.

I nod and his hand kneads my thigh tighter. His other fingers dip into the yellow paint then slowly, with an open palm he presses over my hips to grab my ass. He squeezes and I lose my breath, enjoying the way he brands me.

"Tell me where," he coaxes, his pupils widen with hunger. Both his hands circle the back of my thighs, leaving trails of gold and red as he widens my legs. Still on his knees, he brings the zipper of my jeans closer to his mouth. "Where Margo?"

Slowly, I'm coming undone. The paint is a map of where he touches me, a bold outline of all the places he set aflame. My thighs, my stomach, and my arms. But there's too much emptiness between the marks, too much of me left unsatisfied and unexplored.

"Everywhere," I gasp. "Touch me everywhere."

He's on his feet, moving with a swiftness I crave. His lips are eager on mine, widening our mouths with clumsy fervour while his hand moves beneath the hem of my shirt, gliding smoothly over my ribs and beneath my bra. His every touch zaps straight to my centre. Cupping me in his large palms, kneading while he holds me against him, his thumb strokes my hard nipple, perked with anticipation, as he draws slow, lingering circles over the sensitive spot. Carnal desperation builds up inside me. Pulling him closer by his belt loops, I rub myself against him, searching for his stiff arousal. His hands trail to my hair and I'm sure there's paint on my face and my neck and every spot he stops to appreciate. I moan.

He pulls away and I chase him with my lips, but he breaks the kiss. In protest, I pout. I wasn't done yet. Not again will he build me up without following through.

Richard runs a hand through his hair, leaving specs of gold. "Okay." He huffs. "Is this okay?" he repeats.

"I answered your question," I give him a sultry smile, peering up from my lashes. I aim to show him just how okay this is.

"Shit, Margo." He crumples against any restraint he holds onto, but before my eagerness snags him, he backs away.

Richard leaves me standing confused while he approaches the sink in the corner. Underneath the water, he rubs his palms in a way that gives me a preview. His stare never leaves my face, and from where I watch him, the hard press against his jeans hasn't calmed. Turning the tap off, Richard prowls closer. His features narrow with lust when he shows me his large clean hands before resuming his grip on my waist. My stomach tumbles, imagining what he plans to do. The considerate care he puts into touching me burns me even hotter.

"I don't need paint to make you filthy." His voice is low as he strokes between my legs.

Backing me up against the table, he clings to my hips.

Dropping back down to his knees, he flicks open the button on my jeans. I hold my breath but don't tell him to stop when he slides the fabric lower until it bunches at my ankles. My knees squeeze together as he stares at my lace thong.

"Perfect," he whispers to himself. Placing his lips on my inner thigh, he pauses, taking in the soft skin before he trails his tongue higher, breathing in the whole way up. He twirls me, facing me towards the table and my hands catch the edge.

"That ass," he groans, massaging, gripping me in both of his hands.

Widening my stance, I arch to give him a full view. His fingers trail the lace band along both of my hips, following the fabric between my cheeks. He kisses the dimples on my lower back, building more desire at my centre. I arch further, inviting him, asking for more. His every touch is slow, maddening. He bends me forward, giving him enough of a peek of my wet seam. As if sensing how close I am, how riled he has my body, strung tight waiting for his next touch, he rubs his fingers over the damp fabric. I tremble, gripping the end of the table as my head falls back.

Hooking into the lace, he thumbs the fabric to the side, and the press of his palm on my back forces me to arch further for him. He licks up my centre and a moan sneaks free, but I can't find it in me to care. I close my eyes to focus on the feel of bliss running through me as his tongue strokes over and over.

He spreads my legs further apart, exposing more of me, and I raise on my tiptoes for him, needing him to take over the entirety of me with his mouth. He curls two fingers and pumps until he finds the pace that makes my hips move desperately for friction, riding his hand. Richard stands, keeping the rhythm inside me as he shifts my hair and pulls the high collar lower. I push off the table to move my backside into him further, letting him strum me.

"God, you're so wet. Your perfect fucking ass. Your perfect fucking pussy." His tongue on my neck bleeds into the bliss of his every stroke, the motions speeding up. I'm at the peak, so close to shattering.

"I'm close," I groan.

He pulls his fingers out of me to circle my clit, and my body responds to him in a way I've never experienced. Pulled to an edge, a long moan escapes. A shudder raptures just as I cry out, louder. Black dots prickle my vision, stars twinkling through me as I ride my release. My legs give out. Richard's head presses against my temple, catching my pleasure in his hand and holding me against him. He's panting, wound up by my body. So fucking hot. Our interlaced fingers against the table squeeze.

I meet his stare and we hold each other for a while, watching as we both come back down. This man has the power to make me crumble and for a moment, I wonder what it would be like if I didn't have to let go.

"You wasted a good pair of jeans," my voice is rough.

He sighs a chuckle. "We can throw them in the wash. Not that I mind my handiwork."

Turning in his arms, I sweep over his body. The outline on his pants is hard to ignore, and I'm about to rub my palm over it, but Richard drops down to a knee. Holding the waist of my jeans for me to step into, he trails them up my legs as I bend down to pull them higher, refastening the zipper.

"You're gorgeous," he says.

"You're not what I expected."

"Neither are you, Mystery Margo."

15
Wild Night

Paint crusts my hair into noodles of yellow and red. My reflection probes me, scouring over my flushed cheeks, swollen lips, and the way my laugh lines can't seem to relax. I lean closer to the mirror and pick a fleck of colour from my brow, but it's hard to ignore the face in front of me.

She's happy. *I'm happy.*

Richard's whispered compliments between kisses drew attention to the parts of me I spent the majority of my life fearing weren't perfect. My stomach, thighs, and the large birthmark on my collarbone, he appreciated, adored, and marvelled at. It was when I shivered that he had packed up the blankets and pillows we hadn't used and declared we were moving to the house.

We ran against the heavy winds and the layer of blankets Richard threw over my shoulders in addition to my jacket, but nothing protected me against the pellets of ice that pricked my face. As my boots stomped through each layer of hard snow, he held my hand. He strung curses while he pulled me through the weather that had worsened since he last risked leaving the barn for food. And despite my hair and glasses taking the brunt of the storm, my heart skipped and thawed my insides. It was when we entered the house and he pulled me into his arms that I realized everything outside of my body was cold.

"Take a shower and warm up. I'll show you where everything is," said Richard, what feels like hours ago.

A folded towel glares at me from the closed toilet lid, reminding me the shower is running. Undressing, I observe how my body slithers in my reflection. My nipples are hard and my seam puffed. Drops of dew collect on the crown of my head and strands of hair stick to my neck from the humidity that thickens the air. Slipping into the shower past the glass divider, the hot water runs down my back, loosening the muscles as it trails away. Puddles of yellow pool at my feet as I work the paint free from my hair, and reaching for the soap bar and shampoo in the rack, Richard's face enters clear in my mind. His hands groping over my chest, running down my backside, bending me over.

I debate turning the water's temperature to cold, but the steam continues to build around me, matching the warmth that liquefies my insides. Richard and I cleaned most of the paint from the barn floor, enough that the drops and footprints couldn't reveal what actually went on. But we both knew. Richard unravelled me and caught the pieces.

I wait for the regret to slam into me, but Richard is kind and attractive, patient and smart. I haven't had sex in years and my body refuses to come down from the high. The fear that kept me hidden and bent over a desk was ironically exactly what it took to break its hold on me.

Richard unlocked a boldness that I kept dormant. If I hadn't signed up for Secret Santa, we'd only have our fleeting encounter at the tree farm. I would have never truly met him. I did try to back out by not picking up my match's information, but in the way that is very Richard, he put in the effort where I only seemed to focus on my job. And yes, it was more anxiety than my moral compass that made me want to back out, but when I saw Richard in the parking lot, everything stopped being a lie. I should have kept my distance, asked him to the New Year's gala, and left him alone, but everything about him drew me back.

I sigh. Forcing my mind to clear as I clean the traces of Richard's touch from my skin. Yellow and red washes down the drain.

Pounding the shower knob closed, I wrap the towel around myself, my curves causing the cotton to lift and brush short on my thighs. Any bit of movement risks exposing me again. My balled-up jeans and scrunched turtle neck lay on the floor, but I refuse to wear the crusted clothes. Putting the painted arrows back on my body would indicate what went on in the barn. Gathering my belongings, I intend to ask Richard to use the laundry, but when I open the door, I yelp. I do not expect to find him waiting.

Leaning against the far wall with his arms crossed over his wide chest, Richard's brows shoot up. His eyes drop to the dangerous edge of the towel just long enough to hide the spot he took his time exploring. Recalling the same moment still painted as stars behind my eyelids, his gaze travels up to my face, darkening with every inch before piercing into mine with a hunger written clear for me to read.

My wet hair starts to curl on my shoulders and my face is bare from any makeup, but he doesn't seem to notice, he's enraptured by me and his fascination tingles against my skin with an unfamiliar sensation that calls my nerves to the surface. Standing taller, I prop my chest up, stealing his attention away from where it dropped back down to the cotton on my thighs. Confidence takes over my body, wielding my limbs in a new way, and I present myself as if I earn the stare of this beautiful man and deserve to revel in the reward.

"A little inconvenienced here." I hold up my balled-up clothes. "May I toss them in the laundry?"

"I'll take them."

Richard steps closer, brushing his fingers against my arm when he scoops the clothes away from me. He pauses, marvelling at the spot as if he senses the lick of electricity he just sent across my skin. Caught in the storm clouds rolling over his gaze, I watch the brown turn into black then deepen and narrow. His large frame towers over me and his concentration lifts higher, lingering on where the towel squishes my breasts. My lungs hold still, waiting, expecting him to move closer, to drop the clothes he carries in exchange for my hips, but he's stock-still. A man of restraint and undoing, the desire flickers over him, and presses against his jeans. And suddenly, as if it takes all his willpower, he turns on his heel with force, charging down the hall with a purpose and my pants dragging on the floor.

Motionless in the washroom doorway, the chill entering from the hall raises goosebumps along my legs. That's what I tell myself. The forming bumps have nothing to do with Richard requiring distance as if he doesn't trust himself near me. My toes knead into the rug.

With a breath, I calm enough to give my feet the go-ahead to explore the house. Richard showed me the guest room in passing when he had brought in a bag of clean gym clothes. Padding in the direction of the blue accented bed from my memory, I pass photos of people I've never met.

Hung on the wall are small wooden frames of vacations, trips to beaches and one on a cruise ship with the faces of a laughing couple cut off. They're in every picture. A faded ginger-haired man and a woman who let her dark hair lose colour with age. Arnold and Louisa. By the stairwell, I notice one photo with Arnold and another man. The second figure has a wide face and a hint of a familiar jawline, but it's his curled dark hair that gives him away. Richard's father. They stand outside a storefront with their arms tossed over each other's shoulders, holding a certificate.

The fondness Richard has for Arnold extends back to the business, the supply store Richard worked at growing up. It's where the skills for carpentry drilled into his body and the knowledge carved into his mind. Like Armen and Eric, Arnold is another member of Richard's family. My insides flutter with admiration for how easily he introduces me to the important people in his life.

Back in the room, I spot the gym bag and help myself to a shirt. Tossed over my body, the polyester fabric doesn't cover more surface than the towel and sticks to my curves more than the thick cotton. Using the damp towel, I bend forward and wring the leftover water from my hair.

Richard clears his throat, hard.

Tossing my head back and standing straight, I see him. Hovering in the doorway with one foot in, Richard is frozen, staring at the back of my bare legs and tousled hair with strangled appreciation. Bent over, he glimpsed all of me, on full show beneath his not-so-long-enough shirt. I cross my legs and pull at the bottom hem, willing the fabric to grow longer as a fresh blush crawls over my face.

This is silly, he's already seen those parts of me naked. He's seen me in a towel. And what he had done when he did have me in his hands flickers over his expression, but he doesn't dare to move closer.

"I hope you don't mind, I helped myself." I kick his gym bag and he glares at it like it's the cause of his torture.

"It's fine." He frowns.

"I mean, if it's not." A new wave of bravery sweeps over me and I prowl closer. Transfixed, Richard watches as if I have power over him, and the thrill of being desired makes me want to use it.

My arms cross, and slowly, taking my time, I roll the shirt up my body. Every curve of my skin is revealed inch by inch until I'm bare in front of him. Holding out his shirt, I challenge him to take it.

He sidesteps my offer.

In a swift movement, he grips behind my thighs and my back hits the mattress. Richard crawls over me, his thick arms flex on either side of my head, causing his veins to bulge. The sight heats my every surface. His lips trail across my collarbone and up my neck while I work at his belt and aim to unhook the button. He's hard beneath my hands and I slide under the band of his briefs, searching for the solution to the growing ache that toys with my body.

My hips are wide and he hasn't moved from where he holds me, content exploring me with his tongue, taking his time while I wither beneath him. As if guessing my nerve endings reach for him, he builds me back up. He presses himself into my hand, craving me with the same intensity, but his pants are on and my wrist fails to reach beyond the bristle of hairs leading to the treasure I'm aching to discover the weight of.

"Richard," I groan.

"Not yet," he murmurs against my throat. His tongue circles the crevice beneath my ear, sending sparks along the edge of my vision.

"I want you," I huff, dropping my hands at my sides.

He chuckles darkly against my neck. "None of that."

Pinching my chin, he catches my pout between his teeth, feeding my hunger a sample of what I crave. Throwing my arms around him I tug him closer, pulling him against me. I should care that I'm completely naked while he's not, and somewhere in the back of my mind the voice of Margo screams this isn't fair, but widening myself, rubbing against him, the sensation of him on my sensitive nipples, everything feeds into how bad I want him.

As if sensing where I wish he'll touch me, Richard kneads my breasts and breaks the kiss, lowering his mouth to my aroused nipple. A swirl and the slight suction arch my back and my hands rope into his curls, forcing him to stay there while I move my hips looking for the friction that will help send me over.

"Richard," I whimper.

"Nuh uh, I said I'm going to take my time." His voice is like honey against me and I melt, warm ecstasy pools between my legs.

"Please."

A growl escapes him and he stiffens harder against his jeans, straining to come out. He likes when I beg.

"Please," I say again. "Please, please."

No longer able to resist, he plunges his fingers into me. I gasp. He pulls out, rubbing my centre, circling, before pumping back in, quickly unravelling me as I ride his hand. I'm close, I'm there.

His warmth abandons where he pressed against me moments ago. I'm alone and the absence of him leaves me suddenly cold. Peering down my splayed body,

Richard stands at the foot of the bed. The hollows of his cheekbones are sharp as he takes in the scene before him. His eyes gleam. Using my hips, he pulls me to the edge of the mattress. The frenzy of his touch tears my insides apart, I'm utterly at his mercy and I shiver in the bliss of having his full attention. He kneels before me, and my legs throw themselves over his shoulders. My back buckles when he trails a kiss between my folds.

"You taste sweet," he moans.

Bringing me back to the peak with his mouth, he changes focus. Thrusting his fingers while his tongue licks delicious circles and flicks over the nub with a whirl that makes me see stars. The flat of his tongue rubbing and the weight of his forearm across my torso keeps me in place as he sends a burst of light through me. His name repeats over and over as I reach my climax. I clench my thighs and ride out the tremble that erupts through me. An echo of a voice, so similar to mine, lingers in the room.

But I'm not done yet.

Sitting up, I yank at his shirt and he guesses exactly what I want. Undressing Richard is a whip of limbs and a tangle of fabric. I can't get to him fast enough.

"Holy shit," I freeze.

Sculpted in front of me, Richard's abs are in full view. I can't help myself, I lean forward and slide my tongue between the ridges as I roll his jeans from his hips. He springs free, a length that made my earlier statement premature. I lick my lips.

Vines of ink wrap around his bulging thigh, the muscles flexed and waiting to lunge for me. A tattoo mural of trees and a howling wolf extends from his right hip down past his knee. The detailed shading close to his manhood is sexy, awakening a primal attraction. I spare no thought to the meaning, only wondering how long the artist had spent on the section on his inner thigh.

My hands travel up his stomach, over the soft hairs leading to his ribcage and hook around his neck. He urges me back onto the bed, his mouth back on mine. The contact with his naked body sends a thrill through me. He slides between my open legs and the sound of a wrapper rips over the sound of our mingled panting.

"This okay, Baby?" he asks, his cock in hand, the head pressing to my entrance.

"Yes," I breathe.

Impatient, I pull him lower as I open my thighs wider, bringing myself upward to take more of him. I expect the small sting, I welcome the short pain as I take him deeper.

"Fuck," he groans.

He drives himself until he's buried and I'm full. A moan escapes from where it builds in my throat and he stares down at my bouncing breasts with hooded hunger. He takes two handfuls of my ass, guiding each thrust, helping me bring myself higher as he grinds deeper. Arms still around his shoulders, I dig my nails into his damp skin as he works to bring us both over the edge. Everything is magic, a high I'll ride with Richard for as long as he keeps looking at me with the intensity of the sun. I'm safe here, eager to release for him.

I roll my hips and a surge of heat flares as he presses deep inside me. He holds himself there, slowing his pace to revel in the slick sensation of each slide, but I speed up and Richard complies, matching my rhythm, thrusting into me as I rub him inside, against the spot that grows tighter, and tighter, my insides begging against the full force of him. I'm there.

"Yes," I moan. *Keep going*, I want to say as my legs fight, not ready to give in to the pleasure. Our skin smacks together, a clap for how wet he makes me.

He brings his hand between us, rubbing the button that makes me lose all sense of control. I cry out. "Yes, yes, yes!"

His touch transports me to a different plane. My insides are liquid and I fight the urge to melt beneath him. I'm putty in his hands but he's gentle with his touch, offering me the softest press of his lips while I come back down to meet the green flecks in his glossy gaze.

He's not finished and from the way he squeezes my ass, I suspect what will bring him to his release. I slide out from under him and he watches, his heavy-lidded gaze drunk with desire, but as I turn over, planting my hands and knees, I bend to invite him back into my dripping sex. Richard takes in the view in front of him and adjusts himself between my legs.

"A fucking gift," he pants. He enters and it takes all my strength not to sink into a puddle in front of him. I'm full, so satisfied, each time his hips connect with my thighs another orgasm threatens.

"My mystery gift," he growls in pleasure. "Show me how I unwrap you. Come on, Baby. One more time, cry my name."

He pulls back and gives one solid, deep, and hard thrust. My eyes roll and my back sinks for more, welcoming the delicious movement, letting him bury inside me. Our bodies pull apart and come together, synchronized in a way that confirms we are meant to be joined. His hard muscles and soft curves fit in perfect bliss.

Sliding out slowly, he adjusts his legs to place them on either side of mine and my knees press together, tightening myself for him. Wet and swollen, I relish in the next patient glide of him, bending lower on my forearms for him to hit my target. He surprises me with a quick pound and I whimper, gripping the sheets to hold myself steady. Filling his hands with my ass, he lets it drop and jiggle around where he waits.

"You're so fucking hot bent over for me, Margo."

Saying my name in awe and wonder emboldens me to pull forward and back, rocking against his length until I hear his reluctant grunt. Peering over my shoulder, his stare is already on my face, and I don't look away, watching as he takes over the pulse of our bodies.

"Look at you, riding my dick. Does it feel good, Baby?"

Words, thoughts, everything releases. Lost with the shudder that rakes through me.

"Yes!" I gasp, hitting a third orgasm just as he tenses, leaning back to pump himself deep as I tighten around him.

His ragged voice says something. My name, I realize. I watch as he unravels. He falls forward, joining me while our hearts crash with the most incredible feeling of being complete.

Bending to kiss my shoulder blade, his lips linger to soak me in before pulling away to clean himself off. Without him, the air is cool against the spots where a sheen of sweat formed. Collapsing on the mattress, I lay in a state of neither here nor there, and it's only seconds before he's back in the room and laying next to me.

A pair of grey sweatpants hang from his hips and, pulling me against his bare chest, he slips the covers from beneath us to throw over my naked body. I happily give in to the feel of him. Too worn out to take over my own movements, I let him cradle me. He keeps his arms around my waist and my back pressed up against him, relaxing into the shape of me.

Blissful fatigue creeps into every muscle, my hair is damp from earlier, and my body relaxes satisfied. Wrapped against Richard, the warmth of him against my bare skin loosens any remaining nerves.

"I'm happy I found you," he murmurs into the back of my head, his nose lingering at my collarbone.

"Me too," I sigh, wiggling closer against him.

It's all I can say because this time I'm not avoiding a lie, not when the truth carries more weight.

I'm falling in love with Richard.

16

Morning After

The roads are clear when I wake, but nothing prepares me for how little I want to get up from our makeshift blanket cocoon. Curled against Richard, catching the long lines of his lashes and his mouth parted slightly in sleep, my heart leaps up my throat. The lines on his face are smooth, and my chest fills with joy seeing him at utter peace with me in his arms. It almost hurts to wake him.

But my alarm rings loud on its preprogrammed schedule and slices clean through the moment. The anxious sound doesn't deter Richard from pulling me closer and planting a deep, long kiss. The press of his hips against my bare back gives away how little he wants me to go.

Update: the mole on his ass is cute. The size of a dime and light brown, his grey sweatpants deserved to be yanked down for a better look.

And I do the rational thing. I spare a late morning to show him my appreciation… twice.

Richard drops me into the real world. The low office building is a mockery of the fairytale I just left, and to cover my alibi, Jane agrees to bring me home after work. I bite my tongue, hearing how insane I sound as a grown woman sneaking around my parents as if I didn't have a night full of mind-blowing sex. It's the one time lying is a respectful thing, I tell myself.

Responding to the last of my flagged emails and confirming the guest count to the banquet hall, I push off my desk at the same time Jane hangs around the door and taps a knock that sounds oddly like a wedding march. Wearing a black leather biker jacket and knee-high boots, the ends of her short black hair gelled in wisps, she looks like she belongs on the cover of Rolling Stone.

"Well, well, well. This is the face of my friend who has finally gotten laid."

"Jane!" I hiss and pop my head into the hall expecting to discover the rows of cubicles suddenly full. They're not, I'm still one of the few employees putting in overtime.

"Relax, no one is here." She falls into the seat in front of me and her stare is heavy on my face.

"What?" I untuck a curl from behind my ear to hide from further scrutiny. Might as well have a large glowing arrow pointing at me that reads: *just had the best sex ever.*

"Nothing. Seriously, I was joking earlier but you do seem different. Happier." She taps her chin in thought. "But your hair looks like shit."

A laugh bursts out of me. "My backup brush is in my car!"

"Any reason it looks like you spent the night asleep on the forest floor?" The click of the door sounds when Jane gets up to ensure we stay alone, safe in my office. "Or maybe it has to do with a certain someone whose name rhymes with lick-hard."

I snort and am insanely happy I'm not drinking anything that might shoot from my nose. I put down my water bottle. "That hardly rhymes."

"Ah yes, but I haven't heard a denial coming from your end of the desk." She props herself on the corner and jokingly scowls, trying to appear like a convincing detective rather than a nuisance.

"Jane, we attempted camping once. You know I don't sleep on forest floors." I tap an already straight pile of papers on my desk. I spent our first and last camping trip sleeping on Ruby's backseat.

"Margo, stop deflecting. You call me on my day off to come in and drive you home because you were trapped in a snowstorm with this mystery tree farm man. I deserve some juicy details."

I sigh because I know she's right, but it's been a long time since I dated anyone and I have no idea where to start or what I am or am not allowed to say. A part of me wants the moment to exist as just mine for a little longer.

And what is too much detail? I imagine Richard's gaze piercing into mine from behind, the way he almost collapsed as he finished. My name on his lips.

Yes, too much detail.

"Fine. We did it." I facepalm.

Yup, Margo, you managed to reduce your age to a preteen who whispers in the play yard.

"I knew it! Tell me more. Did you rock his world? I knew you had some type of sex kitten mojo hidden in there." She waves a hand over my repeated outfit, washed from any evidence of paint except for the stitching on the ass pockets. "Margo it's been years. He better have respected your goddess body." Jane folds into the seat across from me and sits perched at the edge.

"Goddess body?" I balk, mortified and ready to die from embarrassment. "And it was nice."

Sexy. Delicious. Thorough.

Jane drops her chin to communicate, *Nice? Seriously?*

"Okay fine, Jane it was incredible. I hadn't expected it and he was—" Patient? Aware? Hot? "Honestly, nothing like Tristan or anyone I've ever been with." Not that I have a long list.

"I'd hope not. Scheduled Sex-Thursdays is no one's idea of romance or a hot time." Jane scoffs at the detail I once let slip from my time with Tristan. "From my experience with men, they only care about what they're doing so that they can get off. Being with a woman, she knows you as thoroughly as she knows what it takes to please herself."

"Okay." Not sure I want to hear details about her and Aubrey, but I am pleased she's willing to share.

"My point is Richard is grown. He's not some guy you met at a campus party. He should answer to your needs."

My needs were heard and my mind still reels with pleasure. Jane and I hadn't breached this level of girl talk before, and jittery excitement has me leaving the land of self-consciousness and spilling my favourite details. Jane's eyes are wide and her mouth open, stuck between shock and a smile— a shile?

"Girl. Four times?" I half-expect her to jump across the room to hug me. "I'm impressed. I should meet this guy to give him a high five."

"He's honestly gorgeous," I sigh.

"Show me," she snaps towards my phone on the desk.

We spend a lot of minutes scrolling through his Instagram. Jane pauses on a younger photo of him and Eric with a dog outside of Arnold's barn, the caption a set of numbers and a wilted rose. She nods her approval, fantasizing about the bits of his life we don't know yet from the picture of him with a guy covered in tattoos, one a group photo of hockey players and it's hard to point out which is Richard with all their helmets, and another where he's on the beach with sunglasses and his abs on full display.

The jackpot is in my phone album, and I show her the photo of us outside of the bakery, frozen in our laughter. My head tilts back to take in his height, but he gazes down as if he has no problem seeing all of me. The expression he wears…

"This photo. This is the one you should make your screensaver." Jane taps my phone, stealing it from me to send the candid as an email. A few seconds later and the attachment lands in my inbox.

"I've never personalized it before."

If this was to solidify my fake dating life, I wouldn't hesitate. But this is me and Richard, and the small act heightens my reserves. Many people have photos of their significant other and children as their desktop background, but something about the switch seems permanent, a statement, even though I have the ability to delete it.

Standing, Jane bumps my chair with her hip, rolling me away from my keyboard. After a few clicks, Richard and I are enlarged from corner to corner. No longer the beaches and forests of Mexico, I have to admit I do love the photo.

My phone dings in her hands, and she shows me the text that banners along the top half of the screen.

Allison (café): Hey girl, your cookies are ready for pick up. Give me a heads up when you're on your way!

4:18 pm

"Well, that's our sign to close shop." Jane rubs her palms on her thighs as if she was the one who just finished a full productive day at the office.

Hooking my purse over my shoulder, I close my laptop and watch the other monitors go black.

"Thanks for driving me home," I say to Jane.

"Are you kidding? Totally worth the hot goss. Aubrey is going to lose her shit, though." Jane's brows scrunch as she thinks it over. She shrugs. "Eh, she's happy for you."

"I'd hope so," I release an airy laugh.

"I'll do my best to relay everything but I can't promise I'll share as vividly." I gasp and she punches my arm. "I'm kidding! Seriously, this gave my little gay heart weird satisfaction."

"Honestly Jane, you're another kind of wild," I mutter as we approach her car in the lot, thankfully closest to the door.

"Funny, I was thinking the same thing about you," she calls, her head peeping over the roof of the car as she holds open the door. "Sex kitten."

She ducks into the vehicle but I still hear her cackle. I roll my eyes but I'm smiling. There's something freeing about sharing vulnerabilities with a friend. Last night changed me, it opened me. I'm grateful for Jane's support, even more grateful she agrees to drive me home.

Outside of my house, my first step is finding my backup hairbrush in the centre console. A cry of victory bubbles just as Jane pulls away and I force the bristles through the knots, cursing myself for breaking a cardinal rule I followed since high school. I fell asleep with wet, uncombed hair.

Rather than going inside to announce I'm home, I start the engine and throw the car into reverse. Driving to the café, I steal a few more moments alone. Over the past few days, the importance of impressing Harvey and Hyup Media became secondary. Late nights were spent outside of the office and no longer exchanged for my stuffy bedroom with stacks of folders. In the New Year, I'll invoke a new filing system. My final checks will no longer act as anyone's fallback for not handling numbers with efficient care. The time I spent in the real world, I put myself out there. And then there is Richard. My heart swells at the possibility of having him longer than his original expiry.

Is this what life is meant to be like? I park my car thinking maybe I can have it all. The job, the boyfriend, a family. Everything is possible.

I told Jane how Richard made me feel last night, but hadn't told her how he made me *feel*. I'm not sure why I held that bit of information back. To learn my heart is open and that I'm capable of putting myself out there emotionally as well as physically will thrill her. Not that she has doubts. No, Jane reinforced the solid guard around my life because she knew I needed backup and that I wasn't ready, but years of dating Aubrey made my friend a closet softy. Jane's support is unconditional. She's ready to fight for me in whatever battle my heart wages, but secretly wishes I find someone.

Announcing my feelings to Jane before I have the chance to tell Richard is a bit premature. When I say the words aloud, he deserves to hear them first. I'm certain Richard guesses how I feel. Last night was emotional on many levels and the attraction we share is hard to miss like sparks in the night bursting from our fingertips, sending static with every touch. But I want to tell him. I'm excited to release the build-up of happiness swelling inside me. I want to say to him, out loud, that I'm falling for him.

Reaching the café, my feet practically skip, and I realize I forgot to warn Allison I was on my way. Hand on the door, I don't know what prompts me to peer past my smiling reflection to look inside.

But there, in the small coffee shop, sits Richard. And he's not alone.

Across the small table for two sits Allison. Her palm cups his forearm and I can practically measure the space between them with the thickness of my small fingers. Tilting her head back, Allison laughs. And Richard pats her hand where it rests, each tap in rhythm with the loud drumming in my ears.

Perhaps last night wasn't as obvious to the both of us as I might have thought

17
Cold Shower

On the other side of the window that separates us, Richard leans in. Close enough that Allison is able to smell his cedar wood and spice scent. He shifts, turning as every word pours from her with overbearing enthusiasm. He hangs on as if she's the lifeline and he's drowning.

My stomach sinks but dread shoots up my throat. Internally, I fight between the shock of what's in front of me and the growing sensation that I'm right no matter how wrong I wish I am. Not Richard. Not the guy who accidentally let go of me while we slept and then woke up to pull me back into his arms to recover from the mistake.

No, not again. Not like this.

But like a car wreck, I struggle to look away. I'm swerving from my lane because I lost track of the road. The path I told myself to focus on when I signed up for online dating is a missed exit.

Allison's attention never strays from his face, and I understand what she sees. I spent last night analyzing where the hard edges softened from sleep. While awake, I found myself adoring the way his entire body reacted to the mention of his friends, so unlike the intensity he had when we discussed woodworking, what he studied, his faith, and his childhood. Richard opens himself up at the mention of the people he cares about as if they are an extension to who he is.

He plays with his mug, rubbing his thumb up and down the handle. I'm curious to hear what they talk about, but even if it wasn't for the ringing in my ears, my weak backbone wouldn't withstand an entrance. From where I stand, I see his throat bob.

Allison cups his cheek, the movement is confident and awestruck as if it answers a question.

His crow's feet is on full display, his expression transforming in a way I haven't yet learned. And it's not even for me. I have to witness his delight through a window.

Fast on my heels, I refuse to glimpse how their exchange might deepen with a shy nod or an intensified stare. The kind of expression he gave me. Richard always teeters on the edge between confidence and uncertainty as if he distrusts his instincts but respected mine. One thing is certain when he leans in closer to Allison, I can't bear the sight of him kissing someone else.

Richard and Allison.

How hadn't I seen the signs? But maybe I had and chose to ignore them. The red flags swung and I ducked.

Richard never told me about his job at the café, never let on that he truly knew Allison. That should have been my first warning. Who forgets to share where they used to work when making a recommendation for something they sold? Unintentionally, I learned the truth from Armen. Further confirmation that I don't actually know who Richard is, and he was willing to hide parts of himself from me.

And what did Eric say at Richard's place when we met? Glad it was me on the other end instead of— who? Who would have been on the other side that would have had the ability to make sure they matched? Who did Eric assume I might have been?

Allison. But why would Eric suspect she rigged the system?

You're the new girl. Again, Nora's jab dings in my head. *He did more than work.*

Richard said he broke up with one of his exes because she didn't know what she wanted, but what if she's ready now? What if Allison hopes to rekindle? What happened to make Eric suspicious of his friend's Secret Santa enrolment?

And what does that mean for me? There is much of Richard's life that I don't know yet. And I stupidly believed I had him figured out.

Hot anger lashes through me when I pull out my phone. Richard wouldn't do this, but my thumbs don't believe me. I press send.

Margo Diaz: Hey, what are you up to?

5:21 pm

I'll give him one minute, one minute to answer. I glare through the window, watching as Richard pulls free from Allison to answer my text that brightens his phone screen on the table. With an aching dread, I watch him type, waiting for my phone to vibrate with some form of explanation.

Richard Vixen: Just working, you?

5:23 pm

I stare at the lie. The familiar feeling of wanting to deny what's in front of me claws through my chest. My throat is raw as if my inner screams had somehow burst out.

I stomp through the slushy sidewalk and fight the urge to turn around and burst into the café. Dating Richard was always only meant to be temporary. Richard was never meant to become more. I had barriers, my rationality. But then I saw my Secret Santa was him and my rationality evaporated out of me. And in the window of hope came the daydream, slowly widening the gap with the possibility that Richard was truly a good match for me.

But good guys don't exist, and if they do, the Staceys and Allisons snag them out from under us.

My eyes burn and I blink fast, avoiding the angry tears that threaten. *I will not cry. I will not cry.*

Richard made me believe he was different. Last night was— I thought...

But I refuse to finish the sentence. What *did* I think?

There's no proof an algorithm figured out my perfect match. The computer made a guess, it couldn't have anticipated the man on the other end of the screen was a liar and a cheat. It's not like the questionnaire asked, "*Are you single– completely, as in: not seeing anyone else you might hold hands with.*" I once read an article about how a guy struggles to stay loyal in the day and age of swiping left and right, having women constantly at their fingertips.

Quickly I send a message to Allison.

> **Margo Diaz:** Can't make it today, something came up.
>
> 5:25 pm

I hope she reads my message in front of Richard. Hope they both stare down at my name on her screen as it dawns on them that they're doing a really shitty thing.

> **Allison (café):** No worries, let me know when you're able to come by!
>
> 5:27 pm

I grit my teeth.

Allison is the creator, the brain behind the matchmaking service, she would have known Richard signed up, right? Maybe he didn't tell her about his match or maybe this is new for them both and he told her the match didn't work out. *Our* match.

The last assumption lingers.

I'm humiliated.

A fool.

Richard is no better than Tristan and Allison is just another Stacey in a world of affairs.

My breath stutters when I inhale. That's not fair. Allison kindly helped me and she doesn't deserve me lumping her in with the Staceys of the world. Unless Allison's generosity stemmed from pity. Stacey had known what she was doing when she involved herself with Tristan. We were openly dating in the office and signed the appropriate consent forms, forms she would have come across as someone who worked in Human Resources. That was my first lesson that sometimes people don't respect the boundaries of other's relationships. And Stacey won, she got the ring after all this time and I got the emotional damage. Part of me always hoped one of them would screw up their relationship built on lies and secret rendezvous in offices. And yet, Tristan stayed faithful to her. I was the one who wasn't worth his loyalty.

I pound my finger into the crosswalk button, again and again, prompting the light to change faster, willing myself an exit from downtown. The place I wish to avoid for at least a year.

Crossing the street, I ignore the gazebo. Regret tightens my muscles and dismisses any appetite. Avoiding the rainbow-painted benches and the tree decorated in ribbon and ornaments, I beep for my car.

"Margo!"

I freeze.

Turning slowly, without my agreement, my eyes find him in an instant. Richard runs towards me. His sneakers tap into the puddles and the peeling fabric soaks. His chest heaves. The same shoulders I dug my nails into last night shrug with nonchalance.

"I saw you across the street." He jabs a thumb behind him.

"I saw you, too." I keep my hand on the door handle. His brows pinch together, probably wondering what I mean, what I *saw*.

"Listen, I can't do this!" I shout.

"Do what?"

Do what? Maybe I label us prematurely, maybe last night doesn't mean anything to him unlike how intimacy changed everything for me. I swallow down the sting. His cluelessness, fake or real, is another reason why this has gone on for too long.

"I get it." I throw a hand in the direction of the café. "You were signed up as a prank and wanted to see what would happen. You got lucky last night and that was a bonus."

"What? No, that's not what—"

"This isn't working." The plan. Richard and I. I shake my head.

His reasons won't change the way everything feels as if it slices in two. If he tries to convince me against all I saw, I won't be able to exit calmly. This is too much, too fast. I thought I was ready. I got too caught up and I forgot my goal. I'm mad at myself for caring. I'm mad at Richard for being an even better liar than me.

I gave a man a chance and it ended the same.

He's about to speak, but I keep going, releasing the truth as if to remind myself of my purpose.

"I signed up because I wanted a date to New Year's." He stares, stunned, and I laugh, bitterly.

"Where is this coming from?"

"I don't want a boyfriend," I clarify. "I just needed a date."

I should regret the words as soon as they're out. A flash of pain crosses Richard's face before he cools his expression back to ice.

"You wanted a date because you didn't want to go alone or you wanted a date because you wanted someone to share the moment with?" God, why does it matter?

"I told my ex I had a boyfriend. I couldn't show up alone." My tone is flat and he stares at me for a long time, debating what he sees as if I'm suddenly a stranger. Good, let him get used to the distance.

"Was any of this real?" He crosses his jaw.

"No." My answer is sharp and he winces at the blow. "It was just convenient."

My gut spews venom as if the wound inside me grew infected, rancid after all these years from the hurt and torment I chomped down. Richard is with Allison. The nerve he has for asking if the last few days, the texts, if any of this is real. I'm some type of experiment to him. He lined me up next to someone else and ran his comparisons.

"I knew something was off whenever you pulled away," he says, but he isn't angry. No, that would require his mask to betray anything he might be feeling.

I shake my head, but he doesn't dare interrupt. He waits to hear what I have to say with a blank expression, but whatever I might share has already lost his interest. His once patient gaze now hardens into orbs of dirt brown flecked with the smallest black stone in the centre. Somehow this is worse.

There's nothing more for me to explain. I will not be the girl who begs for a man to pick me. The girl who is gaslighted and accused of not giving the relationship her all. Not again.

"An algorithm made the choice for you for crying out loud!" And yet he still chooses someone else. I scoff because the irony is too perfect for my life. "You didn't even sign up."

My damn voice cracks and Richard steps forward. "No, I didn't sign up. My ex created my profile and—"

"Don't." I cut him off.

Another ex determining our paths. How messed up is that?

His ex, Allison, the creator of the anonymous dating service. Did she control who ended up with who? My blood runs cold. What if I was never Richard's match, just someone meant to drive him back to her?

I don't want to hear how she won him over or how a few dates with me might have proved to him that his leftover feelings hadn't completely gone away. Each time I pulled away because of an unexpected soft touch or too personal of a question, without knowing, I sent him back to her.

Yanking open my car door, I slide behind the wheel. "Just don't, Richard."

For a moment, his mask slips. His cheeks are hollow and his brows pinch like he's the one wounded. I face forward and avoid the reflection in the mirror. Turning around will only prove what I assume. Richard still stands there, watching me drive away. I cut him off.

Something wet drips from my chin and that's when I realize I'm crying.

18
Walk of Shame

Music blasting, spreadsheet open, I force myself back into a familiar rhythm.

A buzz shakes my phone against the wood surface of my desk, and when I glimpse who the text is from, I flip it over to hide the screen.

Richard Vixen: We should talk

9:56 am

But there's nothing to say. He wants closure, and too much time has passed for him to brainstorm excuses. The same way Tristan never gave me answers but wanted my forgiveness. If I stay away, Richard is powerless, impuissant to convince me I imagined what I saw.

The amount of times I heard someone say, *I don't understand why people cheat, just break up.* After Tristan,

I had asked myself the same thing. Why did he stay? If he wanted to make it work, why keep hooking up with Stacey? Did he really love me?

A bolt of pain shoots through my chest; the residue of a time when fraudulent veracity knocked my feet out from under me. It was years ago, and Tristan hadn't realized I stayed late to finish my application for the newly vacant Director of Finance position. He called Stacey into his office for what he later told me was to discuss customer service scripts when addressing brand concerns. Almost an hour went by when the door to his office finally cracked open again, and I perched higher in my cubicle. I was proud of him, proud I dated someone who would expand Lauder Accounting into the marketing realm and I praised him for his innovative ideas and believed he would give the company a modern edge under my referral.

All of that crumbled when Stacey lingered with her back pressed against the doorframe, peering up while Tristan adjusted his collar. In what felt like slow motion, she had reached on her toes to kiss his cheek. Because my mind chose to lengthen the moment with prolonged torture, I couldn't confirm if Stacey froze under my will or if she truly held her lips against him for achingly long seconds, taking him in the way someone drew out a goodbye. Though I was sure of how she looked at him and I witnessed him stare back, when Tristan saw me across the office, the scene transformed. He shook her hand and strutted to meet me, helped me with my bag, and threw an arm around my shoulders. I convinced myself I imagined it, and when I gained enough nerve to ask, he made me believe I *had* imagined what I saw. When the whispers began, he told me they were rumours.

You're with me. Of course, that's not true. I love you. I would never hurt you.

You believe Gulia over me? People are bored with their lives. They should mind their own business.

Not this again. I thought you said you trusted me.

I should have trusted in myself.

Worse was I forgave Tristan, believed him. Dated him for a year after the incident. And begged even when he chose her.

There are many things that I had never understood, and it's easier not to listen to Richard than to potentially forgive another liar. I refuse to let him suck me back in.

I won't let that happen again. I'm smarter, older. Years have trained me for this, and if someone left me again, I promised myself I'd be fine. Richard entered my life a few weeks ago, his smug smile, his brows arching in a silent question, his fingers on my skin. None of this should affect me so thoroughly.

It doesn't matter anyway because I'm the one no one picks.

"Mi Chiquita Hermosa," Mom taps on the already open door. I hadn't realized I stared at the screen, but I'm relieved I opted for my glasses instead of contacts. Contacts irritate my eyes when I cry.

"Yes, Mom?"

"I brought you some cookies." She holds a dish of cinnamon-powdered shortbreads. Her attention darts around the room before finally resting on my face. "Margo, *Mi Cielo,* what's wrong?"

"Nothing." I sigh. "I have to finish the seating chart for this gala tomorrow."

Mom nods, not believing the source of my distress but giving me space to sort myself through. She ambles closer, places the plate on the free spot by my nightstand, and tucks a frizzy curl behind my ear. "You were born bright, my Margo. You will shine tomorrow."

She plants a kiss on my head.

"Thanks." My voice is stiff.

"Remember the New Year is meant to celebrate achievement and growth. Your father and I will miss you tomorrow, and I'd hate to imagine you spending the night—" she stops, connecting the reasons for why I brood in the lamplight, glaring at a chart of circles and names.

"Alone," I finish, choking on the word.

"*Mi Cielo*," she whispers, her arms wrapping around my neck, leaning my head against her chest. "This is about that boy?"

The room blurs and my damn chest betrays me, raking up lungfuls as if my throat is a broken straw. Not waiting for an answer, Mom combs through my hair with her fingers, over and over, the rhythm coaxing me, steadying me. A shaky breath escapes when I pull off my glasses to rub the tears clustered on my lashes.

"He's not coming to the gala." Finally, the truth comes out, crisp and sharp as if I'm the one who needs to hear it. Mom nods as if understanding the full story in the small admission.

"Love is not easy with a bruised heart, but life will always remain the greatest gift. And what is the point if not for your emotions to guide you?" She presses her lips to my forehead. "My Margo, you've always had so much love. You try to keep it locked away but it still drives you. If he is meant to be yours, your heart will tell you. You are rare, *Mi Cielo*, the right one will see."

"I love you," I whisper and she wipes my cheeks.

"I love you most."

She wedges my hamper against her hip on her way out, silently reigning in her judgement of the messy floor full of abandoned sticky notes, a scatter of colourful sprinkles on the hardwood. A pang of shame tightens my throat. For as long as I can remember, I did my own laundry. I'd squeeze in a few loads, sort through Raph's as well, and run the cycle in the evening to save on hydro. But even the clothes spilling out of my closet spiral out of control. Dad always says he knows how I'm doing based on the state of my room. I'm a mess.

Mom doesn't nag or huff, she collects my clothes in comforting solidarity. The small relief lifts a weight off of me as if she carries away the clutter of darkness from my week. The bubble of peace bursts when her footsteps thud down the stairs but a faint residue lingers.

If he is meant to be yours, your heart will tell you. I stare at the clean corner of the hardwood. The organ in my chest thumps in protest. If Richard was never mine, why does it feel as if I just lost a huge part of myself, yanked clean out of my centre?

Richard isn't good for me. The statement tastes like a lie worse than the one I told. And isn't that always the case? Girl trusts guy, guy deceives girl, girl then has the rug pulled out from under her? My inner Margo wriggles against the barrier I built, not wanting to raise the question that will break my confident streak. What will people say when I show up to the gala alone?

I decide I don't care. To the staff that witnessed my low all those years ago, I will not give them a repeat. I'm Margo Diaz. The department and clients have grown because of my hard work, my hours, and my dedication. No one else's name is attached to my accomplishments. I did this on my own. I'm valuable. And Mom is right, I've played the shining star employee for almost ten years, and tomorrow is my time to claim the spotlight once and for all. I don't need a beating heart to do it.

Tomorrow.

The promotion, the gala, the last-minute details. Like an executioner's sword, too many loose ends hang over me, threatening to take my head. But all I can pay attention to is the crack in my centre that has kept growing since last night.

Even if Richard didn't pick me, Lauder Accounting will. I'll make damn sure of it.

Scowling at the plate of Pan de Polvo cookies, I curse. The dusted cinnamon sugar reminds me I'm not done with my job yet. I have to go back to the café to pick up the order.

— ▢▢☑ —

The drive downtown is slow. Partially because the courage I built up fades the closer I get to the destination. I'll go inside, collect the sugar cookies and leave. A quick exchange that hopefully doesn't involve Allison. With luck, Armen will greet me from behind the counter. Unless he knew Richard's games all along.

Embarrassment coats and twists my insides. I can't bring myself to doubt the friend who smiled with wide brown puppy dog eyes, eager to meet someone new. I refuse to believe Armen is an accomplice, and if he is, then there's no hope for my trust radar.

Make it to the café, collect the cookies, drive home, put together the last notes for my speech, and hopefully avoid crying into my pillow. Completely doable. I got this.

I push open the door and the faded scent of cinnamon does little to calm me. The aroma reminds me of Richard and twists my insides more. My hormones are no longer sure if the familiarity should fill me with exhilaration or dread and before my mind makes the decision, the chime of the bell alerts the two men huddled together at a table. In unison, they glance up from their shared phone, their curiosity notably morphing into recognition. Instantly, I'm struck with the feeling of being someone else's topic. I gulp.

I do not have this.

"Margo!" Allison pops up from behind the counter, carrying a carton of milk. "If I knew you were coming, I would have grabbed the cookies from the back. Just give me one second."

Crimped hair flows down her back in a mane of black. Confident, Allison unfastens the knot around her waist and instructs the two men at the table to watch the door. Like a chain necklace tossed in a pocket, my insides knot to the point of no return. Both ends of the chain reach for my car while the rest of me roots here, hopelessly tangled with the running suspicion that the two men know exactly who I am.

Allison takes more than one second, possibly three minutes, and I keep glancing at the couple. *Crap, I looked again!* But here she comes carrying a large box of assorted cookies and despite my refusal and dream of escape— I practically throw the money at her, Allison opens the flaps to reveal her creation, expecting feedback.

"Wow." I pick up a cookie in the shape of a star, then a camera, then a clapperboard. The icing is like art, carefully drawn and in the exact colour theme of the gala. Alternating between red, black, gold, and some brushed with mica glitter. "You really went all out."

"Do you like them?" Noticing my lack of enthusiasm, she frowns at the box, peering inside to try to see, and doubting her talent.

"Yes, sorry. No, they're amazing. Honestly!" Her expression pinches at the shrill sound of my voice, and I desperately glance at the exit. Reaching for the box, hoping to show her how much I adore them, I hug the cardboard closer.

"Is the packaging not what you expected? If you'd like a discount…"

A wave of guilt slams into me. Truthfully, I'm more in awe than disappointed by Allison's expertise. My night devoted to imagining scenarios where I'd tell Richard exactly what I thought, had wasted time. Especially when I found myself caught in a daydream where things could have ended differently. Sometimes where they didn't end at all. But in those imaginings, I hadn't blamed Allison or myself for his actions. After Tristan, it took me a long time to stop hating Stacey, and eventually, I stopped internalizing my disgust and blaming myself for the betrayal. No longer wondering what I should have done differently for him to believe I was enough. Stacey was the temptress and she owed me no loyalty. But Tristan did; he was my boyfriend. And Allison, she's smart, creative, and stunning. It's not her fault Richard lied to me, either. She may not have known and he could have kept her in the dark. Richard is the one who did me wrong. He's the one I trusted, not the coffee shop owner.

Suddenly, I'm stuck. Uncertain if I should tell Allison that Richard isn't who she thinks he is.

"Allison, thank you so much for these." I nod, slowly. My tongue dries as if I somehow sucked in a mouthful of cotton. "Listen, I have something—"

"No worries, if I had known they were for Richard's girlfriend I would have closed the café to get them to you sooner. Well, not really, but I'd consider it." She nudges me playfully, but I'm struck frozen in spot.

Girlfriend? Richard and I hadn't discussed… wait. Did Allison and him talk about me?

I'm tense all over, my entire body solidifies, rigid with confusion. Something sharp and acidic shoots up the back of my throat, threatening to spew in rivets of regret. The pounding in my ears is loud and my pulse kicks into overdrive, picking up on the guilt I haven't yet placed. No, no, no. My breath comes in short tangents, fear spilling through my veins like liquid nitrogen.

"But you and Richard?" I sputter. "I— I saw you yesterday."

It's Allison's turn to look confused. "Yesterday?"

"You and Richard, you seemed close. I thought…"

What have I done?

I saw Richard and Allison through the window, huddled close, her hand on his face and head tilted back in mirth. He had watched, amused by her display, but what if I painted the image with a brush soaked in envy? Had I imagined the whole thing?

Allison frowns. "Richard and I are friends. He helped out at the café for a few days, but he came in yesterday to give a testimony for my dating app. I have an interview with investors in a month and Richard offered to come forward as a successful case Secret Santa worked for."

"A testimony?" I repeat, and she nods slowly, piecing together my conclusions. *As a successful case Secret Santa worked for.*

"Margo, I don't know what you heard but nothing is going on, I promise you. I have a boyfriend and I can show you the recording of our interview if you want. He was quite smitten when he talked about you."

"Recording?" *Boyfriend?* My brain sputters and quits, only able to process with clipped words.

Richard referred to himself as my boyfriend *again*. A flash of a memory enters my mind of Richard standing in the hardware store, his arm wrapped around my waist and a smirk pinching his cheek, declaring himself to Tristan as my boyfriend. Had he meant it?

"Yes." Allison smiles, misreading how the truth flusters me. "Margo, Richard is a good guy. I was there when he found out his ex signed him up for the dating service. She was… a lot, but he stayed committed and took a chance."

When he found out his ex signed him up? My mind

reels back to the parking lot when Richard mentioned how his ex created his profile. I had cut him off, assuming the person who signed him up was Allison, the brains behind the whole system and likely suspect. But if she was the one who made his account, she could have rigged the algorithm to make sure they matched.

Allison doesn't know that Richard told me his ex signed him up, and I appreciate her more for not wanting to spill the events as if he were some small-town gossip headline. The recount should come from Richard, the full story told from his perspective. I'm the one who hadn't stuck around to listen.

Allison's effort to ease the situation and reassure my opinion of Richard, confuses me further. Dread and blame lash together, demanding the rest of the details. I stopped Richard when he was about to explain, convinced myself I already knew the kind of guy he was. And I left him behind in the parking lot right alongside my heart, exactly how I thought he intended to leave me. The fact that Richard met with Allison to provide a testimony for how the service worked. My insides riot.

Allison continues, unaware of the turmoil sloshing through me. "He deserves happiness more than anyone, and he came in yesterday morning ready with his review. Nora, my sister, called me and we arranged to meet up last night. He's really helping me out. I'm happy for you both."

My brain latches on one detail: Yesterday morning.

Richard must have come by as soon as he dropped me off at work. The pieces of the puzzle come together as if I played upside down the whole time, never truly having the intention of seeing the full image until it was done.

My mind spirals with all the bits of truth Allison lays flat. If I had listened to what Richard wanted to say, had spared a moment to learn how everything fit together, I could have spared us both from hurt.

I screwed up.

Winds of Change

Richard hasn't replied to any of my texts.

> **Margo Diaz:** Hey, I'm free if you're willing to talk still
>
> 11:08 am

That was hours ago. A sinking feeling has dragged me lower ever since.

What if I missed my chance?

I have to explain myself, and to apologize over text is unfair. I refuse to be the girl who sends long paragraphs, and no matter how badly I want to, I never press send on the carefully crafted messages I type.

Caught up in my past trauma, I shoved and squeezed Richard into the mould of Tristan. I tell myself I'm over what happened years ago, but the statement is half true. Tristan hurt me and though the sting is a memory and no longer a physical pain, the rejection left a shadow on my dating life. If someone can surprise you by leaving suddenly, then someone can slowly pack up their things from your apartment and move them into another woman's house without you noticing until it's too late. Over time, my hurt turned into bitterness, and seeing Tristan every day added a layer to the wall I built, hardening and reaffirming my strength. If I protected the cavity that held all my dreams and affection, I'd survive.

At least, that's what I told myself.

But I left a tiny door for Mom, Dad, Raphael, Jane, and Aubrey. The same door Richard wiggled in and brought along his friends. After his past relationship, he has his own support team.

The difference is my small circle of undeniable trust and love became part of my guard, and this is why I never agree to drinks with Bianca, why I spend nights at the office rather than picking up a hobby that might introduce me to new people, why I play music over my thoughts and sing loud enough to drown the worries that bounce around my skull. Tristan abandoned me and found someone he thought was better, and I held on tight to the last bit of our future he left in the shards of our could-be life— my job.

"Maybe you are cut out for marketing." Logan's voice slices through the room and breaks the staring contest I've been having with a magenta tablecloth. I had ordered red.

He struts in, wearing sunglasses in the dim-lit banquet hall. I half-expect a team of Hyup interns trailing him in a fluster of notepads and held-up recording devices. He definitely walks as if he expects the entourage.

Did he come to oversee me? Logan has no involvement in the gala. Not the decorations, the budget, the guests. His company's part is to attend, not to arrive on the morning of the party to provide unhelpful feedback. If I ignore the fact that he's wearing shades, his self-importance riles what remains of my patience. I clench my jaw.

"Understanding what your company does has nothing to do with balancing books," I retort.

I realize too late that my understanding of Hyup Media may determine who will win the promotion. This whole time it's felt as if Tristan has had one step ahead of me in the running. His marketing knowledge earns him Logan's interest.

Not giving Logan the satisfaction of my misspoken remark, I cross my arms to guard myself. His sneer confirms I say the wrong thing, but that doesn't stop him from moving closer. The air swirls with his heavy cologne and grates against my skin. I'm certain I'll develop hives.

"Miss Diaz, I'll have you know that Harvey and I will consider candidates fit to represent both Lauder and Hyup. I've heard praise for your confidence, but numbers often lack vision. I hoped the gala would introduce me to the wide skillset I read about in your cover letter." His insult is clear. Straightening his sleeve cuffs, he brushes me aside with the lint he picks off his wrist.

Logan's presence only makes my irritation grow. Why come here? Why check on me and everything I arranged as if I need supervising, yet no one is assigned to help? He can't have it both ways. Either I'm able to handle this alone or I require a sitter.

"I've managed planning the gala quite fine on my own. My *confidence* is what brings me in front of my team and clients, ready to deliver. Bad or good news, the numbers are proof. *Vision* may be how you sell the idea, but numbers are the promise. If I had known decorating was a test, I'd say my focus would be better spent on the sell-through. Tell me, Mr. Hymn, have you settled on our offer?" Tilting my head, I do nothing to hide the edge in my voice.

I know I step into dangerous territory. Hyup Media may be my client and as part of the board, I took part in the negotiations, but Harvey and Logan had kept the lawyer terms private. The gala is meant to impress him, and though I claim ignorance of this being a test, I had always known. I planned to use the grandeur to showcase my organization and yes, my design skills. Both seen as assets to the marketing agency we aim to buyout.

Logan considers me with a narrowed sweep. For once, he remains quiet. I meet his scrutiny, readying myself for the lecture and another passive warning. No matter how well I party planned, he already decided I was just a numbers girl, a rule follower without a creative bone.

"We have good news!" The banquet hall coordinator, a tall woman with tied back greying hair, bursts into the room. She stops when she notices I no longer wait alone. "Sorry to interrupt. Margo, we found black tablecloths in storage."

I watch Logan's face, expecting a delayed remark to feed the tension, but his expression is guarded. Turning away, I let the woman's announcement sink in when my attention snags on the cart pushing folded linen. Relief takes over.

"These are great! Thank God you were able to find something. Should we start removing the other cloths from the tables?" Stepping further from Logan, I spare only a short glance over my shoulder. In the dim light, his skin is the colour of dehydrated mangos. "If you'll excuse me, Mr. Hymn. I have my hands full."

"Of course." He offers a slight bow to dismiss himself, but his sneer returns before he reaches the door.

Checking over the final arrangements, discovering they made an error on the number of vegetarian dishes required, I sigh in relief when I tick the last boxes in my planner. I move to help the waitresses and waiters redress the tables because if I stand still, I'll stare at my phone or the place along the span of the room where I imagine large wooden letters spelling out *Hollywood*. The banquet hall is bare without the vision Richard gave me, but I waste no breaths dwelling and throw myself into a roll call of decor and dietary confirmations.

Logan is wrong about me. Confidence and numbers aren't my only skills. I'm also good at risk management.

— ☐☐☑ —

Kicking off my boots at the front door, I'm grateful they land on the mat to avoid a lecture from Mom. But my mood plummets further when Jane texts me to tell me she and Aubrey are running late. I hoped to update them about everything I screwed up. I need Jane's hard truth and Aubrey's soft encouragement. Ideas and scripts of what I want to hear replay and bounce through my mind. I wasted too much time pouring myself into Lauder Accounting as if it could provide me with the emotional connection I desired. I protected myself from developing relationships with coworkers, avoided going home, and now I have no clue how to unwind and let loose.

Jane Jones: We'll be another hour, Aubrey's dress doesn't fit. She hasn't worn it in years and decided tonight was the time to try it on

2:34 pm

Aubrey Kennedy: I didn't think my boobs were still growing!

2:34 pm

Aubrey Kennedy: 45 minutes - tops! I'm borrowing something from my sister

2:35 pm

Jane Jones: And I'll make her try it on before we leave

2:36 pm

Aubrey Kennedy: Stop making me look bad

2:37 pm

Jane Jones: You could never look bad

2:37 pm

Their messages ring like ping-pong. I fight the urge to point out that they're texting when they're most likely sitting beside each other. Their cuteness is a sore spot, but I remind myself these are the two people who rebuilt me after Tristan and I erupted. They couldn't have predicted I'd become the Tin Man.

I sigh, hanging up my jacket and debating if I should fall face-first into the front closet and lock myself inside.

"*Mija*?" Dad calls from upstairs.

"Yes?" I close the closet door, unfortunately with me still on the outside.

"Can you come here?"

My blood pressure spikes and I follow his voice up the stairs. My first fear is he swung out his back again.

"Dad, are you okay?" I call, but I step into his bedroom and he's not inside. Cold sweat forms between my shoulder blades and my pulse beats loud in my ears. "Where are you?"

"Come, come, come Mmmm-margo!" Raphael squeals. He sounds as if he's across the house. Their voices echo down the narrow hall.

"Raph? What's going on?"

"Just come!" yells my brother.

Their shouts come from my bedroom and the hairs raise on my arms. "What are you two doing?"

My steps are slow but sure, worried but already deciding it's my job to confirm they're okay. What did they find in my bedroom? Why would they look inside anyway? A vision of Dad on the floor fills my mind. Mom is working which means I'll have to assist Dad, pick him up and somehow carry him alone. Inhaling as I turn the frame, I tense, readying myself for a sight I'll have to quickly solve before Raph senses my panic.

The scene in front of me distorts the image of calm. Heaps of clothes pile on the bed, tossed aside carelessly. Raph sits cross-legged on the floor, peering up while Dad forces his shoulder into the side of an armoire that wasn't there when I left this morning. The wooden closet half-conceals the window, unwilling to budge against the weight of my father's nudge.

Speechless, I stand in the doorway while Dad grunts from the impact. The bone of his shoulder thuds and Raph squeals with delight, taking pleasure in the show playing out in front of him.

"Dad, stop!" I bark, or at least I try to, my voice barely comes out above a whisper. Still, he hears, turning to hit me with a grimace he hopes comes off as sheepish surprise.

He steps away from the armoire, leaving the piece of furniture in full sight. That's when I smell it, the scent of wood shavings and oak, dusty yet calming, bringing back reminders of the barn I visited a few days ago. The air is missing the hint of men's cinnamon body wash I've come to expect, but I push the thought from my mind before the void in my chest lashes.

The armoire is exactly like Abuela's. The small three drawers at the bottom, two large wing doors with carved flowers, a curved top. The metal handles are too small for my adult hands, but I hesitate, trying to pull at the memory to compare if they're the same. Different, they have to be. Inside, the hanger is empty and the cabinet is too narrow for me to curl up inside, but I sit down anyway. My legs hang over the edge. I trail my finger along the thin back wooden wall, feeling the seam and searching for the place where I drew my initials. But this is a replica, a new version still carrying the smell of stainer and sawdust.

"Margo?" Dad's face peeks around the door.

"Dad," I croak. Tears blur my vision but I keep them trapped in my throat.

A piece of my childhood stands in my bedroom and I wasn't sure anyone remembered the armoire except for me. There's no denying the small bit of my past showing up when I doubted myself is a coincidence. Life is full of signs. Signs like the ones a certain small town coffee shop posted in every window. Signs like the messages that dinged on my phone back and forth as a stranger became someone I know. Gestures from the universe in the form of peppermint mochas. The armoire is love, family, it's me.

"*Mija*, I'm sorry your present is late." Despite my tears, Dad smiles down at me. "Do you like it?"

"How did you know?" I wonder, tracing a floral pattern in the wood.

"Since you were little, you've stared at every closet with disgust." He chortles. "The idea came to me a few weeks ago when I ran into a man at the hardware store. I thought, *This man makes things from wood, that front closet always pissed off Margo.* Then I asked him." He shoots a concerned glare at Raph, noticing he cursed.

"Abuela used to let me read your books inside."

"I remember," Dad nods. He waves towards my brother, calling him to his feet.

Raph stands, his small hands fiddling with an object. "Here."

My brother leans against my shoulder, his mop of black hair falling over his eyes as he squints at the title of the ragged book he hands me. *El Llano en Llamas* by *Juan Rulfo*.

Finally letting them fall, my tears streak and roll off my face. I always stole Dad's books, unable to read the content but loving the covers and the idea of understanding what they were about. I spent hours imagining the story on the inside just from the colourful images on the front.

A Spanish professor in Canada, Dad reversed his job from teaching English in after-school and weekend programs. I always found the idea amusing, but the job offer and money had moved our family here and we never glanced over our shoulders. Dad and Mom dreamed of a better life, and Abuela followed her only son without hesitation. Together we rebuilt our home here, and slowly as the days passed, the excitement of living some place new outshone the memories of my first house. But I never forgot the coconut trees, the brown ceramic tiles, or the armoire that acted as both a closet and my clubhouse.

"I love it," I wipe my nose on my sleeve. Gross.

"Open it." Dad bobs his chin towards the book, shuffling his weight between his feet. His eagerness draws him closer when I flip the front cover. His gaze tracks my shaky fingers as they trace the edge of the page and scoop the folded envelope inside.

My brain connects the dots but my pounding heart demands I see the contents for myself. Unfolding the blue cover of the envelope, strips of paper stare up at me. My name is printed next to a designated airline and a flight number dated three days from now. I gasp.

"We're going to Mexico?"

Dad no longer holds back his excitement. He blurts, "Surprise!"

"Wait, all of us?" I separate the pages, reading over the names of my parents and brother. We're taking a trip to Mexico. *Home.*

"Yes, after talking to you, we decided it was time to bring Raph. Your mother's cousins have tried to get us to visit for years. It will be nice having the family together." His arms are ready when I run to him. His shoulder absorbs the leftover tears and foundation that washes down my cheeks.

"Thank you." My gratitude is muffled.

The family I haven't seen since I was young, the faces online who follow and like every birthday and milestone photo posted on social media, welcome our visit. My throat tightens with excitement. Married young and pregnant, Mom hadn't spoken with her family in a long time and as an only child, Dad had little reason to return, but the passing years hadn't erased the lives they lived there. This gift is for us all.

My parents witnessed me struggle after Tristan but never once had they considered flying us to another country. The gift is a timed coincidence, the universe's way of signalling my true priority. Time to reconnect with where I come from. A step back from work to take a break and learn to balance family. Timing is everything.

"Your mother is going to be mad I showed you without her." He rubs my back. "Please act surprised."

I laugh, moving away and wiping my eyes. Leaning the book on the back wall of the armoire, I scoop Raph into my lap. The scent of cedar wood hugs us. "Do you like it, Raph?"

"It smells weird." His nose wrinkles. I ruffle his hair and then push the black strands away from his forehead.

"How did you get this upstairs?" I grimace, considering Dad and his bad back, but the urge to scold him is pointless to follow through, my delight is permanent.

"Oh, I didn't bring the thing up. I barely moved it an inch." He points at the half-hidden window. "Your mother will hate this here. I should have told him to place it somewhere specific, but I only thought to move your dresser when I saw where he left the armoire. I tried to empty your clothes and move everything for you, but the gift was a closet, not redecorating." His dimples are bright and Raph turns in my lap.

"Dad said I'll get to fly!" Raph's wonder is adorable.

"Yes, you'll ride in a plane!" I glance between him and my father, bouncing my knee.

Details of Dad's story remain unaligned. The wood is too strong in the air. The delivered furniture was dropped off without requiring any assembling out of a box, handmade by a carpenter he ran into at the store.

"Who did you hire?" I aim for indifference, a modest interest and appreciation. Nothing to give away the shiver sliding down my spine.

"A local guy, he lives outside of town. He used to own a hardware store, runs a farm now." Dad shrugs.

Okay, many people run hardware stores. Anyone can be a carpenter just outside of town. There are plenty of barns around Bolton.

"Funny story, remember that kid who helped us at the tree farm when I took a tumble?" asks Dad, rubbing the back of his neck.

My mouth goes dry, but I manage the slight dip of my chin to confirm I'm listening.

"Small world, the boy's got talent. Arthur, the guy who runs the business, said he hired an assistant, someone he hopes to take over when he retires. You know me, I wanted to make sure I met the boy, that everything was in good hands." Dad grows animated as he unfolds how the encounter played out. "He did good work."

To demonstrate his point, Dad rubs a hand over the wood, smooth from splinters. And to ring home the irregular thud going on in my chest, Dad says, "You should get to know him. You'd get along. Richard is his name. He was nice enough to offer to drop the closet off with a few friends. Do you think he'll come back here to move it if we call? Your Mother says you're in need of a date for the countdown."

He means to make me laugh, it's not his fault my throat is iced over. Dad's joke sits in the air without purchase. Raph flips through the pages of the *El Llano en Llamas* and I'm transfixed by the book fluttering closed until he grabs the cover to repeat the motion. Everything whirls to the concept of fate.

Richard was in my room?

His friends helped him. Armen and Eric?

Saved by the doorbell, Dad appears unbothered by my silence. Jane and Aubrey are outside, the buzz in my pocket confirms my suspicions. Dad snaps towards Raph, who crawls out of my lap, leaving the book behind. Together they answer the door, and I'm grateful for the small moment alone.

Richard stood in my *bedroom*. What had he thought of my piled binders and bulletin of sticky notes, arranged in a palette from light to dark with matching annotation pens? Did he judge my green walls and the doll that perches on my bookshelf full of textbooks? Notice the unopened romance novels on the bottom shelf, the half-finished paintings resting against the floorboard by my closet that I had every intention of finishing but never found the time to?

Dad hadn't thought to move my current dresser, which means the clothes thrown across my mattress happened after Richard and his friends left. Well, at least there's that bit of silver lining.

But the armoire. I trail my fingers over the grooves of the face. Dad must have shared a photo with Richard for him to craft something similar. Dad shared a bit of my childhood, a bit of me with Richard. Richard built me my armoire.

And he knew. He would have recognized my father when Dad claimed he wanted to finalize details. If Dad saw him, knew his name, they had spoken, they had reminisced.

All this time, Richard kept the secret from me. A gift from my father that he spent his time piecing together.

Suddenly, I recall the sheet covering a large rectangle. A flash of fear sparking on Richard's face. Could this have been in the barn? Had I been close to unveiling my dad's Christmas gift?

My vision blurs just as Jane's voice crowds into the room, a loud presence my head and heart want to burrow in.

"What the heck happened here?" Jane curses.

"Tell me you know what you're wearing, we're not about to find another dress. Margo, did you not read our texts?" Aubrey means it as a joke, but her voice pitches close to hysteria.

When I turn, my expression must be worse than I think. Fresh tears pool, and Aubrey's hug envelops me. She coos, "Oh Honey, we will find you something to wear."

20
The Pre-party

Jane sits on the edge of my bed, lifting a jacket sleeve I'm sure she's never seen me wear.

"Oh, Honey," Aubrey sighs, the same go-to sentiment she's repeated over the last ten minutes. She shifts closer to put her arm around me and I lean in, wiping at the raw skin under my bottom lashes.

They let me cry until I run out of tears and my sleeve protests against absorbing any more snot. Neither of them try to ask what happened again, not when the first time resulted in a fit of hiccups and choked gasps. Winded, the bits of my heart blocked the way to my lungs.

The tears finally stop, but crying puffs my eyes.

"Fuck, my face is going to be swollen tonight. I have to take out these contacts." I rise, almost hitting my head on the top of the armoire Aubrey and I nestle into.

Focus on a task. The New Year's gala is tonight and I can't afford to fuck it up. Not with Harvey watching, not after what I said to Logan and a promotion hanging over me just out of reach. Make it through tonight, and tomorrow, and the day after that. One step in front of the other.

Jane shoots Aubrey a look that seems similar to her *I told you so* sneer, but I'm unable to guess the meaning. Aubrey shakes her head and scowls her *shut up, it's not the time* look. I leave them to their charades to remove my contacts and put in some rehydrating drops.

Running cool water over my face, I pat a towel, holding myself in the dark while I breathe into the cotton. The cloth almost hides the smell of freshly cut wood from my hands.

My heart quivers. No, it's my phone.

Sliding on my old cat-frame glasses, I read a text from Bianca asking if she should bring anything to the banquet hall from the office, she's about to set the alarm. I quickly type out a reply, sending her my address. She's a good worker, a decent friend I've kept at arm's length.

I keep everyone at a distance to spare myself. The one man I trusted, I crafted this wild backstory to justify why he wasn't all that great and how I'm the same fool I was years ago. Of course, I told myself Richard couldn't be patient, kind, creative, smart, funny. No, something wrong with him had to exist. And if he is all those things, then there's definitely something wrong with me that he will uncover with time. And if he doesn't see why I'm wrong for him, someone else will show him. The prettier blonde who works in HR or the cool café shop owner with amazing eyeliner.

He would learn eventually.

But Richard made me an armoire. He offered his help with party decorations. He remembered my preference of dessert coffee. He wanted to give Allison a testimony for her matchmaking service, saying on the record… what? That it worked? We worked?

I am the problem because I never had the intention of liking him. When I felt a bit of happiness and woke up like the leading character in a life where I could take on any obstacle with my wit and strong will, I searched for the cracks. Through the pieces left unhealed, an overlay of fragments like stained glass, I morphed what I saw. I fabricated a fake scenario where Richard doesn't like me.

Glaring at my unanswered text, I debate spamming him. Spewing out my reasons paired with a huge apology. But there's no guarantee he will read what I have to say.

I hurt him when I said none of it was real. My insecurity lashed out and made me the person I accused him of being: a liar.

But he believed me.

A shudder rakes through me.

Jane and Aubrey's whispers bounce angrily from my room.

"What are we going to do?" asks Aubrey, her worry causing me to linger in the hall.

"Nothing." Jane's response is clipped and edged, a kind of warning that only Aubrey gets away with challenging.

"Nothing? I haven't seen her cry like this since…"

"You're the one who encouraged her!" Jane whisper-yells.

"Is it a crime to want to see our friend happy? She has to put herself out there, all she does is work. We're her only friends." Ouch, but she's not wrong. Aubrey goes on, "Besides if I recall you came home excited when you heard their date went well."

Aubrey's irritation points towards Jane, and her girlfriend isn't someone to accept blame lightly. Before they end up in a fight, I reveal the real problem: Me, standing in the doorway.

My two friends notice the shift immediately. Aubrey's attention falls to her knees where they cross on the ground at the foot of the armoire. Jane shrugs.

Shame rolls through me and suddenly I'm very tired. My friends had my back, they nursed me to full strength after the first heartbreak and I count on them to get me through whatever shitty days are in my future, but bickering because they accuse each other of knowing better when I am still learning sounds absurd.

Nudging the pile of clothes aside, I sit between them.

"None of this is anyone's fault except for mine." Aubrey opens her mouth to object, but I hold up a palm. "I don't mean the terrible mistake of blind dating, I mean the lie."

Inhaling, I make sure they're both paying attention. Holding their gaze for long enough that they understand I'm serious, I dive into the story of my overreaction to Richard and Allison, me letting my insecurities morph a harmless encounter into a mirror of my past, Allison later telling me he was at the café to offer a testimony, the unanswered texts.

"You had a vulnerable night," Aubrey reaches for my hand. "You took a huge leap with him and that was just your mind's way of backpedaling when you got cold feet."

"You saw a convenient out. Do you regret sleeping with him?" Jane's black brows almost touch, but other than the small change, it's hard to read what she's thinking.

"I don't." A memory of Richard pulling me against him the next morning causes my stomach to somersault. His kisses trailed my collarbone and down my spine. Every touch was careful as if he wanted to savour me and convince himself I was real.

"Even when I got mad, I wasn't ashamed about sleeping with him," I say. In all the spewing rage, I hadn't once wished to take the night back. Opening myself up and Richard's gentle acceptance is the bit of truth my mind could never deny.

"Good, because you shouldn't be." Aubrey nods.

"I got defensive and said things I shouldn't have. I was mad at myself for caring about him. I remember thinking I should have known better, but the thing is, I don't know if I was fully in denial about his feelings or if I was in denial about my own."

I spent many years avoiding dating because I never wanted to repeat what happened with Tristan. When I saw Richard and Allison, a part of me wished I was right for missing out on all the times I could have dated and shared moments like the ones Richard gave me.

All the years I could have had experiencing great sex and someone to drink peppermint mochas with. If all guys are cheaters then I was right to stay away. I hadn't missed out. Better to find out about him now rather than later, right?

Wrong. I was so wrong.

The sledding, the hardware store, the barn, they made me happy because they were with Richard.

"And how do you feel about him?" Aubrey's eyes are like saucers, peering up at me with the same hope she had when I told her I signed up for Secret Santa.

"He's great. No, he's pretty fucking perfect." I point to the armoire. "He made that. My dad hired him, but he knew it was for me the whole time."

For a second, I fear I sound lame. He gave me a present that my dad paid for. My friends don't know the childhood attachment I have for the furniture, Richard doesn't even know. But just the thought of him putting in the care for something this large, knowing while he sanded and stained that the armoire was meant for me, making sure every detail came out flawless. Aubrey meets me at the same conclusion.

"And you pushed him away before he could tell you. Oh, Honey." Aubrey wraps her arms around me. "Pushing your fears onto people is not a solution. The whole point of signing up for blind dating was to land a date for New Year's, but as much as you wanted a fake relationship to protect yourself, Richard was always real. You deserve to find someone who makes you happy. Not every man is Tristan." She turns to Jane who remains oddly quiet.

"I think you underestimate how great you are because one asshole convinced you that you weren't enough," says Jane. "And yeah, whatever, you don't love Tristan anymore, but he still has you believing you're second place. He's the one who wasn't enough. I've said it many times before but maybe now you'll listen. Margo Diaz, Tristan didn't deserve you. He had you and didn't know what to do with you. He was a guy who didn't know what he wanted and you were collateral. But Richard, he was honest about his intentions. He built Hollywood letters for you and this masterpiece of a closet. We might forgive him for leaving it in front of the window. The point is, you dated someone who wasn't ready, but now think about how fucking great it'll be dating someone who is."

Aubrey stands from the floor and crawls across the messy mattress to her girlfriend. Sitting in her lap, Aubrey plants a long peck on Jane's mouth. Usually the image for *no hard feelings*, Jane melts against Aubrey's touch. Her heavy-lidded gaze follows her finger as she twirls a strand of red hair around her black nail, completely in love.

"That," says Aubrey, "was well said."

I shake my head to move my heart back down my throat. The day Jane found me was the best and worst day of my life. The worst because my most vital organ was just ripped out and I was hiding in a bathroom, and the best because Jane was who found me. Soon after, I met Aubrey and they welcomed me into their home with open love. Seeing them happy after all this time is proof of good people and kind hearts.

They love me unconditionally. Throughout the years, they never abandoned me. I received an invite to every one of Aubrey's art shows, the time Jane wanted to learn guitar and had to perform at the annual concert, when Aubrey crashed her car into the garage and called me instead of Jane because she wondered if she could push the airbag back in, when Jane broke her arm at a rollerblading derby, when Jane needed stitches because she punched someone with a beer bottle in her hand, when their cat died, when Jane showed me the ring she bought. My friends have always been here and wanted me alongside their adventures. Margo and all.

Knowing I have them makes the hurt bearable.

The doorbell rings and after a few seconds, Dad yells up the stairs.

"Send her up!" I scream. Aubrey hangs with one arm from Jane's shoulders, the both of them wear mirroring masks of confusion.

"I hope there's room for one more, I texted Bianca to come." Keeping my face neutral, they know this is a big change for me. I'm opening myself up, I'm growing.

Aubrey squeals. "Yes, yes, yes! Now we have an even group for shots."

Bending to open her bag, she reveals a four-pack of Twisted Shots. Entering with a dress held over her head, flowing down her back, Bianca freezes at the sight of alcohol.

"Wow, it's that kind of night already?" Bianca hesitates, and I help her with her dress, hanging it on the edge of the door.

"Glad you came! Don't mind them, the good drinks are downstairs," I stage whisper.

Jane and Aubrey are in a silent standoff. Aubrey grows more annoyed while Jane leans back on her elbows, clearly enjoying herself.

"Why does it matter if there are four of us?" asks Jane.

"Because there are four shots." Aubrey waves the pack in front of her girlfriend, close to her septum piercing.

"But you know I don't like fruity drinks." Jane raises her brows. "You always drink mine."

"And now I don't have to beg Margo to have another one and end up drinking all three. You know I'm a lightweight."

Jane smirks, most likely remembering all the times Aubrey begged our Uber drivers to pull over for her to puke in the bushes. "Yes, I'm aware."

"Exactly, and now we have Bianca to help. Hey, Bianca! So nice to meet you!" Aubrey scoops her into a hug, her red hair whipping me in the face as she comes barrelling.

Bianca and Aubrey drink all the shots while I curl my hair. At least, that's what Jane says when she comes into the washroom and closes the toilet lid to take a seat. Crinkling her nose, her piercing hangs in full view, two red diamonds at the end of the horseshoe.

"I think Aubrey hijacked your new friend."

"That's okay, Bianca is a nice girl." Releasing the iron, I twirl the ringlet around my finger to fix the shape. "I'm just sorry my room is a disaster. What an impression, huh?"

"Nah, you're okay. Bianca is probably relieved that the uptight manager of the office is secretly a slob."

"Hardy-har-har."

We fall silent until Jane decides to break it. "You're okay, right? You had some type of breakthrough."

But Richard still hasn't texted me back. I'm not forgiven.

I sigh. "I know. And I'll give him a few days to respond. I'll try again, and if he's not ready to talk, I'll try my luck with Tinder."

She rolls her eyes at my attempt to joke. "Margo, it's his loss if he doesn't hear you out and give you a chance to explain, but whatever happens, I'm here. Okay?"

I swallow, unable to face her in the mirror, I focus on twirling the iron. "Thank you. I just really hope I get a chance to explain."

"Me too." She places a hand on my shoulder. "But in the meantime, let's land you that promotion."

I shift closer to her, resting my head against her knuckles. Her support sends a shot of confidence through me. Tonight, my emotions take the backseat. I have a client to impress.

The past month whirled by with too many lies to track. I wasn't honest with the people at work, my parents, Jane and Aubrey, Richard, or myself. I crafted this story where I had a boyfriend because somewhere in my mind I believed I required someone next to me to complete the picture of success. I let my insecurities dictate my qualifications as a friend, daughter, manager, and girlfriend.

The goal was never to fake a relationship but to prove to everyone watching that I could have it all without actually taking the risks to get everything. Pouring myself over paperwork each night came with the excuse of extra pay, but really it was that I didn't have to sit at home alone on the couch. Blasting music filled the nights when I could have been out dancing or singing karaoke at the local bar.

The truth is, I spend too much time worrying about what other people think of me. Somehow my success measured my value. Achievements decided my worth.

Tonight, I'm showing up to the gala and proving I'm more than qualified. I dedicated a lot of years to Lauder Accounting. For once, I'm taking ownership. Standing in front of a room, I'll demand recognition. Tonight, everyone will know Margo Diaz put together the event without a committee at her flank. I'm not only a numbers girl.

Jane slinks out of the washroom unnoticed. She probably escaped during the odd minutes when I started ogling myself in the mirror while I gave myself a mental pep talk. Re-emerging from the washroom, the women who've had my back over the last month are dressed and glamorous, taking the theme of Old Hollywood to the next level.

"Holy crap, Jane!" I say. In a slim gold dress that ripples off her small frame with a slit that cuts to her thigh and open-toe heels that have ribbons up her calves, Jane is the poster image of a goddess. Seriously, I want to bow.

"Right!" Aubrey kisses Jane with a quick peck. "She's no Marilyn Monroe, she's better."

"Yeah, and you are?" Jane challenges.

"Hot." Aubrey shoots back matter-of-factly.

"Well played," says Jane, grabbing Aubrey's hand and planting a kiss in her palm. The black dress Aubrey borrowed from her sister is open-back and form-fitting, making her scarlet hair pop against her pale skin and red lips. Her long legs do wonders.

"Cu-uuute!" cries Bianca, observing their display.

"Girl!" I shout. "Twirl for me!"

Blushing, Bianca stands and obeys. She earns a round of whistles in her floor-length silver dress, making her blue eyes appear more grey. With matching gloves pulled to her elbows and a side bun, she fit the theme. It's when she pulls out a vintage short face veil I decide I'm keeping her.

"What about you?" asks Aubrey.

I close the door, revealing the shimmering sequin red dress hanging at the back. Aubrey gasps, touching the shimmering sparkles.

"Dolores del Río is my inspiration. My Abuela used to watch all her movies on repeat. She's known for having bad luck with men." I duck when Aubrey swats my arm.

"Bad luck? What happened to your boyfriend?" asks Bianca, and Jane's stare lands on my face, wondering how I'll approach the truth.

"I lied. I don't have a boyfriend. I was seeing someone for a bit, but it didn't work out." Laying out the dress on the bed, I fight against the tears choking me. I said I will stop caring what people think, but I don't want Bianca to judge me.

"Bummer. I got dumped before Christmas, we can be each other's dates."

Yup. I'm keeping her.

"Who is Dolores del Río?" Aubrey marvels herself in the mirror at the back of my door.

"Here, I Googled." Bianca holds her phone up, then she squints at me. "You kind of look like her."

"Let me see." Aubrey crosses the room. "Oh, you do! Especially now that your curls are contained, sorry. Wait, look at this photo."

She holds up an image of Dolores del Río in a gold dress. "You totally have to wear Jane's dress."

"Yes! And Marilyn has a red sequin dress. I remember seeing it online once. Let me find it." Bianca makes quick with her phone. "You have to swap. This is iconic." She turns on Jane as if she expects the lady in gold to object.

Truth is, Jane is used to changing outfits whenever Aubrey demands they have to coordinate and forgot to mention what she was wearing *before* Jane got dressed. My friend tilts her head at Bianca's serious tone, debating how she should take the accusation. Lifting her shoulders, she drops them and turns to me.

"I'm game if you are?" asks Jane.

I trail my fingers over the sequins. This isn't goodbye. *I'll have another chance to wear her*, I tell myself, not yet ready to part. I have no attachment to the dress aside from the fabric matching my favourite shade of lipstick and the success of ordering something online to happily discover it fits. Besides, Jane's dress is gorgeous.

A hesitant nod is all Aubrey waits for from me before she shoos Jane towards the bathroom with the red dress shoved against her chest. Bianca seizes the chaos to rummage through her bag. Revealing a bottle of clear liquid, she twists off the cap and thrusts the bottle toward me.

"You look like you could use a drink."

Aubrey gasps. "We shared Twisted Shots when you had this?"

"I wasn't going to turn down shots, but our girl needs all the help she can get tonight." The bottle suspends between us, hanging readily for me to take it from her.

"She has us," Aubrey counters, but chews her cheek. "Okay, sip some courage. You have a speech to give in an hour."

In one hour, Logan will have the show he craves. His warm welcome and his last display of power before he hands three-quarters of his company's shares over to Lauder Accounting. Pinning me against Tristan, standing me up in front of our combined offices, I accepted Logan's challenge and now I'll show him what I'm capable of. Onstage and in the spotlight that will try to reveal my every flaw, I'll present my claim on the promotion.

A swig of fire burns down my throat confirming the drink Bianca offers me is vodka. My insides warm and loosen. The past month sucked me dry. It's nice to have a drink.

Feeling the instant effects of alcohol loosens me to Aubrey's charge. Jane and I swap dresses and I'm inclined to agree this is a good idea. A warm cloth pressed under my lids soothes the puffiness and Aubrey's skillful artistic touch comes in handy when it's time for my makeup. She paints thin lines of yellow metallic wings in the corners of my eyes and blots highlights on my cheekbones and nose. My lotion has a shimmer that rubs into my tanned skin, sealing any cracks with a fine glitter up my legs and arms.

I'm a woman who flows like liquid gold.

Broken or not, when I step on the stage, there's no doubting how powerful I am.

21
New Year's Resolutions

The stage is like a beacon. Logan's sneer might as well come from a judge's corner.

Across the room, sitting at the table reserved for board members, Logan slouches in his seat with a lazy arm tossed over the back of the empty chair next to him. My chair. He's entertained, listening to Harvey's warm welcome to him and our collective guests before Tristan and I deliver our individual gratitude for the passing year.

Instantly snapping into boss-mode when I entered the banquet hall, I had rehashed the final details with the coordinator, but each time the woman with the tight bun answered my repeated questions, my attention flashed towards the display next to the dessert tables lined against the wall. The fire of vodka in my gut dried up. I haven't been able to look away.

HOLLYWOOD

Every letter is carefully aligned as if the gap between each had been measured. LED lights shine on the inside edge of the wood, hidden and casting a warm glow on the back wall. The red paint was bold in the setting sunlight that peeked through the balcony windows while guests arrived, but now under the night's shadow, the letters fit in perfectly with the lowered ambiance of the room.

Richard delivered them sometime after I left the hall during my morning rounds and before I arrived to check over the last touches as if he knew to avoid me. Just the idea of potentially running into him, smelling the scent of cedar wood on his skin and knowing he is the craftsman of my Abuela's armoire replica, had evaporated all the alcohol from my blood.

The room greets me at the mic with respectful applause, but none of the faces I spent hours arranging on a chart capture my focus. My attention snags on the Hollywood letters as if they deserve the appreciation I voice.

Delivering a speech to a roomful of people may sound nerve-racking to most, but when I was young, Abuela made me stand in front of the television and read her my homework. If I stumbled she would draw a circle in the air to tell me to start over. If my voice lowered from fright or uncertainty, she would point to the sky. Abuela's English improved but she could never string a full sentence. When I read to her, I suspected she wanted to learn, so I'd do my best. I'd perform.

That's kind of what standing in front of a banquet hall rehashing our successful year to the employees of Lauder Accounting is like. I rehearsed the numbers before tonight, but the speech is completely my own, hitting key topic notes from memory. My confidence in our staff, my work, and the company gives me an edge. Unlike Tristan and Harvey, I take my entrance without cue cards and wish everyone a great time before the countdown.

"Let's soar into the New Year like our last quarter everyone," Tristan hollers into the mic.

"But first," interrupts Harvey before the guests resume their evening. "I have an announcement."

My stomach drops. Announcement? What topic is important enough to interrupt the flow of drinks and excitement? I remember the reason for the gala, the reason tonight had to go perfectly.

Immediately I spot Jane at the table located near the back of the hall, strategically placed close to the bar. Our gazes lock. Next to her, half-turned from her neighbour, Aubrey sits ramrod tight. Together they freeze in a shared image of alarm. They must sense my tension from where I wait.

Is Harvey announcing who will receive the promotion? Again, my attention shoots to Logan, smug and rubbing together his palms as if Harvey is about to reveal the winner of a game show.

His eyes meet mine, and I can't pull myself away. His expression morphs into one of pride. Different from his usual cockiness, he straightens and raises his chin. A glimpse of the CEO he aimed to be before he lost his money.

My stomach tumbles where it falls and my mouth goes dry. Forcing a calm exterior, the feedback of the microphone blends into the ringing in my ears. This is the moment Logan hinted at in the elevator. The burn of vodka shoots back up my throat and I force myself to swallow it down.

"As leaders of the board and an embodiment of hard work and dedication, Tristan and Margo have proven their talent. Without them, this evening wouldn't have been possible. Please give them another round of applause." Harvey pauses for the ovation.

My tongue coats with sharp anger. Tristan left me alone to sort out all the details and plan for the gala. How dare Harvey put us on the same stage and expect me to share the praise? On the other side of the hall, the Hollywood sign mocks me from where it stands, bringing in the rustic theme of the gold and black party decor.

Over and over I'm compared. Next to Tristan, next to the woman he cheated on me with, the applicants for Secret Santa, the traditional notion of a woman in her twenties starting a family and maintaining her career. I'll admit, I leaned heavily on the latter in the last part, but I have baggage I prefer to keep hidden and goals targeted through checklists in my agenda each morning. Family is my greatest priority and work is my passion, but love, that remains unanswered. Richard proved it's possible, that I'm ready to put myself out there, and this week taught me the rhythm required to balance.

Harvey speeds through his company vision of Lauder Accounting tied with Hyup Media, his deep, elder voice unrelenting for his age. He's a leader I couldn't abandon,

I trust him too much. Harvey trained me and promoted me since my internship in my first year. It's no surprise he captures the crowd with his brief introduction of what to expect from the firm in the New Year. All I'm certain of is that I can have everything I care about. The job, my family, love. And this is my moment to reach for it.

Standing off stage, Bianca waits to assist with the audio setup once the speech concludes. Something flashes across her face when Harvey circles back to the mention of restructuring and I recognize her annoyance in the brief flare. If anyone has witnessed my sacrificed time, it's the other woman who also shows up and does her dues each day in hopes of receiving some recognition. It's Bianca who pops into my office to let me know everyone else has left.

Frozen with the chill of envy, I listen to Harvey reel in the growing suspense. "You are all familiar with Hyup Media, our loyal client and a huge part of the success of our marketing and sales department expansion." He waves to the table where Logan sits. The spotlight turns his skin a deeper shade of orange than his usual fake tan. "Before we cheers to the growth and success we expect to see in the New Year, I would like to bring attention to these two candidates, who will help lead our teams as we make the transition, but it is with pride that I announce the new Chief Financial Officer."

I risk a glance at Tristan and my chest puffs when I see he's just as nervous as I am. This is good, this means he doesn't know any more about Harvey's plans than I do.

"As we expand the marketing branch, there is someone I want to draw attention to," continues Harvey.

All the moisture leaves my mouth and it's hard to swallow. As I feared, Tristan is the Marketing and Sales Director, he has more qualifications to oversee the buyout in his title alone despite the hours I put in to assure the entire firm operates with accuracy, submits reports on time, and the procedures I implemented to increase efficiency. Just last month I caught the error in Delilah's audit, and—

"Margo Diaz."

My breath escapes my throat and clogs my ears.

Did I just hear my name?

Harvey turns his shoulders in my direction, calling me into focus for the rest of the large crowd. He said my name.

"Margo Diaz has shown a combination of dedication, hard work, and commitment. Her talent as Director of Finance has proven her ability to reach goals and encourage others to achieve desired success. And I desire a lot of success." The room offers a weak laugh while any sound I aim to make remains in my chest. He's giving me the promotion.

"Give it up for Margo," Harvey waves towards me and the guests offer a string of claps. Someone whistles from the back and I'm sure my heart stops beating altogether. I offer a curt nod to my boss and the crowd. Harvey runs his fingers through his salt-and-pepper hair, breaking the character of seriousness. "With that, let's eat. Enjoy everyone!"

The lights dim and the DJ turns the volume higher on the dinner playlist. A jazz melody greets the air just as the delicious waft of garlic and herbs calls from the kitchen.

"Lauder Hyup!" Logan shouts from his table, his hands cupped beneath his nose. He pronounces the company 'louder hype' and I already anticipate a decline in client retention because of the god-awful play on words. A few of his board members copy his chant.

"Congratulations, Diaz." Harvey steps down from the podium to shake my hand. His grip is solid and part of me is endeared he doesn't offer me a delicate clasp.

"Thank you, Sir. I'm honoured. I won't let you down."

There's so much I want to say, to thank him for. As the youngest candidate at the time, he took a chance on me when I first interned. And again when I interviewed for Director of Finance after Tristan broke my spirit. Harvey played a key supporter in my career.

"I know you must have campaigned for me," I continue. I haven't released his hand yet and he must notice the sweat that accumulates on my palm. Dropping my arm, I wring my fingers to keep them busy.

Harvey picks up on everything unsaid. "Actually, Mr. Hymn came to me this morning with his final decision and requested I make the announcement. He said if anyone was going to deliver a promise, it would be you."

As if hearing us from across the room, Logan offers a curt nod, raising his champagne flute in the air as a silent toast. Repeating my words from earlier to Harvey, Logan must have truly heard me.

"Margo, you've done a lot for the company already." Harvey pinches me with a stare, requesting my focus. "I want you to know, I fully support his choice. I see your hour logs and I wanted you to know with the promotion you'll receive help. Starting next week, we will find you an assistant."

I gape. An assistant? No more late nights spent triple-checking numbers. I'll have someone to file the accounts receivable and payable, the small tasks that turn overwhelming with quantity. I will fully focus on operations. Now with the buyout, our business strategy is essential to manage. The opportunity to shape the firm by implementing an improved employee structure.

"I may have someone in mind," I say, stealing a glance towards Bianca. Harvey rubs his chin, considering. "Also, next week I'm not in the office. The tenth is my first day back. I decided to extend my holidays and spend some time with my family. I'll be out of the country."

I hold my breath. The declaration is bold, but considering I rarely use my vacation time and spent the week working when the firm was meant to be closed, he isn't in the position to decline me of my contract. Plus, it's Mexico.

"Good for you," Harvey admits, clapping my shoulder. "We will flesh out more details of your contract when you return to the office and schedule a powwow. All of this can wait another week. My wife made sure to remind me that tonight may be a business gala, but it is still a party. I sense her frowning at me now." He feigns a wince and I laugh.

"Enjoy your night."

"You too, you did an amazing job." He nods to the Hollywood letters and a blush climbs my neck for reasons he cannot guess.

Just when I think I'm unable to accept any more compliments without exploding, Bianca rushes up to me when Harvey steps down from the stage.

"Eeeek, you did it! Congratulations!"

"Thank you," I manage. I'm eighty percent sure I'm frozen in some other life at the moment. After a quick hug, she moves to dissemble the microphone and the podium.

The din of the room picks up and Harvey moves to greet the tables designated to Lauder Accounting staff and their families. He leaves me standing alone with Tristan, who collects his papers from the podium Bianca rolls away. As the event host, I should make my rounds too, but something nags me, snags me, and tugs me down from cloud nine to root me to the stage. The surreal feeling of Harvey's recognition and the fade of the applause leaves space for thought. Happiness should spew out of me after winning the promotion of CFO and the reveal of receiving an assistant. But all of the excitement is void when the person I want to tell is not in attendance.

"Harvey shouldn't have announced the promotion here," I admit, catching Tristan before he joins the guests.

Logan is the culprit for the evening's events, but Harvey followed the plan through. Pride over the promotion blooms and then fades, understanding the Sales and Marketing Director would have also had the qualifications for the new position. Yet to gloat brings no satisfaction. I still half-expect the ground to give way beneath me. Missing the easy way Richard pulls me from my shell, the emptiness inside me grows to consume any leftover thrill.

Tristan's brows shoot up and I hear it in my voice as well: doubt. I'm finally recognized, but beneath the shadow of my ex and Logan's games, I question my credibility. If the roles were reversed and Tristan had won the position while I stood behind him... The idea pinches my lungs. I should feel great that I finally beat him, that Tristan knows what it's like to fall into second place, but I'm starting to understand that comparison is a dangerous game.

"Margo, you must know you earned it."

Shock explodes from where wariness festered moments ago. His congratulations is unexpected. Tristan's brown eyes widen, and the shade is dull and absent of any green.

Scanning over the little changes age brought him, the few strands of white hair and the new lines folding his skin, I do the math. Tristan must be thirty. A grown man ready to settle down and get married. When was the last time I observed him with anything other than disdain? Have I truly been the only one stuck in this loop of hate, feeding it with my energy each morning as I strut by the mouth of the cave, his office?

"Thank you." I nod. I replay his words, searching for a hidden meaning that doesn't exist. Was he congratulating me? He actually sounds genuine.

His stature is confident, his hands comfortable in his pockets while he stares across the room at his soon-to-be wife. There's a warmth in his gaze, and I fail to recall a time when he looked at me that way. All these years and

I let myself be miserable while he moved on. He perks up and watches Stacey with a fondness that reminds me of Richard.

"Guess I just have to try harder next time." He shoots me a smirk to tell me he's joking, a remnant of the boyfriend I use to know. "You're great at your job, Margo. And I think I want to spend the next year with as little stress as possible."

"Right, you have a wedding to plan. I can't imagine anything else less stressful." He rolls his eyes.

Why am I trying to joke with my ex? I guess it's happening. And it's almost civil.

Tristan groans. "Stacey wants to invite her extended family from England. There's like a million of them. I suspect she wants a big family too," but he doesn't sound turned off by the idea. He's truly happy with her.

"I never said congratulations on the engagement," I swallow.

"Thanks." He shrugs. "What about you, where's Richard?"

He has no idea how his words pierce me. Tristan may recognize Richard from his past, but the man I spent weeks with had left behind a deep sadness as if I've known him my whole life. I feel the absence of him, aching my joints and resting at the back of my throat.

Time to stop lying. Tonight proves the animosity between us ran its course. Tristan screwed up but he found Stacey in the process. It's like what Jane said, I'm collateral damage. But if Tristan stayed and I forgave him, I wouldn't have met Richard and I would have always wondered what it would have been like to be put first. I have nothing left to prove to Tristan, not anymore.

"Richard isn't coming." The small admission getting easier each time I say it, but hurting the same.

Tristan nods, not prying for more details. His expression remains unfazed and relief unties the knots in my stomach because, for some reason, I expected him to judge me. Probably the same way he expected me to gloat when I won the promotion. We've silently fought head-to-head for a long time, it's nice to call a cease-fire.

Luckily, Bianca saves us before the comfortable quiet turns awkward. One day, the past will no longer affect Tristan and me, but standing on a stage at a New Year's party is not that day. I'm not sure if exes are capable of friendship, but the idea of not hating him sounds somewhat nice.

"Margo, they're starting to bring out the food and want to confirm who is receiving the vegetarian dishes." Bianca's panic is clear. Since we arrived, my friends have given themselves roles to make sure the night goes seamlessly, and Bianca fears she will screw up with any small mistake. She's basically me reincarnate.

"Thank you, Bianca, I'll go there now. And I appreciate your help," I add, and she beams.

"Oh, no problem! I have to make sure every table receives a bottle of champagne for the countdown. I'll catch up with you later for a dance?" She shimmies and I laugh.

"For sure," I shake my head and turn to Tristan. "I have to go, but we'll chat later."

"Okay," says Tristan, but he's looking towards Stacey. This time, when no emotion flares up inside my chest, I'm grateful.

22
The Countdown

Dishes add a burst of colour to the black tablecloths and gold centrepieces. Red meats, vibrant vegetables, a tomato sauce that smears the white plate, I have to stop myself from groaning with pleasure.

"Show me your ring, Darling." Harvey's wife, Janice, reaches for Stacey's wrist. "Marvellous."

Stacey blushes and whispers her thanks, then the two women dive into details about wedding timelines and when to place a deposit for a venue. Wedged between Tristan and Logan, the two men discuss a movie that recently hit theatres. I sip my champagne, appreciating the bubbles sizzling on my tongue before cooling my throat. The topic of my ex's marriage, the way I'm pinched between a bro moment while Harvey strategizes across the table with Hyup Media board members, none of this bothers me. I'm sure faking interest in a movie isn't hard— when did I last see one in public? And I certainly can join in with Stacey and Janice's talk about wedding details— I have experience, I planned tonight's gala.

No, the void in my stomach that I fill with bites of filet mignon is for the empty seat across from me. The chair that the table designated as the purse holder and where Logan hung his tie on the corner in exchange for an open collar as soon as the formalities were over. My plus one.

Frills of golden streamers and feathers wisp from the gold-painted centrepiece vase. I opted for the taller assortment to allow the table to comfortably view one another. Now I regret the clear path to my heartache. The empty seat.

We had shifted the name cards for Logan to sit next to me instead of Harvey. No one minded. No one asked what happened to my date. Thankfully the drama of my single life hasn't entered the conversation. The perks of being a business professional.

Except, I want to scream.

Without the focus of a promotion— which I won *yay, me*— I'm left with the sinkhole in my chest that started to form the more I gave myself a chance to have a relationship. Late nights were spent painting decorations, grabbing coffee, shopping for materials, and talking about memories we had forgotten.

Lauder Accounting was my life for years, but I forgot what living was like until Richard.

As if sensing my thoughts, Stacey calls my name. "Margo, you have to tell us where you bought the sign."

Her lips purse sourly, probably hearing how awkward my name sounds coming from her mouth. Next to me Tristan tenses, but Logan continues his rant about an unrealistic skydive without noticing. The newly engaged couple share little confidence in how I'll respond to their direct consultation. Probably wondering about the limits to our ceasefire.

"A local carpenter in my town. Our town," I correct when I glance at Tristan. "I can pass along his contact information if you'd like. He's truly amazing. His father used to own the supply store and now he's woodworking full-time." *Shut up Margo*, no need to tack on more detail than necessary.

If Tristan and Stacey notice how I swoon, they choose to say nothing. "Yes, please! I'd love that!" Stacey smiles with teeth then turns back to Janice. "Imagine if we had our names written across the length of the field?"

She's having an outdoor wedding. I wait for the sting to hit, but nothing comes. I'm too busy buzzing at the prospect of a potential hire and recommending Richard. How many other guests have envisioned large letters for their next event?

Patting my mouth with the napkin from my lap, I dismiss myself from the table with an excuse that I have to check with the DJ about the playlist. The current track is perfect, a light bass paired with a mix of mainstream pop, the kind of overplayed songs everyone recognizes but wouldn't belt unless they drank an excessive amount of cocktails from the open bar. Walking the length of the room, I verify all guests eat peacefully. Another perk: when you attend a company gala the people you invite aren't likely to get hammered and jeopardize your safety deposit.

"Hello, Margo. Everything is great." Sheryl, Harvey's receptionist, holds her wine glass up to me as I visit tables.

"A receipt is preferred, but if you submit your bank statement with the highlighted transaction, I will see what I can do. I'll make sure you get reimbursed," I tell a junior accountant who hired a babysitter for the evening. Harvey promised to pay for any sitters and transportation expenses for all employees to ensure his staff attended tonight.

Efficiently, the waitstaff clear the dinner plates and the dessert table opens. Coffee pots line the wall next to the large trays of sugar cookies and a late-night menu. Finally, the music rises to invite guests to the dance floor. Exhaustion makes an entrance, weighing my shoulders. The night is almost done. Soon, I'll return home and lay in the bed the girls helped me clear before we left.

The beat thrums beneath my feet with another idea in mind. Each step is more sober than the last, bringing on the wave of fatigue that usually hits when I haven't committed to a full night of drinking. I spot Aubrey and Jane on the dance floor. Aubrey sways her hips like the seductress she is, stealing glances from every male within a ten-foot radius. I surprise myself by turning away. Let them enjoy their night. They've done a lot to help me and earn a little hip grinding.

Lauder and Hyup employees, along with their friends and families, mingle throughout the hall. Palpable excitement hangs heavy in the air as the year ticks away. The promise of new beginnings is like the bubbles of champagne brimming close to the rim, about to tip over. In the glow of the large Hollywood letters, a haze falls over the guests, and they bask in the mystery of what's ahead.

That's the thing. No matter how careful I was, no matter how great I am at planning or analyzing trends to predict growth, there will always be things outside of my control.

Sometimes a service promises you exactly what you get. Sometimes you don't believe it. And sometimes the hot guy you saw at a tree farm the week before ends up tipping your world from its axis and amping up the speed until it's spinning. Dazed, adrenaline mixed from thrill and fear paired with nausea, is the kind of toll Richard has on my nervous system. Of course, the press of his hands against the small of my back, breath on my neck, teeth on my collarbone, and fingers in my hair melted me down like gold. My heart, tarnished from disuse, demands all the light and love, ready to glitter in the effects of happiness.

Digging for my phone in my purse, I cave. The space I promised Richard, albeit without his knowledge, is too vast. He welded closed the cracks in my shell and then shattered the wall completely. He can't leave another gap. He needs to know I'm sorry for overreacting, that I lied more than once, the biggest time being when I said nothing was real.

11:11

A choked chuckle bursts from my lips. Of course it is.

If Richard's right, and there's something lucky about this exact minute, then please let the universe hear my wish and prove me wrong when I type out my text.

A photo of the letters we created, Hollywood bright in its glory, sits beneath my last message asking him to talk.

Margo Diaz: They look great! Thank you

8:58 pm

Margo Diaz: For everything

8:58 pm

Regret takes over with the realization that Richard could have bailed, could have abandoned the project and left it unfinished, but he delivered and pulled through. He held true to his promise. He finished painting the letters and installing the lights. Richard was committed, he was always all in.

Please, please, please, give me another chance. I clutch my phone, willing the device to reply for him.

"Margo! Come dance?" Bianca wraps her arms around my shoulders, hanging over me. Her nose scrunches at my phone, my message to Richard still sits on the screen. "Come on, Girl. Put that away and dance with me. We're supposed to be each other's dates, remember?"

Happy for the familiarity of her sweet raspberry and vanilla scent mixed with vodka, tears form for a different reason. Bianca's kindness bursts into me. She patiently waited for me to let her in, and here she is, distracting me from the guy I lied to her about. All she wanted was my friendship and I pushed her away, but if she is able to forgive me, then maybe Richard can, too.

I sniffle and her arms fall away from me, spinning me to hold my wrists. "No, you don't. No crying. We are not saying goodbye to the year with tears."

"Margo?" Jane's voice reaches us before she and Aubrey do.

"Oh, Honey!" Aubrey wedges next to Bianca.

The three people I adore watch me with similar expressions of love. God, they're amazing. Throwing my arms wide, I pull them towards me. Huddling close, stealing their warmth, I let them hug me back.

"Thank you," I whisper. I don't have to explain for what.

Aubrey kisses my temple, Jane rubs my back, and Bianca squeezes me tighter. Stepping away from them, I wipe where a few tears leaked.

"In case you forgot, Margo, you're a badass." Jane bumps my shoulder, the faint scent of whiskey follows her movements. I wobble on my heels and a small sad chuckle breaks the tension pulling my veins taut.

"Let's not forget, you totally ate up that promotion," chimes Aubrey.

"An overdue praise in my opinion. Margo, you're already running shit." Bianca beams. As the only one part of Lauder Accounting, her compliment hits differently. Jane and Aubrey have witnessed me carrying loads of folders to their movie nights, but as a member of my team, Bianca knows my performance. The first thing I'll do when I return from my trip, is put her name in the running for my assistant. I hope she accepts.

"The night isn't over yet, let's go!" Aubrey claps to move us onward.

"I can't, it's getting too close to midnight. I have to sort out any last details with the DJ for the countdown, and then call for cabs for any guests who plan to head home to their families." Not that I have a lot of party planning experience, but I've gone to weddings and events before to know that normally parents and older folk wait until twelve o'clock and say rushed goodbyes. They aim to return home by a quarter-after.

"Jane and I will do all that," says Aubrey, and Jane's brows shoot up. Aubrey loves a good movie moment, and to spend her countdown on the phone organizing cabs is her confirming just how much I mean to her.

"Aubrey, I won't ask you to skip the countdown." Not when she actually has someone to kiss.

"You're not asking, we're offering." She turns to Jane for approval. Her girlfriend pecks her cheek. "Besides, we're going to make out in the coat check closet."

We laugh, and with a hug from each of them, we promise to see each other in the New Year. There's always one person who makes the joke (it was me). Bianca and I leave them and hit the dance floor just as the bass builds.

Arms in the air, I sway my hips, releasing the tension that has stiffened my back since the second I saw Richard in the café talking with Allison. I sent my message. I sent my olive branch. While the ball bounces in his court,

I belt lyrics to a *Whitney Houston, I Wanna Dance With Somebody* remix.

Sweat drips down my back and my curls return to their usual fro-like state, but I no longer feel like crying. Bianca dances in circles around me, bending backwards to fist pump while giddiness and laughter break free from my sad haze.

The countdown starts at 59 seconds. Bianca holds my wrists, refusing to break apart as we twirl to the music like girls in a schoolyard. 30 seconds. Everything floats through me, no longer from the emptiness I coaxed. As the entire crowd begins to chant 29… 28… 27… every fibre in my body wrings with adrenaline as if the new year will burst in and change my life forever.

15… 14… 13…

Bianca tilts her head back to shimmy jokingly to the music and if I wasn't yelling numbers at the top of my lungs, I'd thank her for the distraction. Richard is far from my mind, but for a moment I accept his place behind my eyelids, smiling at me as if watching me dance is both amusing and adorable. As if he's standing in front of me, reaching to push my hair from my face, whispering—

"Hello, Margo."

10… 9…

23

Fireworks

His large palm cups my jaw, drawing my face towards his. Eyes growing dark, he spares only seconds to gaze into mine, but the stretch of time is infinite. I'm in a mix of brown and green, every bit of me pours into the fall. I'm putty in his hands, waiting for his lips while his nose trails down to the tip of mine, his breath teasing the space where my mouth parts.

"Tell me it wasn't true," he whispers, his half-lidded stare pleading.

Desperation rolls through me as I fight for the right answer. I'm unsure of whether he means the whole relationship or what I said to him in the parking lot. Both are lies I wish I never told, but one of them I'm grateful for.

"I'm so sorry," I say, but my voice is swallowed by the shouts of the countdown.

My breathing loses all sense of pace. Deep inhales and shallow releases while my heartbeat hammers loud against his chest. His fingers dig into my hip while the others keep me suspended, long enough for me to make certain he's really here. Arching my back, I plead him to seal the gap.

3… 2… 1…

The kiss hits right when the cheers erupt, and a part of me— the Margo at the back of my brain— appreciates the execution of the countdown, but inside I'm wild. The distance of physical space is nothing compared to the separation of time. Days apart left me starved.

And it happens. Fireworks. Like tiny stars trapped in my veins, our languid touches smoulder and meld.

I thought I could never forget his touch, but my body reacts as if it survived years without satisfying a craving. Richard tightens his hold on me, winding into my hair, cupping the back of my head to bring my mouth closer to his, deepening the swirl of our tongues. Every taste of him is familiar, but my memory did no justice to the feel of him pressed against me.

Pulling away to tug at my bottom lip, Richard crowds over me. The hard flex of his arms, the press of his chest, the angle of his hips. My body is on fire.

Sound is lost and the brush of bodies is absent from the champagne bubble we float in. He tastes like mint and sugar, and I chase his mouth unwilling to break the kiss as he pulls and separates completely.

"Margo," Richard murmurs, the edge in his baritone voice persuading me to open my eyes.

His mouth is pressed in a lopsided line, but the

corners curl with humour. His five o'clock shadow is shaved, showcasing the hard edges of his jaw and knife-sharp cheekbones. Peering down with half-lids, the dark clouds that storm mirror what brews in my stomach. He waits. For what? I'm not sure. My mind is lost in the fog that accumulated when he arrived.

"Richard," I answer, huskily. A sound rumbles in his throat and he glances back down to my lips.

"I'm not entirely confident with groping in front of your coworkers." His grin says otherwise.

I sigh, untangling my grip from the curls at the base of his neck but resting my arms on his shoulders. Sparing a second to wonder if holding him is okay, Richard answers when he stops cradling my head, shifting his hold to my waist. No longer pressed flat against his body, the air between us manages to somehow tighten. One glance at his stormy gaze, still focused on my mouth sends a lick of heat through me. Like moving two magnets close to one another but not letting them touch, the energy flares between us with an attraction we force ourselves to avoid for the sake of public decency.

"I suppose our make-out window has an expiry. Though no one has provided quantitive feedback for how long one is allowed to kiss after a countdown," I say. He licks his bottom lip and I track the movement. The glistening plump surface is inviting.

"Bummer. I'm happy to offer my services as a test subject."

The right words haven't accumulated in my brain yet and Richard keeps us sensible, leading the shuffle of our feet among the raving crowd of interns who holler over the music that grows louder. The bass picks up and hammers in my chest, but somehow he finds the beat to keep us moving.

Richard is here. All the apologies I rehearsed, the opening lines I hoped I'd have a chance of saying. He's here. And my mind erases, empty like the blinking cursor in a blank document. And he kissed me as if he made a promise for the New Year.

"You came," the thought sneaks out. "How did you get in here?"

"A woman at the door named Jane, a friend of yours, I assume?" His voice hums with mischief, raking deep in my belly. "She gave me a high five and said she recognized my photo from Instagram. She let me in." He peers over my head to skim the crowd to where I assume Jane and Aubrey manage the doors.

Embarrassment should bloom inside me over Jane admitting we stalked him online, but a satisfied thrum takes over, silencing any unease. Richard's here. He answers his physical arrival, but I struggle to make sense of *why* he's here. He dropped off the letters without saying anything and he hasn't replied to my texts. If he wanted to talk and wanted to come as my date, he would have. So why is he here?

Our feet stop moving.

"You left me hanging until the last second," I chide, my hurt and confusion distorting my tease. We face off in the middle of the dance floor, the distance no longer a temptation but a barrier against the truth. Explanations are owed from both of us.

"All night I rushed to finish the Hollywood letters and install the lights. The guys helped. We forced the paint to cure with a fan, but I'm pretty sure the red stain on the truck will last for a while. Not that Arnold will mind. But after I dropped off the letters, I spent all afternoon running around looking for a suit. Nothing was open!" Richard grunts. Stepping back, I inspect what he's wearing for the first time.

A black suit with narrow lapels that sharpen his shoulders and broaden his chest. The dark fabric pulls at the shadows in his eyes and the dark curls around his face. On his cuffs, two ruby links flicker in the spotlights. Richard is dashing, I realize. Not hot or sexy, though those are good choices too, he's built with aged confidence. Held with a kind of respect that shapes the air around him, a charisma that pulls me close, and a comfort that promises safety. Richard doesn't wear a suit for authority, he looks like he walked out of an episode of *Bridgerton*.

"You should always wear suits," the thought seeps out without warning. He tilts his head back and laughs.

"Margo, do you see yourself? That dress is driving me crazy." His gaze sweeps up my body.

The shimmer of gold hugs my curves different from how it spilled down Jane's lean body; a detail that made me slightly embarrassed to wear it in front of the entire firm when I put it on. But Richard's gaze trails the slit up to my hip, peeled open to glimpse the smooth tan skin of my thigh, and releases any insecurity I might have had. The dress really does do wonders for my backside and boobs. I wanted him to see me like this. And his reaction exceeds any daydreamed scenario I might have forced to the back of my mind to entertain sad-Margo.

Pulling me against him to resume our slow shuffle in the middle of the large crowd, he plants a kiss on my forehead, sparing seconds to linger and sniff my hair.

"You're beautiful," he murmurs. "Fucking perfect."

My cheeks warm, and it's fitting to place one on the source— his heart. His pulse thumps fast in his chest. A hint of how nervous he is.

"I knew you wanted to talk," he goes on. "I saw your text. Obviously, I did. But I couldn't let you break it off without one last gesture. I wasn't sure if I was still invited, and I took a chance. If I couldn't get in for the countdown then I planned to sneak in and find you while the place cleared out."

"What?"

My mind whirls with the timeline of events. Richard assumed I wanted to break it off. From how our last conversation ended, he guessed I agreed to meet him for closure. I hadn't communicated well. He came tonight to make a final plea the way I planned to make my own.

But kissing me at midnight wasn't his only gesture. The Hollywood letters, the armoire, the sled, the peppermint mochas. All the details about me he paid attention to. Richard has shown me from the start how he feels.

And I told him it was all a lie. My lungs shrink, unable to pull in air.

"No, Richard, I'm sorry. The day at the café, I should have realized that you and Allison weren't a thing. I should have trusted you." He balks at the mention of Allison, but I press on. "I've been carrying around this fear in my head that I'm not built to date anyone. Truth is, I was scared of being the girl who lost the guy to someone hotter, again. I thought," *That I wasn't ever going to be enough. That you were too good for me.* "I pushed you away, and I'm so, so sorry. And what I didn't admit until it was too late is that a small part of me was hopeful when I signed up for anonymous dating. I feared if a guy saw me or met me at a glance, I wouldn't have been his first choice. I spent years thinking of myself as second."

I want to explain more about Tristan, about bailing to pick up my Secret Santa match, but understanding dawns across Richard's face. He reads me clearly.

"Listen, I owe you the full story and I want to tell you everything." Richard drops his chin to look at me, hitting me with the weight of his remorse. He forces a deep breath, ready to charge on before I have the chance to interject and tell him it's fine, we will work it out.

"You deserve to know what happened." He runs a hand through his hair. "My ex, she wasn't a good person. I knew it for a while, and Armen and Eric were glad I was free. Surprisingly my brother was the least shocked about the matchmaking service. But Margo, none of that matters, and I would have told you eventually. Or, I guess it does matter in the timeline of things, but it doesn't matter how it all happened. Jerrica thought the algorithm would prove she was perfect for me, but I met someone who truly was. You. And— fuck. I know I'm explaining this all wrong. I know I should have told you right away. But talking to you brought back my hope.

Armen, Eric, Tyler, they were happy to see me putting myself out there. And you got me to call my parents when I told you they moved to Florida. Back at the tree farm, you convinced me to make the effort because family is important. I saw your mom panic over your dad falling, your crying brother, and then you stopped. Do you remember what you said to me?"

His words pour out of him and my brain whirls with the spill of events how he saw them. I knew he remembered me and my family from the tree farm. The whole incident was scary, but I hadn't known I left a big enough impression for him to call his parents. What had I said?

"I don't remember," I admit.

"All you said was that I should reach out to them, but seeing how your dad's injury shook you reminded me of all the people in my life that remained, all the people I love. You showed me. At the farm, you reminded me what it was like to have someone need me. The matchmaking service was just another confirmation that I was meant to be with you." He waits for me to reply, but a response isn't feasible. My silence cracks his expression into one of desperation.

My problem has always been the insecurity over how I saw myself. I refused to put myself out there because I anticipated immediate rejection, and when I did make the effort, I convinced myself it was temporary. My deal with Richard was only to bring him to the gala, not long term. A small goal to checkmark in my agenda.

I never factored in that anonymous dating would present me with someone like Richard. And I panicked.

"You're not second. Not to me. You're so beautiful, Margo. When I first saw you at the tree farm, you struck me silent. A pair of green eyes over a thick scarf." The memory of our first encounter plays between us, heavy with unspoken desire.

"You said I reminded you of family, that I made you call your parents, but you're the one who showed me how to balance. I had fun and I didn't think about work while I was with you. And my dad, he got me plane tickets to visit our hometown," I pause, realizing my trip to Mexico equals a full week without Richard, without figuring out what all this means.

"That's amazing! Margo, you should go." Laying in bed, I had spilled the details of my first home to him. "You should connect with your past, get away from the office to rediscover what makes you special." His gaze is intent on mine, pleading with me with an openness that clogs my throat.

"The armoire, Richard, it's beautiful."

"You're beautiful. My inspiration for giving something my all. I had you stuck in my head for weeks. And your lips," he pauses to kiss me as if remembering they're in front of him. "The same red lipstick. Even before I showed up to meet you that night, your voice constantly ran through my head. And then you were there, waiting in the gazebo. A fucking gift. Everything fit together. I had met someone smart and caring."

Happiness blooms inside me. Richard has always seen me as my best version. And because my good news hadn't felt complete without him. I announce, "I got the promotion."

The last bit of pride shifts in my chest when Richard blinks, stunned. Satisfied with his surprise, I release any lingering doubt. I am the Chief Financial Officer at Lauder Accounting.

Richard reaches for me, circling my waist and lifting me up. The room swirls as we spin, mixing in with my delighted shriek. This. This is what I waited for.

He places me down, my heels hitting the dance floor in two light taps. Bending low, he nuzzles me, mumbling into my hair.

"I'm so fucking proud of you. My Mystery Margo, I knew you could." He kisses my forehead. "You are first. For me, you are first."

My mind sings with gratitude I struggle to explain and I turn away, trying to hide the tears threatening to spill. But sitting at the edge of the dance floor, Bianca, Jane, and Aubrey make no effort to hide their staring. The three women watch as if Richard and I are the finale of their current binge. Behind them, sits a set of familiar faces. Underdressed in jeans and a sweater, Eric snacks on chips from his cupped hand. Armen waves.

Our friends, our group of supporters, wait for our happy ending. How had I missed all the love already present in my life? Holding Richard, and from the way he grips me tight, I know we will be okay.

"Richard, all of it was real. Every moment with you. I shouldn't have said otherwise." Somehow this is easier to admit while seeing him.

"Margo." He sighs the breath he held. "It was all real for me, too."

We stand, no longer attempting to sway our feet as the dance floor clears from guests. In an embrace that feels like the fusion of two souls, I welcome the warmth of his body and allow the last pieces of my shell to melt away. In Richard's toned arms is where I'm meant to stay.

"Margo, there's only you, and us. And I'm not letting you go. That's if you'll have me still?" He shifts closer, his fingers pinching tight into my hips.

Something vibrates against my collarbone on the inside of his suit jacket. I peer up at him, wondering if he will let go of me to answer his phone, but his grin is lopsided and the sheen on his skin glows beautifully in the coloured lights.

"An alarm," he admits, but his stare focuses over my shoulder. "It's 12:34. I wanted to make sure I made my wish for the New Year."

He set an alarm for the time I believed in. I don't tell him my 11:11 wish already came true, that he is here and I have faith in him and all the fates that push us together. It was meant to be Richard all along.

"And what is your wish?" I whisper.

"I'm not telling." He shakes his head, but the crook of his lips tangles my insides. "I'm still waiting for you to answer to see if it'll come true."

My heart flutters. "Yes, Richard. It's you and us. I'm not letting go either."

Acknowledgements

When I first started the Holi-FATE collection, I hadn't expected the idea to branch out past a single book. Different characters called out to each reader, which made me sit back and uncurl all the overlapping strings. Each character has a bit of me inside of them, but if it wasn't for my support team, I wouldn't have known the true emotions of witty side characters, close knit friends, and found family. There's so much love in the world and we all experience it differently, but the main take away is that we learn and grow together.

Thank you to my alpha readers who left their exclamations in the comments and drilled home feedback I wasn't ready to hear. You helped push my idea to its final stage. Angelina Bolosko, Tanvi Singh, and Emily VanderBent, you all truly have main character energy and I'm lucky to be part of your story. Thanks for lifting me up. I can't begin to thank you properly for your encouragement and praise. Having such talented minds and genuine help in my corner is a blessing.

To Marissa Miller, I have to acknowledge you separately because it was my drive home phone calls with you that saved this book. Thank you for straightening every spiral and digging me out of every pit. You are my favourite brainstorm buddy and I'll forever be grateful you came into my life.

My Mexican Muse, Vikki. It's been over ten years of dessert-coffee runs and I love you to pieces! Thank you for your support in all realms, but thank you especially for getting your father on the phone for Spanish translations and food tutorials. You make me laugh constantly, and you let me word vomit for hours. Our friendship knows no bounds!

To my personal support team— my family. Please skip chapters 14 and 15. But seriously, thank you for always insisting on being the first to buy my book, to attend signings and markets, and for always making me feel like my dreams are possible. I love you.

And my readers, hello! It brings me so much joy to know my book had made it in your hands. WOW. Thank you for walking this path with me. I wish you all the love and magic (and peppermint mochas) every day of the year.

Thank you,

TS

Richard's story starts in...

Look out for Holi-FATE book one!

1

The First Snowfall

If asked where I was four years ago, I would say happily renting in Vaughan, driving my high school car to my part-time night school classes after a full day of chilling with the guys. Jerrica changed that.

She changed a lot of things.

For one, I'm stuck in the city without a car, relying on subways to drive me to my condo in Liberty Village. The carefree life of an undergrad is over. Gone are the late nights and long cruises through backroads to loud music. I don't recognize who I've become.

Cold air nips at my bare neck and I curse November for bringing the winter early. With my hands in my pockets, I join the rest of the commuters on the subway platform. I bump shoulders with the shuffling people around me, searching for an open place to stand by the yellow line like we're all a bunch of lambs. Old gum plasters on the ground in dark flat dots and dried stains pool over the asphalt. Do they have sidewalk cleaners in Toronto?

The wind rips through the underground tunnel and I clench my fists. Holding my breath, I dream of permanently shutting my lungs against the onslaught of warm recirculated air and sweat. The chime from the subway alerts the doors will open. I mind the gap and search for a seat, but rush hour promises me a standing spot gripping the overhead pole. An older lady with black hair poking out from her knit hat rests against my side, awkward under my arm. I scoot away and bump into some dude's backpack. He glares at me from around his large headphones. Facing forward, he doesn't turn around further to say something. I wish he did.

The lights on the board turn red as we pass the last stops. King to Union. Two more green lights until I escape this cart emanating the smell of wet cotton and body odour. I'm tempted to sniff where my coat strains at my armpit. One more stop. My tie starts to itch and the tight wool fabric stretches across my shoulders while I hold the bar above me. This suit is expensive and the material will smell as if it didn't cost me a hundred dollars to dry clean.

The cart beeps and the passengers who were sitting, collectively rush for the exit. This is the worst part — trying to exit while other people enter. I push against the oncoming rush of the crowd. It's unlikely the doors will close and trap me here, I always feel as if they will.

When I'm on the platform, I glance back and send a prayer for the next poor bastard in a suit trying to go home. Wiping my hands on my jacket to smooth the wrinkles, I fix the buttons on my chest. I forgot the touch of the cool breeze and I almost missed the winter air, chilled from the wind carrying over Lake Ontario. Then the cold brushes my ankles and I catch myself, vowing not to stupidly wish away warmth ever again.

I take the stairs one by one to avoid stretching my legs and ripping the seam on my crotch. Happened one time and my subconscious refuses to let me forget. On a Thursday, no less — I remember this because Thursdays usually sound like innocent days of the week. Whatever God we named the day after decided to strike me with a bolt of embarrassment right in the middle of my legs when I lunged forward to tie my shoe. The uncomfortable day at the office had me close to quitting because I couldn't walk up the glass stairs confidently. I clench my cheeks and watch the cement steps to refrain from any fabric strain.

The vibration in my pocket notifies me my data is back. Except, the vibrating doesn't stop. A steady pulse counts the missed texts against my thigh.

When I pull out my phone, I'm not surprised by the notifications lining the screen. The messages group together to show me the final count. Twelve. All from Jerrica, with two hearts and a kissy emoji. She added those emojis herself.

I read the first text:

Hey, I updated my Christmas list. No surprises this year.

The second:

Daddy's asking what you're getting Mom. I told him you bought her something.

Third:

She doesn't wear gold, only silver.

I don't have a chance to read the rest of the messages before a picture of me, on a beach in Punta Cana with Jerrica, pops up on my screen. I weigh the option of whether I should decline the call then I remember ignoring her usually results in more reading. I answer.

"Hello," I release a breath.

I turn at the corner and angle my back to the wind. Snow starts to fall and the night creeps into the navy-coloured sky. Headlights flash along store windows in wiggled lines and for a second, I hear nothing apart from the whoosh of the passing cars. The yellow hues reflect off the wet ground, turning puddles from this morning's rainfall into a dancing reflection of the upside-down city. Sometimes I'm the one no longer right-side up.

"Did you receive my texts?" Jerrica shouts, out of breath. Probably on the elliptical in her dad's home gym. I imagine her curls in a messy bun, the crop top she checks herself out in, and the leggings that cost me too much money to make her ass look good.

"I didn't have a chance to read them. I got off of the subway two seconds ago." My condo is within sight, nestled between the apartment towers. A window on the small brick building and a twenty-minute walk away from the subway.

One weekend, on a trip to the city, Jerrica had marvelled at the old homes next to the tall columns of single-bedroom condos. The neighbourhood was cleaner than most areas, but her eyes rounded and her cheeks pinched with excitement. Watching her delight sold me on the daydream of settling here. She squeezed my hand while she guided me through the street and swatted my chest when she pointed at the restaurant she read about on some blog. Over dinner, she decided where I'd live. The fantasy formed into an idea and she worked through all the kinks. I provided her with a luxury weekend getaway and her round lips emphasized the promise of alone time. The last part sounded great, but did her happiness require an expensive condo? The following week, her dad cut a deal with the building owner, and I don't remember if she asked me for confirmation. Before I knew what happened, I found myself sitting in a tight room, signing the contract. As for the guaranteed alone time? Jerrica sleeps over whenever the location is convenient for her.

"Oh great, you're almost home. I'll video call you with some Christmas gift options."

It's the middle of November, let me digest Thanksgiving first.

I don't say the remark aloud. Not after our recent argument when I tried to remind her I have a family, too. All Thanksgiving night, my brother acted out whipping gestures behind her back after we force-invited him to her parents' house for turkey. After all, my brother and I are a family of two to her three, plus her extended relatives, who all share the same judgemental trait. I'm pretty sure her aunts show up to take inventory of the decor while their husbands appraise their value. There's a different vase modelling on the front table at each event. A showpiece from her father's antique collection, not a typical market find. The art pieces come from places where private men in suits send their assistants to hold paddles and play with their money. An impressive find worth displaying at the next event. And Jerrica demands I buy her mom something equally show-stopping.

"Can we worry about this later?" I ask. My stomach growls and I debate if I should stop at the burger place on the next corner.

"Online shopping takes time, we have to place the order before everything gets delayed." She makes the wheezing noise she does when she fakes shock at my response. "Richard, when do you expect we buy something then?"

I read the menu in the window. Twenty dollars for a burger and fries doesn't sound bad. I got paid today, I'll treat myself. I open the door and the bell above me dings to tell the cashier he has a customer. The warmth inside the small restaurant is different from the subway but smells just as sweaty. A couple sits by the window, picking at a basket of fries over their unfolded burger wrappers and I'm sold by the way the two patties stack beneath cheese, lettuce, and all the other good stuff. My mouth reacts to the fries before my stomach can speak up again.

"Hello, welcome. What may I get for you?" The cashier's grin unveils overlapped teeth and one jutted incisor. Short white hairs prickle out of his wrinkled chin.

"Hold on, Jer." I push the phone away from my mouth, cutting off whatever she says. "I'll take a regular burger, everything on top. Hold the tomatoes and bbq sauce, though." The man nods and turns to the grill.

"Are you even listening to me?" Jerrica starts again. "I'm trying to figure out Christmas, and your help is appreciated."

"Yes, I'm listening." I grab my empty cup and move to the pop machine.

"So what did I say then?"

My anger surfaces and I don't care. A second to myself isn't unreasonable. She sends me a million texts knowing I finished work an hour ago and rode the subway. She asks for my money and expects me to buy whatever flashy necklace her mom will hold up to the crowd for shock appeal and never wear. All to show the extended family Jerrica has a loyal boyfriend who cares for the leading lady of the house. The pitch of her voice is what pierces the hold I have on the weight I've been carrying all day. A build-up of words brim over the seam of my lips, and I let them pour out without hesitation.

"Why do you ask for my input? You're going to tell me what to buy anyway."

She gasps and the mechanical groan of the elliptical in the background stops. I continue, not wanting to lose the momentum of my anger. "I don't understand why I have to buy your mom something anyway. She's not my mom. Use your father's money instead of mine. I'm tired of busting my ass for you."

"You wouldn't have money if it weren't for my father, so who are you to throw that in my face?" And the song begins. Opening with high-pitched indignation.

"Okay, tell him I say thank you and I'll see him in the office on Monday." Eh, what does she want me to say? He's not my boss, he runs the IT Department.

"You're seeing him tonight…" She speaks slowly, a warning in her voice.

"Uh. No, I'm not. Try again." The cashier waves me over with a foil-wrapped burger. The fries pour onto the tray and my mouth waters. Pinning my phone against my shoulder, I reach into my suit pants for my wallet. Jerrica rants while I tap my card on the machine and turn to leave with my dinner. The seat by the window looks welcoming on the opposite end of the restaurant away from the couple. Not because I care about their opinions towards my conversation. I feel bad and I don't want to ruin their evening by forcing them to overhear my drama.

I slide onto the wooden stool and shove a fry in my mouth. The snow falls in clumps but refuses to stick to the pavement.

Jerrica enters her third chorus of *how could you* when the familiar melody turns to her one-hit wonder *after everything my family has done for you*. Without fail, she circles back to I'm ungrateful and delivers the reminder she made me who I am. The phrases I've heard repeated over the last year no longer drop rocks into my stomach.

We didn't used to argue this often. There was a time when I did whatever I could to make her comfortable. What she'd never admit is that the iconic cityscape she wished for, created a barrier. The wild nightlife scared her, and the distance grew from an ache to a nuisance. I'm tired of hearing her complain about what I'm doing wrong. I'm a blemish to her. She picks and picks until the gash is too large to ignore. She didn't realize the scars she left behind and didn't understand we'd argue less if she left the little things alone.

"Listen," I cut her off. By the lord, she actually listens, too. "I'm inviting the guys over tonight and it's best I don't see you this weekend."

I peel back the wrapper, exposing melted cheese and fallen shredded lettuce.

"We have plans this weekend. I'm not explaining to everyone where you are again. You can't keep doing this every time." She's borderline whining.

"I'm not coming, figure out how to tell them. I'm done, Jerrica." I bite into the hamburger and my stomach groans at the first real food since the company luncheon of finger sandwiches.

"Done? Oh, yeah. For how long this time?" She mocks me. She knows our breakups don't last long.

Her challenge spikes my blood pressure. Why have we danced on and off for over a year? Why am I fooled by the little efforts to win me back only to return to her dictating my existence? For how long, she asks.

This time, I'm determined to leave her.

"Forever. Merry Christmas, Jerrica." I say around the next bite, before swallowing.

After all the yelling and the silent days apart, my defense usually wore down and she'd barge in to kick over the foundation of each wall I built. I have nothing left to say anymore. No strength to pick up the pieces because they've long eroded into sand. I'm tired of thinking of new creative ways to defend myself. I'm not angry or sad, what I feel doesn't matter. Whatever reservoir of energy I held onto, is long depleted. I have nothing left to give.

I hang up and throw my phone onto the table.

The snow pellets against the window, and I watch as

the little flakes melt from the heat into droplets. Another bite and I reach the pickle. The two girls across the restaurant lean close together to watch an online video on a shared phone. The sticking of winter tires on the road is loud over the kitchen exhaust fan. Bicyclists and foot traffic rush overtime to return home from the cold. The snow continues to fall.

I dumped my girlfriend of three years in a burger restaurant.